BESSIE

Cathi Bond

MONTREAL PUBLISHING COMPANY

ISBN: 978-1-7386548-6-4

Bessie/Cathi Bond — 1st Edition.
April/2024

Any references to historical events, real people, or real places are used fictitiously. Names, characters, and places are products of the author's imagination.

Front Cover: Nelligan Design

Montreal Publishing Company
montrealpublishing.com

*For all of my family, far and wide, in the country
or the city, on the earth or in the grave.*

"It was the best of times, it was the worst of times, it was the age of wisdom, it was the age of foolishness, it was the epoch of belief, it was the epoch of incredulity, it was the season of light, it was the season of darkness, it was the spring of hope, it was the winter of despair."

– Charles Dickens

A Woman of Good Standing Trilogy

Book One

BESSIE

A Woman of Good Standing Trilogy

Book One

Cathi Bond

ONE

Dancing Day 1920

E lizabeth Hunter, known to all as Bessie, sat with a group of friends on the stone stairs of the London Ontario Normal School awaiting the results of their final exams. Bessie had decided to cut her long, lush, black hair into a new bob and was twisting a curl with the finger of her right hand. The others appeared nervous, but not her, she was too busy thinking of the party planned for that night. "Your mother is going to have a fit," one of the girls said, reaching out and giving Bessie's hair a playful tug. Bessie laughed. "I don't care, this is the 20th century. It's my hair, and I'll do with it as I please."

The group of young women, ages eighteen to twenty, had spent the last year in the city, living in a boarding house, preparing to be teachers. It wasn't enough to simply pass, they had to do well in all manner of subjects, from history to English, science, philosophy, and arithmetic. Still thinking of the party, Bessie heard the doors of the Normal School burst open, her classmates tumbling out. "They're up! They're posted!" A girl in a mauve cloche hat called out, "Bessie, you aced them! Every last one. Come and see."

As her classmates rushed to check their exam marks, Bessie remained, standing in front of the large glass doors, considering her reflection. At five foot five with jet black hair, a nicely proportioned body, and bright green eyes that could pierce ice, her thoughts weren't vain, but practical, and more useful than any philosophy would ever bring to the life of a woman from her generation: The greater the beauty, the higher the prize at the altar.

Having checked her exam marks, Bessie looked down the empty hall, the feel of freedom beginning to tickle the tip of her fingers, and she thought again of the party.

The gymnasium tables overflowed with garlands of multicolored flowers, the room feeling as if it had been choked with blue and white bunting. The band was playing "Pretty Baby." Sipping her glass of punch, Bessie watched her classmates dancing, their celebration, a momentary sanctuary from the uncertainty of their pending futures. The song ended and the band started playing, "Everyone's Crazy on the Foxtrot." Behind her, through the loud, pulsing music, she heard a man clear his throat. She turned and looked.

"Will you give me the pleasure of dancing with me?"

Bessie smiled. The young man, tall and handsome, was bowing so deeply she thought he might be able to kiss his knees. Tilting her head in agreement, and knowing it would be considered an act of incivility to refuse, she took the stranger's hand and followed him to the dance floor.

"And your name would be?" she asked.

"Hannibal."

What an odd name, she thought. He doesn't look foreign. His eyes are so bright blue. "I'm Elizabeth," she replied, thinking that sounded grander than Bessie.

"I know," Hannibal replied. "One of my friends taught you history and claims you're the best student he's ever had."

2

Bessie smiled as she followed Hannibal foxtrotting around the room. She knew she'd done well in school, but to be called the best was another boon from this already record-setting day of personal accomplishments.

The song shifted to Al Jolson's, "A Dangerous Girl."

"Would you like another dance?" Hannibal asked, hoping for a yes.

"Certainly, I would," Bessie replied.

"And just warn me, please … are you a dangerous girl?"

"I think I could be," Bessie said, smiling, prompting Hannibal to seize her by the waist and twirl her.

They danced more, oblivious to all, Bessie with her dress catching the warm air, enjoying the ease of Hannibal's movements. She caught a glimpse of the chaperones, their eyes wanting to ensnare. So Victorian, their judgement, she thought, so passé, and where is the fun in that? This nineteen-year-old girl, however, on the road to becoming a professional woman, had chosen to let go, for all to see.

A Charleston began, and Hannibal asked Bessie again. She accepted, and off they went, knees and elbows all akimbo. He flipped her over his back and pulled her between his legs. For a slim man, she thought, he was quite strong.

When the song ended, they stood catching their breath, and to Bessie's surprise, everyone started clapping, understanding something was unfolding in front of them. Bessie, unable to restrain a smile, knew she should sit down, but it seemed a shame to end such a perfect night by doing what was expected of her. Feeling empowered and unencumbered by the rules, she kept dancing, feeling as if the two of them had been together for years, ignorant of the stir in the room they were causing.

Exhausted, the couple exited the dance floor and headed outside for a stroll.

"I had such a lovely time," Bessie said, as they walked down Elmwood Avenue.

"I did, too—and oh, my real name, I have to tell you, is not Hannibal, it's Edward. I just finished a PhD with a specialty in the classics. Which explains the strange name," he added with a smile. Bessie listened as Edward explained he was there to discuss history with an old friend who taught at the Normal School. Edward's focus was on ancient battle techniques, and in particular, Hannibal's, the great Carthaginian general that had fought during the Second Punic War. Hence, the nickname. "Hannibal refused to admit defeat," Edward continued, "and he rode elephants over the Alps to take the fight to the Roman Republic, even though most of the animals died falling off mountains. He persisted, and he prevailed."

"My goal is to educate children," Bessie said, making a mental note to research Hannibal more closely. It sounded like a good lesson in perseverance.

"Mine is to become a history professor," Edward said, daring to take Bessie's hand. She hesitated for a moment, knowing it was improper for her to accept his touch, but left her hand resting in his palm, soaking in the feel of his skin—its warmth and its softness. These are not farmer's hands, she thought, these are the hands of an educated man.

Swinging their arms in tandem, they continued walking beneath the elms and maples, before entering a small leafy park where a wrought iron bench near a fountain was waiting for them.

"Where are you studying?" Bessie asked.

"Toronto."

"I've never been."

"You should come and visit," he replied. "Care to sit?"

"I really should get home, I needed to be in by eleven, and it's past midnight."

"Just for a minute, then?"

Bessie's smile said yes—again.

Taking in the quiet of the night, and the feel of Edward's arm around her shoulders, pulling her closer to him, she couldn't stop thinking how happy she was.

"I think you're the loveliest woman I've ever seen," Edward said, tilting Bessie's chin up toward his. She knew she should turn away, but instead, she opened her lips meeting his own, letting Edward's hands delicately travel over her body. When he kissed her neck, she kissed his back, allured by the faint smell of perspiration seeping from his skin, and the taste of him.

As they kissed there came a swishing of the grounds by footsteps, the brushing of dresses and sashes curious to know more, whispering under the light of a lamppost. "Elizabeth Hunter!" the principal shouted. "Come here right now!"

Bessie jumped to her feet and turned to see her classmates standing behind the principal, the chaperone, and her landlady, a look of deep disbelief etched on their faces, mouths aghast, pointing fingers, heads shaking in condemnation.

Edward spoke, and yet, Bessie did not hear his words, frozen in the realization she'd become disgraced.

One of her classmates yelled, "Hussy!"

In a trance, Bessie started to walk to her boarding house, wanting to escape them. Wanting to escape him.

"Do you realize what you've done?" the principal called to her.

Yes, she thought, she'd destroyed everything she'd worked so hard for, spitting in the faces of her family, the rules of God, and the United Church she believed in so fervently.

In her room, tears rolling down her face, she undressed slowly, slipping into her nightgown. To disappear into sleep was the only thing she wanted.

Assaulting her mind were images of Edward trying to defend her. She had told him to go away and had screamed for him to never cross her sight again, whoever he was, Edward or Hannibal.

Why didn't I resist? Hadn't I promised myself to remain pure until marriage?

The night's events continued to roll around in her head, compressing her heart as much as her body.

Under the covers, she thought of her humiliation. The revelations. The losses. "I made a mockery of chastity and polluted myself with sin," she whispered in the dark, "and it will never happen again."

TWO

Autumn 1930

"Don't run!" the teacher called to the grade three students quickly fleeing the one room schoolhouse, breaking into the sunshine.

"Teddy Barnes," the teacher said, settling her hand on his shoulder, "the reading will keep until Monday." Reluctantly, the boy closed the history textbook. Marco Polo and his acolytes would have to wait until another day. Gathering his pencil and scribbler, he headed for the door.

From the baseball diamond, his best friend, Bill, yelled, "You're on my team!"

The boys picked sides for a quick game of baseball, and Bill MacMillan, wanted, as always, Teddy to be on his team. "You're pitching!" Bill said as he stuck his fingers in one of the patches that covered his trousers.

The boys played and scuffled, the way they do when alive with rivalry. But not Teddy. When he was shoved, he didn't push back.

"Why do you always let them get away with stuff like that, shove you and push you around?" Bill asked, his shoes tied around his neck by mismatched laces, his books casually tucked under one arm. With the sun going down they were headed home, the breeze on their faces, untouched

7

in the current moment by the harshness of the times. Following the stream, they continued walking barefoot, splashing the hardened skin of their feet through the shallow waters. Working shoeless in the fields all summer had changed the boys' feet, transforming them into leather-like things.

"Dad always says there's no good in fighting," Teddy said, picking up a flat stone to skip across the water.

"The kids'll say you're yellow."

"I don't care," Teddy replied, picking up his pace.

"We got a whole bunch of new lambs in. You want to come see them?" Bill asked.

"Sure."

Teddy didn't want to hurt his friend's feelings. While Bill loved to farm, Teddy couldn't bear to think about living out his days on the land any more than he liked to fight. He just didn't care about farm animals. He knew the thought to be wicked and ungrateful, that it would most likely send him straight to hell for not honoring his mother and father, but no matter how many times he desperately prayed to God to make him want to be a farmer, all he ever thought of were ways to escape. And so far, the only avenue for him to do that, resided in the magic of books.

When a horn sounded in the distance, both boys turned, looking to the concession road where an old pickup truck with slatted wood siding was speeding toward them, billows of dust trailing behind it. Mooney acted as conduit between the farmers and the local egg grader. Bill waved his hand and Mooney replied with another short honk of the horn.

"Mother says Mooney can't be trusted," Teddy said, adding, "a few times he's short changed her, claiming that some of the eggs were broken."

"I can imagine your mother, hands on her hips, telling him, 'They weren't broken before they got in your truck, Mr. Mooney!'" Bill mimicked.

The boys laughed and imitated the man, the way he reached into his pocket and fished out a penny or two, grumbling about how hard it was to make an honest living.

The truck screeched to a halt by the side of the road and Mooney leapt out. "It's your mother," he yelled, his hands finding his knees, bending over almost double to catch his breath. "The baby's come."

THREE

The Christening

The CN train moved west through long fields of corn as the purser took Ed Barnes' ticket. Since Black Monday, he could ill afford the fare. The government promised economic mechanisms would soon right themselves, but life had only gotten worse: banks were going bust; people were being tossed out of their houses; jobs had all but dried up—even Ed's scholarships were being compromised. Yet, he knew to be grateful for what he had, other young men and women had nothing to hope for, their dreams on indefinite hold. Ed's future, at least, was still bright. I'll make do for right now, he thought, while the great minds that run the world economy figure things out. He didn't care much for the business of politics, anyway. He only wanted to teach history.

Ed had yet to meet his nephew, Teddy, and his brother's wife, Elizabeth. He'd missed the wedding, and Teddy's birth, using his exams as an excuse. Still, he loved his brother, Charlie, and this time there was no acceptable reason for missing his niece's christening. While he'd never formally met Teddy, they'd established a regular correspondence. So much like me, he had thought when reading Teddy's letters, nothing about farming, solely about the world of ideas.

The train whistle sounded as the taxi's wheels struck the open metal tracks covering the bridge. Ed could see the wide expanse of the Grand River churning below with its armies of trees, their branches clenched together in tight balls of brilliant orange, red, and gold.

Ed had arrived home, a place he'd not been back to for a long time. Even with the economy being bad, the farm still looked prosperous. The house, especially, looked to be in good condition. He smiled, recalling Charlie's written description of his wife's capability to stretch a penny. "She's Scottish to the core."

He knocked on the door and poked his head inside, "Hello?" his voice volleyed. Stepping inside, he looked around and thought, the house still looks the same as when he was a boy, the furniture, the light fixtures his grandparents had brought over from Scotland. Walking farther into the house he felt as if he'd been swallowed by a spring bouquet, the parlor flooded with cheerful yellow daffodils, the hallways awash in dusty pink roses. Only the paint and wallpaper had been changed.

Ed walked into the kitchen and reached for an apple from a bowl on the kitchen table. Taking a bite, he decided to go up to his room and get some reading done. The more I can get done now, he thought, the more time I'll have getting acquainted with everyone.

He slowly climbed the stairs wondering where his brother's family had disappeared to—christening preparations, perhaps?

Ed entered his old room with a feeling of nostalgia until he saw all traces of his previous life there had been washed away, and in its place, a nursery, pink and soft, reconfigured by the presence of a little girl. Gone were Edward's books, sports pennants, and even the old blue beanie he'd worn all frosh week.

He walked back down the hall, and seeing his parent's bedroom door slightly ajar, he poked his head inside. There was a woman fast asleep on the bed with a little girl sitting awake beside her. Quietly, Ed tiptoed in.

The baby gurgled, her eyes wide open. Look at you, he thought, alert little creature with cerulean eyes and Charlie's bright red hair. He brought his finger to his lips, attempting to shush her, but the baby gurgled again. He twiddled his thumb in her face and she reached out to grab it. "Shh," he whispered. "I'm your Uncle Ed."

The woman stirred, bringing her hand up to the side of her face to brush away a stray lock of long, black hair. With a green and white gingham sundress twisted around her hips, and the mark of the bed sheets imprinted on one of her cheeks, she appeared to have stolen time from her day for a nap with the baby by her side.

When Ed saw her face, he stepped back, his eyes wide, his brain at first not understanding. Can it be?

"Hannibal?"

He remained silent, in shock, until, realising her fright, he lifted his hand. "I'm sorry. I didn't mean to scare you."

She propped herself up, bringing her arms, lightly tanned and slim, tightly around her waist. The dance. The school. The humiliation. It all came back, uncontrollably, her heart racing. She took the baby in her arms. "What are you doing here?"

"This is my parent's house."

Her eyes narrowed.

"Bessie, I'm Charlie's brother."

"What?"

"Haven't you seen pictures of me?"

"No, she said, startled. Charlie didn't keep memories lying around. After his parents passed, he removed most of the family photos, and she'd never asked to see them. "You weren't at our wedding? Teddy's christening? Who *are* you, really?" Her anger beginning to rise. "You ruined my life, you know, and now ..."

"Your life seems fine to me, and my name, Bessie, is Ed Barnes. Surely Charlie told you about me? I'm a PhD student in Toronto, remember? I told you at the dance."

Bessie looked away, her mind trying to process Edward standing before her. She knew Charlie had a younger brother, Ed, who'd left for university years ago, but she had never connected his Ed with her Edward. Why would she have? There must be thousands of Edwards roaming universities campuses.

"Bessie, I looked for you. I found out where you were staying and I went there. The landlady said you'd packed your things and returned home, but she wouldn't tell me where that was."

The baby had fallen asleep, her head resting in the nook of Bessie's shoulder. She caressed her hair. So, he had come round to find her, she mused. And he still looked the same, better maybe. Ed—such a normal name. Hannibal was a better one.

"Mother!" a boy called, running up the stairs. "Is he here?"

"Yes," Bessie replied as Teddy appeared in the doorway.

"I'm Teddy," the boy said, thrusting his hand out to grab his uncle's, who thought while shaking the boy's hand, I've never known a boy with such a firm, honest grip. "And I'm your Uncle Ed."

"Teddy, why don't you show your uncle where he's sleeping."

"She's a pretty girl, Bessie," Ed said. "What's her name?"

"Elizabeth, but we call her Bette for short."

As Ed nodded, Bessie discreetly scanned the man she had once known. That's where Teddy gets his coloring, she thought, and his build, too. Stunned by the impromptu of the encounter, she wondered again, why hadn't Charlie told her about Ed? Why hadn't she ever asked? But she knew one thing, Ed wouldn't be staying for very long. He just couldn't.

Teddy left his bedroom to let Ed unpack, and Ed sat on the extra bed. What a horrible piece of luck. He'd never forgotten her, no matter how many girls he had asked out. Her eyes. The way she felt in his arms. Nobody else had come close. He'd written the head of the Normal School trying to find out where she was teaching, but there was no Elizabeth Hunter listed. She wasn't registered as teaching anywhere in the province. He'd even bought a road map, borrowed a car, and driven around the London area asking in every small town and school he came upon if they knew her. It occupied every weekend of his life for at least a year, but he never found Elizabeth Hunter. She had vanished.

The family sat around the kitchen table eating scalloped potatoes and ham. Charlie had insisted on something special in honor of his brother coming all the way from Toronto.

"How are people in the city doing?" Charlie asked.

"Bad," Ed said. "Out here you can grow your own food to eat, and you've got a cow for milk and wood for heat. The city people don't have that. There's a lot of begging."

"I wouldn't beg no matter how hungry I was," Bessie said, ladling another spoonful of potatoes onto Charlie's plate. "I think the Prime Minister is right. I think they're looking for a handout. Lord knows we can't afford to be giving money away in times like these. We need somebody keeping an eye on the purse strings of the country."

"I imagine you wouldn't know what you'd do unless you were in the situation," Charlie replied.

He'd never gone hungry before, but Charlie was starting to feel the pinch in his wallet, and his gut said it was going to get a whole lot worse before it got any better. He wasn't even sure how they were going to afford seed for next year. "How are things at school?" he asked his brother.

"Times are hard there, too."

Bessie looked up from her place across the table. "We don't have any money."

"Bessie," Charlie said, surprised that his wife would be so direct.

"If he needs money, we just don't have it," Bessie replied, "I have to tell the truth."

Teddy looked at his father, wondering why his mother was being so mean to Uncle Ed?

"I don't mean to be rude, but this farm can only generate enough income for one family, and since you made your choice years ago to move to the city and take on all that studying, you can hardly go changing your mind now," Bessie said. "More ham?" she asked.

"Please, I don't need your money. I've got my scholarships to see me through, and when I graduate, I'll get a job."

"This place is half Ed's, too," Charlie said.

"He hasn't farmed it. He hasn't wanted to have anything to do with it and he can't come back when things are bad wanting his share," Bessie said.

"I was just explaining the way things are to Teddy," Ed said, slowly chewing the ham. "I don't have anything to worry about. By the time I'm finished school, this whole mess will be over."

"That's what people say, but then they find their back up against the wall, cap in hand," Bessie said, cutting herself a piece of meat. "I just think that it's important we discuss these things. We can't sweep them under the rug."

"Bessie," Charlie repeated, a whole lot louder this time.

Teddy looked around the table. "What's going on?"

"Don't worry about it," Ed replied. "Your mother is right, she should be thinking of her family."

"But you're family, too, Uncle Ed," Teddy said.

"Theodore," Bessie said. "You don't speak until you're spoken to."

Teddy hung his head. "I'm sorry, Mother."

"Have you met any nice young ladies?" Charlie asked, trying to bring a bit of levity back into the conversation.

Ed shook his head. "Too busy with school. And as Bessie so rightly pointed out, I don't have the money for courting."

A silence fell over the table, and Bessie thought about Ed's revelation there'd been no women in his life. How long had that been true for?

Charlie nodded to his brother, and the two men got up from the table and walked out to do the evening chores.

"I apologize for Bessie," Charlie said, stepping inside the barn.

"Nothing to worry about," Ed replied, wondering if he should talk to Charlie about knowing his wife—but how to start that? Bessie clearly hated him, and any chance he'd had with her was gone forever. He looked around—the old paddock still looked the same. "I'm sorry for not making the wedding," he said.

"You were busy," Charlie replied.

Ed nodded, wandering over to the pen that housed a large male boar. What if he had attended the wedding? Could he have stopped it? Charlie and Bessie had been married now for nine years—she hadn't exactly been waiting around for him as he had for her. Besides, she seemed so changed from the happy, spirited young woman he'd danced with. Life on the farm had hardened her. Was it his fault? But the past was dead, and as far as he was concerned, he'd left the farm behind the day he had stepped on the train for school. Charlie and Bessie could have it all, he had another destiny to fulfill.

"How's school?" Charlie asked.

Ed started to explain his thesis but could see that Charlie wasn't listening. His older brother didn't really care about anything other than the price of seed, weather reports, cattle futures, or Massey Ferguson tractors. Ed's fascination with antiquity, in particular Hannibal, meant nothing to Charlie. They loved one another in an abstract dutiful fashion, the way that brothers should, but their passions ran in opposite directions, except, apparently, for Bessie.

The next morning, the family sat in the front row of the United Church in downtown Galt. The church bells rang as the congregation filed into the nave, each member quickly taking their seats. The ladies, all wearing hats, veils, and white gloves, made certain their children sat up straight in the oak pews, and minded their manners. Teddy looked over the church program while Charlie nodded to a friend in the row behind them. Bessie, trying to look nonchalant, looked over the congregates, curious as to who was in attendance and who wasn't.

The church bells ceased to ring, signaling the service was about to begin. Ed looked over at his niece dressed in a fussy baptismal gown Bessie's grandmother had brought with her from Scotland. Such an angelic little baby, he thought. Bessie had bleached the gown, starching it until the dress had become a brilliant white.

Ed felt warm, desperately wanting to loosen his tie, yet, he didn't dare so much as budge in God's house. Every time he walked into a church, all of Ed's grand ideas about Nietzsche, and God being dead, dropped away like deserting troops in the face of an invincible enemy. Inside a church, he felt naked and vulnerable, much as he had as a child sitting through Bible classes and listening to his grandmother assail him with threats from the scriptures. Ed dropped his head—an attempt to avoid being noticed as much as pray.

"All rise," the organist said. The congregation rose on mass, holding their hymns high. The familiar strains of "Guide Me Oh, Thy Great Jehovah" began. Ed started to sing as the choir appeared from the back of the nave, walking up the center aisle, followed by the minister dressed in his long black vestments.

Teddy listened closely to the words he was singing. "Guide me, O, thou great Jehovah/Pilgrim through this barren land;/I am weak, but thou art mighty, Hold me with thy powerful hand;/Bread of heaven, bread of heaven, Feed me till I want no more; Feed me till I want no more." What did the words mean? the boy asked himself. People in the world were starving, Teddy had learned that in school. And now the trouble had reached Canada. As much as it was challenging to understand what the words meant, Teddy knew he was never to doubt God. He was to sing to His glory with all of his soul, all hesitation cast aside. Bessie, upon hearing Teddy's voice, swelled with pride, and she remembered how these same hymns had formed the core of her parents' lives, as they had now, hers. With Bette in her arms, she felt content. They couldn't have chosen a finer hymn to welcome her daughter into the family of Christ.

Bessie stood in the far corner of the church basement, holding court with the baby still in her arms, the other ladies admiring what a fine child she was. The usual array of cookies was more meager than usual, due to the high cost of sugar. A large cluster of children lay waste to the sweets in minutes. Bessie, while exhorting the joys of raising children, kept her eyes on Ed, until she saw two of the county's chief busybodies were about to descend upon her.

Mrs. Little and Mrs. Moffatt.

As president of the Women's Institute, Mrs. Little held significant sway, a bad word from her could seriously impair a woman's standing in the community. Mrs. Little's son, Rusty, sulked around the punch bowl, drinking more than his fair share as Mrs. Moffatt, Mrs. Little's constant companion, stood nervously beside her.

"You are the brother are you not?" Mrs. Little asked.

An unlikely name for a woman so large, both in girth and bearing, Ed thought. Carefully, he set down his cup of coffee, extending his hand to Mrs. Little. "Yes, I am, Edward Barnes. And you are?" he asked, feigning ignorance.

Mrs. Little, annoyed at having to introduce herself, turned away and looked at Mrs. Moffatt thrusting a gloved hand toward Ed. "And I'm Mrs. Moffatt," she added, "Maybe you remember me?"

"Of course, I do," Ed replied. "You're our neighbors. And I know how much Bessie appreciates the occasional use of your phone."

Mrs. Moffatt nodded with a smile. Ed thought she was pretty, but strain had scratched early crow's feet around the corners of her eyes. "How's your husband?" he asked.

"Yes, where is Mr. Moffatt?" Mrs. Little asked.

Mrs. Moffatt, put on the spot, yet again, by an absentee husband who refused to attend church regularly, quickly changed the topic. "You're the historian, aren't you?" she asked.

Ed noticed Bessie glancing their way. He knew his sister-in-law had aspirations to be named secretary of the Women's Institute—Teddy had told him his mother had been stumping to gather support for a nomination, that she'd plied the ladies with her homemade cake and pies, flattered their children, admired their sewing, and complimented the look of their husband's fields. Teddy claimed his mother felt confident in the nomination, as long as nothing went wrong.

"Yes, I am," Ed replied, while checking to see if Bessie was still looking. He looked back at the woman. "Are you interested in history?"

"My yes," Mrs. Moffatt replied.

"I should say so," Mrs. Little added. "If you don't know where you came from, how can you know where you're going?"

"Most wise," Mrs. Moffatt said.

"Indeed," Mrs. Little replied, turning to Ed. Her neck was wide and fleshy. "You should speak to the Institute."

"I would enjoy that," Ed replied, as he turned to look at Bessie who had joined them. "The ladies want me to come and speak at your club," he said.

"Oh really," Bessie replied. "That's unfortunate, because Ed is returning to school later today."

"Maybe I should stay another week," Ed said, "with this opportunity to speak to these young, hungry minds."

"We wouldn't want you to miss any of your coursework, Ed," Bessie added.

"What are they teaching these days?" Mrs. Moffatt asked.

"Communism," Ed replied.

Bessie blanched. The other women looked alarmed.

"Surely they're not encouraging that kind of thing," Mrs. Little said.

"It's sweeping Europe," Ed replied. "Only a question of time before it sets down here."

"There's talk of riots," Mrs. Moffatt said. "The Prime Minister is taking very firm action. I read it in The Daily Record."

"As he should. I really don't want that kind of political talk around the family," Bessie said. "Where's Charlie?" She scanned the room, and seeing Charlie chatting with a group of farmers, she signaled to him it was time to get going. He nodded.

"Very nice to see you Mrs. Moffatt, Mrs. Little, but I really should get the baby home for her nap. If you don't keep them on a firm schedule, there's no abiding by them."

"I'm sure that you know what's best for your children," Mrs. Little replied, cocking an eyebrow at Bette, as the two women stepped away.

"Let me carry the baby, I know she's heavy," Ed said, extending his arms. "It'll give you a break."

Bessie, with tired eyes, handed over the baby. "Why did you feel the need to mention that?"

"Mention what?" Ed asked.

"You know perfectly well what I'm talking about," Bessie said, quietly repeating, "Communism."

"People are interested, Bessie, and just because you don't like it, doesn't mean it's going away."

"I won't have talks about communism in my house," Bessie said as she walked toward Charlie.

"Hey Uncle Ed, do you want to go down to the stream?" Teddy asked.

"We're going to drop your uncle off at the station after lunch," Bessie replied.

"But Mother, his train isn't until later."

"We don't want him missing it. Your uncle is a very important man, and he has important things to do in the city."

"Your mother is right," Charlie replied. "We'll all have a big lunch and then see your uncle off." He put a hand to his son's head. "Your Uncle Ed will be back before you know it."

FOUR

The League for Social Reconstruction 1934

B ack home in Toronto, Ed sat on a bench under an enormous bronze
statue of Canada's first Prime Minister, Sir John A MacDonald, and
he pulled a letter from his pocket and began to read:

September 27th 1934

Dear Dr. Barnes,

*I regret to inform you that while you have successfully completed all the
required coursework, and defended your doctoral thesis with the highest
distinction in your class, the university is unable to provide you with
employment due to the current national financial situation. Should
things improve, I would be very happy to discuss a possible tenure track
position with you at a future date. I wish you every success.*

Sincerely,
Dr. Ian Lancashire,
Dean of History

Ed looked away. What am I to do? There wasn't a single university in all North America that was hiring, and most of them were letting people go.

The pressure was growing, the last of his scholarship money had run out two months before, and while most of his friends had already given up and returned home, Ed had stayed. He'd been living hand-to-mouth in a house with no heat, and little privacy, determined to better his thesis, believing that if it was good enough, he would be able to get a job. But there was nothing now: no job, no money, no options.

Rising to his feet, hands in his pockets, he stared up at Sir John A. "You, Sir John A.," he said loudly, "had a place to go, strode into history, and made a difference. What about me?"

Walking along the stone path heading to the boarding house, he realized he could no longer afford to call it home. He halted his walk as the family farm came to mind—but then, he'd have to deal with Bessie's tart observations about fancy university learning, and no job to show for it all. Ed couldn't bear the thought of groveling before his brother's beautiful wife. However he'd felt about her in the past clearly wasn't reciprocated, and most likely, had never been. In any case, he reminded himself, she's married—to my brother.

Walking, he recalled the times at the farm he'd spent with the children. His presence had been valued, the children, he felt, truly loved him. And with no money to pay for hired hands, Charlie could use his help. Perhaps, he thought, the farm wasn't the worst solution, at least for a while, until the economy improved.

A voice called Ed's name, making him turn. It was Fen Hall, a fellow student who'd been pinning his hopes to the same lost dream Ed had. "Hey Fen," he called, heading toward his friend, and wondering when he'd become the kind of man who hoped a friend would fail so he'd have more of a chance himself. Is that what the Great Depression was teaching the world? Every man for himself?

"Good we ran into each other today," Fen said. "Let's go somewhere we can talk, there's something I think you'd like to hear."

A jungle of homeless people had taken root beside City Hall, next to several large iron vents from which city boilers pumped out heat. Ed and Fen walked through the chaos of canvas-made shacks. "Hey brother," an old man said from the shadows, black rings under his eyes, a bottle in his hand, asking for money.

"I'm sorry," Ed said, "I just don't have anything."

"Fine, fine, fine," the old man answered with a hoarse laugh. "Keep your spirits up, they're the only thing we've got."

They entered the Hippodrome, a smoky vaudeville house across the street from City Hall and the hobo jungle. "There's a group of men putting together a new league," Fen said. He dropped his voice. "Underhill's heading it up."

Ed felt his hair rise as the two friends took a seat at the back of the enormous theatre. Several clowns were putting on a show below them.

"Frank Underhill?" Ed asked. "I worshipped him. The best professor I ever had."

Fen nodded and quietly explained to Ed how Underhill and a small circle of socialist intellectuals were forming an anti-capitalist group called The League for Social Reconstruction to advocate for radical social and economic reforms in response to the Depression. "They want to turn things around."

Ed felt hope, finally, in something.

When Charlie had read Bessie his brother's letter, they'd had their first real argument. A fight, so severe, they had to go to the back of the paddock so Teddy and Bette wouldn't hear them. Bessie didn't want Ed there, under any circumstances. "He's a socialist that will bring ruin to this family," she had said. "And a bad influence on the children." Charlie had countered by pointing out both of their children loved their uncle, and insisting he also needed the help.

"I didn't give up my career as a teacher to take care of a bum," she said.

Charlie rammed a pitchfork into a bale of hay. "My brother is not a bum, Bessie. Ed is a well-educated man, a respected man who has fallen on hard times through no fault of his own."

"But—"

"No buts Bessie. Not one. And you never taught a day in your life. You married me nearly the day you got out of school, so don't you be holding that over my head."

Waiting for the train, Bessie carefully examined the state of her hair in the rear-view mirror, while watching Bette bounce around the back seat, excited to see her uncle. She sighed when the train's whistle sounded. Getting out of the car, she opened the back door to grab Bette by the hand. "You be certain to curtsy when you see your uncle," Bessie told her, smoothing down the girl's cowlick.

"Uncle Ed! Uncle Ed!" Bette cried, pulling away to dance around the platform. The girl's red hair was just as unruly as her temperament, Bessie thought, scanning the crowd. She didn't want any of the neighbour ladies seeing her daughter with messy hair. "Hold still," Bessie ordered, seizing her daughter's hand to fix her hair.

"There he is!" Bette called, pulling free of Bessie's hand once more and running across the platform toward her uncle.

"Whoa there!" Ed said, swooping the girl up and into his arms, "you're nearly as big as your mother," he added, kissing the girl on the cheek.

She giggled and threw her arms around his neck.

"You're going to sleep in Teddy's room," Bette said, "he's got it all fixed up."

Bessie, embarrassed at the public display of affection, quickly walked across the wooden planks, through the throng of passengers. "Bette," she exclaimed, "get down."

"That's okay, Bessie," Ed said, leaning down and giving Bessie a quick peck on the cheek, "it's nice to get a kiss now and then."

Bessie flushed scarlet. "You look well."

"Not as good as you two," Ed said, slinging the prattling girl around on his hip.

Bessie had lied. Ed didn't look well at all. He was rake thin and pale, and for all his fancy university learning, he had the same hunted look like all the wandering men.

A feeling of uncertainty passed over her, and she wondered how long Ed would need their help. She didn't want to help him. She wanted him to leave. And how could he have kissed her like that? She caught sight of Mrs. Little a second too late.

The older woman had seen the kiss, frowned at how improper it was, and leaned in to whisper something to Mrs. Moffatt. Bessie's pulse quickened. She knew Mrs. Moffatt would be on the party line that night telling everyone in the township about what they'd seen at the station. Seeing the two women negotiate the crowd, moving toward Ed, she held her breath.

"Hello, Mrs. Barnes," Mrs. Little said, adjusting her hat while giving Ed a thorough look over.

"Mrs. Little, Mrs. Moffatt," Bessie replied, nodding her head as graciously as she could to both women. This was a terrible state of affairs. Bessie was now the Secretary of the Women's Institute, and gossip about inappropriate behavior would hinder her reputation.

"Hello ladies," Ed said, setting Bette on the ground, and extending his hand. "Don't you both look lovely?"

"Pick me up, Uncle Ed," Bette exclaimed, "I want to go for a ride."

"Elizabeth!" Bessie said, seizing her daughter firmly by the shoulder.

Thinking it might help his cause, Ed suggested to Bessie they drive the ladies home so he might enjoy more of their company.

"It's good to have a well-educated young man back in the territory," Mrs. Little said.

"We once talked about my giving a speech at the Institute," Ed said, "would you still be interested?"

"I think you'll be much too busy with work," Bessie replied.

"Nonsense, there's always time for talk, isn't there ladies? Especially in such provocative times."

"Indeed," Mrs. Little replied.

"I should think that would be lovely," Mrs. Moffatt added.

"Shall we?" Ed said, offering his arms to the ladies.

The moment the clock struck three, and the school bell rang, Teddy grabbed his books, threw his jacket on and tore out the door with Bill in pursuit. "Where's the fire?" Bill called, following his friend as the two boys ran across the field.

"Uncle Ed's home," Teddy replied, kicking it up another notch.

Bill struggled to keep up. Generally, he was faster because Teddy didn't see the point in running, but nothing could slow Teddy Barnes down that day. The boys burst through the screen door, having seen the car parked in the yard.

"Did you bring the radio?" Teddy asked, moving his chair up close to Uncle Ed's.

"The whole set up," Ed said, tapping his trunk. "Stand up and let me get a look at you."

Teddy complied.

"You've grown over a foot since I last saw you."

Teddy shrugged and fell back into his chair. He'd turned thirteen that spring, and was already nearly five foot seven.

"Can you really talk to England?" Bill asked, crunching on an apple.

"Sure," Teddy proudly added, "even Timbuktu."

"Don't talk foolishness, Theodore," Bessie said, expertly rolling out a ball of dough with just enough crust for the top of a pie.

Teddy thought, his mother never called him Theodore, unless he was in trouble. What had he done?

Uncle Ed squeezed Teddy's shoulder. "Sure, I've talked to Timbuktu, and the Taj Mahal," he said, grabbing a piece of fruit from the bowl.

"Wow!" Bill gasped.

Bessie smothered the bed of sweet apples with a pastry. "That is a lie, and Ed Barnes, as long as you're living under my roof, there will be no high talk."

Teddy lowered his eyes to the floor, his mother was frightening when she raised her voice, but terrifying when she went quiet like this. What was it? he wondered. Why was she always so mean to Uncle Ed?

"Do we understand each other?" Bessie added.

Ed was about to retort when he looked down at his nephew. The boy's knuckles were white. "Always, Bessie," Ed said, "after all, this is your house." He turned to the boys, asked them to help him unpack, and together they walked up the stairs.

"You sleep here and I sleep there," Teddy said, pointing to the bed under the window.

"Normally you'd get your own room, but now it's the girl's room," Bill replied, distastefully speaking the word, 'girl'.

Bette strutted in, swinging her Raggedy Ann doll by the arm. "You can sleep in my room Uncle Ed," she said.

"That wouldn't be right," Teddy replied.

"Where's the radio?" Bill asked, as Bette started jumping up and down on the bed.

"Maybe later," Ed said. While he enjoyed the idea of Bessie being down in the kitchen, slamming pots and pans and getting as hot as her apple pie, he knew he couldn't risk Bessie's anger. Charlie had offered him a roof, and he knew if Bessie insisted, he'd be asked to leave the farm, with nowhere else to go.

Amidst protestations from Bette and the boys, he retrieved an old pair of overalls from the back of the closet, got dressed, and headed for the barn. There might be no pleasing Bessie, but Ed was determined to do his best.

Charlie read the newspaper while Bessie's gaze was lost to the sky looking at the stars. He talked about Europe, and a fellow by the name of Adolph Hitler, the Chancellor of Germany. "He's making trouble for the people in Czechoslovakia, and the French, and the Dutch," he told her.

Bessie didn't care about Europe. There was enough going on here without fretting about what was happening across the ocean. What occupied her thoughts had to do with Ed and Teddy. What were the two of them up to?

Charlie folded the paper, set it on the bedside table, and flicked off the light. A long moonbeam stretched across the bed as Bessie swung her leg over his thigh, signaling a gesture he had initiated years before. He felt Bessie's soft, dark hair cover his face, and he felt her lips on his as he wrapped his arms around her, pulling her to him.

FIVE

The Women's Institute

Winter arrived in North Dumfries Township early that year, but Charlie, feeling the cold in his bones, had sown twenty-five acres of winter wheat, beating the first big blow by a scant two days.

Stamping their feet to dislodge the snow on the way into the paddock, Ed congratulated his big brother on his foresight. Since Ed's return, the two brothers had stepped back into their rhythm from childhood: Charlie, the boss, Ed the backup.

Ed talked about history and anything else that came to mind, while Charlie pretended to listen. After several months of small talk, Ed began to run out of things to say, figuring out, too, that Charlie had only been humoring him.

"You ever think about getting a wife?" Charlie asked.

Ed leaning on his pitchfork, shook his head. "I'm still hoping to get a job teaching. And I don't think most of the girls around here would be too keen on a professor. Besides, even if I farm, I don't have a place of my own."

Charlie broke up another bale of hay and thought it true. They only had one farm and it didn't generate enough income for two families.

Tradition dictated the oldest son inherited the home place, and since Ed had always been determined to go to school, that had never been a problem. Yet sometimes Charlie wondered about the inequity. Was it really fair Ed didn't have a place to call his own? He also worried about his younger brother's spirits. When he'd first arrived, Ed had gone to church, and attended the odd dance. But most of his old friends had now married and were busy with their farms and families. Ed still went to church, but other than Teddy, with whom he spent hours in his room talking to, he pretty much kept to himself.

Almost every night, Bessie would ask Charlie, "What do you think they're doing in there?"

Charlie would reply, "I imagine Ed's describing some ancient this or that."

Propped up in bed, reading the Bible—the minister had recommended the Book of Job for inspiration, he looked at his wife.

"It's just not healthy," Bessie said, walking toward the bed, sitting down to brush out her hair.

"Let me," and setting down his Bible, Charlie took the brush from his wife's hand.

"Don't you think Teddy's spending too much time with Ed and not as much with Bill, anymore?" Yet, Ed's bookish ways were encouraging her son's natural academic inclinations, something she enjoyed seeing. But still, she worried. "The teacher said he's the best student she's ever had, and everyone in the community knows he's the brightest boy at school. If you ever got lost in a snowstorm, you could always find your way by the lamplight burning late in that boy's window."

"Good marks aren't going to mean much when he's trying to barter for seed," Charlie replied. While Charlie thought it was wonderful Teddy was spending time with his uncle, he did wonder, when was his son going to start taking more of an interest in the farm? After all, it would be his one day, but the boy either had his nose in a book, was listening to the radio with Ed, or was out in the coop playing with his rooster, Hannibal. Teddy had raised him from a little chick and hoped to show him at the Royal Winter Fair. Morning and night he'd go into the coop to visit Hannibal, and hand feed him specially grown corn.

Teddy, obsessing over Hannibal's appearance, talked to the veterinarian and every chicken farmer who'd listen. As a result, Teddy was seen as a devoted junior farmer with a brilliant career ahead of him. In his mind, however, nothing was farther from the truth. Raising Hannibal had provided a legitimate break from all the boring work, giving him something interesting to focus on.

"Let's go listen to the radio," Bill said, perched up on a bale watching Teddy try to coax Hannibal to hop up onto his finger. "He's never going to do it," Bill added, reaching for a long piece of straw.

"Sure, he will," Teddy said. "I just have to be patient."

Bill groaned, flipping onto his back, "You'll make a fine farmer, Mr. Barnes. Farmers are nothing if not patient."

"I'm not going to be a farmer, Bill. Ever." He didn't want to offend his best friend, but it was time he told the truth. He knew that, to Bill, being a farmer was the best thing in the world. "I want to go to school and be a historian like Uncle Ed."

"But he had to come home because he couldn't get a job," Bill said, spitting out the straw. "My dad says that if you've got land, you've got a home."

Teddy scanned the chicken coop looking at the egg crates destined to Mooney. He looked at the pitchfork, the bags of chicken feed, and the troughs that always needed to be filled. Not for him, he thought. And he remembered the winter when the pump froze and he had to carry bucket after bucket of water from the house. The yard had been like an ice rink, and on the second trip, he slipped, landing on his tailbone. He had howled from the pain, and it had taken three weeks to heal. He hated being locked up in the house during the winter months while his mother played the piano, and his father read the paper, worrying about the price of wheat. You could barely get to church before you had to turn around and hurry back to milk the cows. It all just seemed too hard of a way to live, but he also knew they were fortunate, as they owned their land and could made a living from it.

"Who'll pay your way?" Bill asked.

"I'll get scholarships," Teddy replied.

"But there are no jobs even if you do get educated."

"The Depression can't last forever," Teddy said, "and I'll be ready when it ends."

"Don't you know how lucky you are?" Bill asked. "You've got everything you want right here."

Teddy didn't respond.

Seeing he wasn't going to change his friend's mind, Bill swung off the bale and hit the floor with a bang. "Let's go see who we can get on the radio."

The boys walked out the door knowing all had been said, and that their lives ahead of them would be met by different avenues, and different purposes.

Standing on her tiptoes, wearing her good Sunday dress, Bessie tried to fetch a crock pot located at the back of the top shelf. The family had planned on taking a drive after church, and she wanted to start slow cooking a stew while they were out. Not wanting to take the time to retrieve the step stool, Bessie kicked off her pumps and opened the bottom drawer to use as a boost and climbed onto the counter. It was nice to get a different perspective on her kitchen, and other than a bit of dust on top of the clock, she found herself quite satisfied. Her world looked pleasant from up there, she thought, everything was as it should be.

"How's the view?" Ed asked.

Bessie, clutching the crock pot, looked back.

He thought she looked beautiful, although it was the last place he ever expected to find her. This, he recalled, was the impetuous girl he'd met at the Normal School dance.

"Honestly, Ed, the way you sneak around," Bessie said, wondering how she was going to get down without showing her underthings. Why didn't he just leave? "Tell Charlie I'll be out in a minute," she said.

Ed remained in the doorway. "How are you going to get down? Jump?"

"No, Ed, I'm not going to jump." There was no way down that would maintain her dignity, that much she knew. Moreover, she couldn't afford to get a run in her hose, as she wouldn't be able to get a new pair for a long time.

"Levitate?" Ed asked, leaning against the wall, thoroughly enjoying himself. Bessie held out her hand, there was no other choice. "Please help me," she mumbled. It wouldn't do to be late for church.

The old Dodge crested Cedar Creek Road and plunged down the other side churning its way through the snow. Slowly, they passed through a forest of red cedars, and although nobody spoke, the car was alive with thought. Bessie had enjoyed the service, the minister's talk about their duty to the Lord, and about the importance of living a life of service and humility. If only she could get Mrs. Little to listen to her plan at the Women's Institute, but the only plans Mrs. Little was ever interested in, were her own. Still immersed in the minister's words of guidance, Bessie noticed Ed looking out the window in the back seat. What is he thinking of, she wondered. He looks gone—but where to?

The minister's call for a life of modesty and discretion had angered Ed. How much more modest could he be? When was the Lord going to help? he thought. He'd been there for six months, and nothing had changed—just work and food, food and work, and nothing to break up the monotony except sleep. The letters he'd been getting from Fen contained all sorts of details about the League for Social Reconstruction, but he couldn't help advancing the cause, and it made him feel stuck. "Say Charlie, did you read about the work camps?" Ed asked, breaking the silence.

"Can't say I did," Charlie said. He didn't want to talk about politics, preferring to focus on things within his sphere of influence.

"What are work camps?" Bette asked.

"If you're a man and you don't have work or a place to stay, they make you go there and lock you up," Ed replied.

"That's a bit simplistic Ed," Bessie said. "They're called Relief Camps, and they offer men with no home, a roof over their heads, and food."

"And you're forced to do slave labor all day for twenty cents," Ed replied, "building roads to nowhere. Dig holes and fill them up."

"Slaves?" Teddy asked.

"Slaves," Ed replied, "and any man without a job or a place to stay is being forced to live in them."

"Why doesn't the government help the people?" Teddy asked, knowing Mother and Dad paid their taxes, and understanding tax money had to go somewhere.

"Your uncle is all worked up because he knows that if he couldn't stay with us, he'd be living there," Bessie replied.

Charlie dropped a hand from the wheel and squeezed Bessie's wrist in warning.

"Are you a slave, Uncle Ed?" Bette asked, sitting up.

"According to your mother I am."

"Honestly, Ed, you take things so seriously. Times are hard and we all have to pull together. In fact, I was wondering if you could come to the Women's Institute and give a presentation about what's happening in Saskatchewan. The women are very impressed by your degree. Would you consider it?" Appealing to Ed's vanity was bound to work.

"I guess so," Ed replied. "Preparing a lecture might be interesting." Anything to take his mind off his prospects, which were nil.

The Women's Institute was born from the great success of the Farm Institute. After they'd settled the land, farmers needed a place to ask questions and share ideas about what they were learning, such as how to get rid of the blight and new tilling techniques. Of course, the men needed a place to escape their wives, somewhere they could have a smoke and swap stories about the efficacy of the latest piece of farming equipment. The Institute was a lifeline for the farmers, keeping them connected, and allowing knowledge to be shared.

The Women's Institute was founded on similar principles, only, rather than sharing knowledge about farming, the women were committed to improving the care and feeding of children. Unsurprisingly, the mission was wrought with the need to gossip—who was seen where, in whose company, and now with the Depression running full tilt, who was likely to end up in the poorhouse.

Bessie remembered when the Shepherd family had lost their home. The bank had auctioned off all their belongings, forcing them to move into the poorhouse located in Galt, a big home on top of a hill overlooking the Grand River.

The Galt poorhouse wasn't much better than a prison.

Bessie became pensive. There was nothing worse than the stain of the poorhouse except for being accused of adultery—just the hint of impropriety was enough to damage a woman's reputation for the rest of her life. Her husband would leave her, and if he didn't, he'd have the right, if not the obligation, to beat her. A wanted woman, she would never be again, as no other man would have her. The Women's Institute existed to ensure women didn't stray, and that if they did, the Institute would be there to judge them, reliably so.

Arithmetic equations filled the blackboard behind Mrs. Little as she brought the oak gavel down with a bang. The schoolhouse served as their headquarters and the room was filled with ladies decked out in the finest garb they could afford. Scarves cleverly covered spots where fabric was wearing thin, and weary hats were reborn with a new sash or a splash of costume jewelry.

That night, winter boots neatly lined up in the cloakroom by the door, the women quickly took to their seats. Ed walked in, hat in hand, and after nodding hello to Mrs. Little and Mrs. Moffatt, he took a seat beside Bessie.

Removing her pad and pen from her purse, Bessie prepared to take the minutes of the meeting. Two urgent matters of business needed to be attended. The first, an unresolved motion from the last meeting: Should the Women's Institute start raising money to offer children's public speaking contests? There was a great clamor at this notion. "Children should be seen and not heard," one of the ladies stated. Bessie silently agreed as she jotted it down. She had Teddy nicely in hand and certainly wouldn't endorse him getting involved in any of that kind of foolishness. And Bette? If that child got any sassier there wouldn't be any living with her. No, Bessie did not approve of public speaking contests.

Votes were cast, and it was deemed imprudent to support this venture.

The second motion was Bessie's. Nervously, she rose—with much at stake. "I'd like to propose we initiate a drive to collect food and clothing for the people out in Saskatchewan."

"Surely we should be focusing on matters closer to home," Mrs. Little replied, staring at the clock on the wall, "we have our own troubles."

"That's true, but isn't it our duty as God fearing citizens to love one another?" Bessie asked.

A wave of approval passed through the room. While the Depression had hit them hard, most of them still had a roof over their heads and could grow their own food. It wasn't the same for the people of Saskatchewan.

"I'm certain, Mrs. Little is well aware of the gravity of the situation, but I thought that for the elucidation of the rest of us, I'd bring my brother-in-law in to explain the scheme," Bessie said, "if the idea appeals."

The ladies clapped and Ed rose. Approaching the blackboard to wipe the slate clean of multiplication tables, he began an in-depth explanation of what was transpiring in the prairies. "All their fertile topsoil has been blown away by the relentless winds that haven't let up for years. The livestock has either starved or been slaughtered for food. Nothing grows from the land, except for Russian Thistle, a wretched weed the women boil to feed their families because there's nothing else to eat. The women sweep and dust, yet daily their houses are carpeted in thick layers of dust blowing in through exposed nooks or crannies in the walls. Children share a single set of clothes or wear feed sacks with arm and neck holes cut out of them. Cars and tractors sit idle because there isn't a penny for gas. Entire farms have been abandoned, furniture still in the houses, families having fled to live with relatives in other parts of the country. And yet, for many, there is nowhere else to go. In short, thousands are dying in Canada's heartland. And that's where my sister-in-law's plan comes in," Ed said. "What she's proposing is to gather as much food and clothing as we can spare and send them out to Saskatchewan in a railway car."

"And how will we manage that?" Mrs. Little asked.

"Mr. Wilton Gillespie says he'll donate the car," Bessie said, jumping up, unable to contain herself.

"Mrs. Barnes!" Mrs. Little barked, bringing her gavel down with a bang.

Bessie dropped back into her seat.

"Did you really talk to Mr. Gillespie?" Mrs. Moffatt asked in a whisper.

Bessie nodded. Wilton Gillespie, the wealthiest cattleman in the province, had a wide reputation that spread across the country, and regularly purchased cattle from western ranchers. Once a week, Gillespie cattle cars clattered through the county bound for the east. Bessie had written him a letter asking if he might consider letting the ladies use one of his railway cars to ferry the goods out west. Mr. Gillespie had written back immediately, assuring her transportation could be arranged. When Bessie had showed Charlie the letter, he could hardly believe it.

Looking at the roomful of women, Ed felt better than he had in ages. All eyes were upon him and they seemed keen to learn more. "Wouldn't it be something to see an end to all of this suffering?" he asked. The ladies nodded. "The current government has done nothing but line their own pockets, and they've done nothing for the poor."

Bessie shifted in her seat. The idea had been for Ed to sit down after he'd finished with his presentation on Saskatchewan. But there he was, writing something else on the blackboard. It read: "The League for Social Reconstruction."

What was that?

"There is a way for the country to get out of the mess we're in," Ed said. "What it's going to involve is a new vision, a vision rooted in the idea that a government is there for the people," he added.

"What kind of a vision?" Mrs. Little asked.

"A vision from England," Ed replied.

The ladies sat up. They were all devoted Monarchists.

"We need a new political party," Ed added.

"A third political party?" Mrs. Little asked.

Ed nodded. Bessie didn't like the turn the discussion was taking and began discreetly signaling for Ed to sit down. Instead, he rapped the blackboard with the chalk. "We need the League for Social Reconstruction, a party created by the people, for the people."

Mrs. Moffatt put up her hand.

"What kind of a league is that?" she asked.

"A socialist league," Ed replied, "run on a purely democratic platform."

The ladies burst into an explosion of chatter that sounded not unlike chickens suspecting a fox in the henhouse.

Mrs. Little's gavel came down three times in short succession.

"Order," Mrs. Little said, "order!"

Nobody was listening.

"ORDER!" she finally bellowed, quieting the room. "You may sit down, Mr. Barnes."

"But you haven't even heard about it yet," Ed said, still standing by the blackboard.

"We most certainly don't need to hear talk like that," Mrs. Little replied. "Take your seat."

Setting the chalk back in the tray, Ed reluctantly returned to his seat. Mrs. Moffatt, watching him, couldn't help but feel sorry for Ed, and even worse for her neighbor. Bessie Barnes was shaking, and rightly so. Talk about socialism would spread like grassfire, and by the end of the week, folks would be saying the Barnes family was harboring a communist. Tentatively, she raised her hand. Irritated, Mrs. Little asked her what she wanted. "I would like to second Mrs. Barnes' motion that we initiate a drive to help the people in Saskatchewan."

Mrs. Little glared at her friend, as another woman raised her hand.

"While I don't agree with that young man's politics, I think it's a grand idea to help those in need. Why, the thought of starving children wearing feed bags, that's not right," the woman said, resuming her seat.

"All those in favor," Mrs. Little said, glowering at Bessie who looked down at the pad in her hand.

A sea of hands shot up.

"All those against," Mrs. Little added.

Very few voted no.

"The motion to send a railway car of food and clothing has passed. Let us break for tea," she replied, banging the gavel again.

The sky was so black, Ed couldn't see the horizon. He looked at Bessie for a moment. She was driving them home, not speaking—her silence deafening. Nervous, Ed didn't know what to do with his hands, feeling as though they didn't belong to his body. Quietly, he cleared his throat. Bessie's head quickly turned to look at him, but he kept his eyes on the road ahead.

"What?" she asked.

"Nothing," Ed replied.

For months, years really, ever since the beginning of the Depression, he'd been creeping across an ocean of ice, always careful as to where he stood, mindful of how he shifted his weight, and tonight there had been an audible crack. All Edward wanted was to share the thoughts living in his head, as much as in his heart, and explain to the ladies there might be a way for the country to free itself from hardship. Looking out the window, he thought, is there really a way out? Especially out here, in God's country? He sighed.

I'll tell Charlie when I get home, Bessie thought. Tell him his brother had to leave, that he'd endangered their position in the community, exposing them to ridicule and possibly even contempt. Her hands on the wheel, she glanced at Ed, and she found her mind suddenly changing.

She'd never seen him so low; so helpless. Usually quick with a smile, a joke or a teasing comeback, he had become something of a dark cloud. Moved by his pain, for reasons she was unable to grasp, she simply couldn't bear to worsen his lot. Ed's presentation on the Dust Bowl had been exceptional—until he'd veered into the communist nonsense. He was a fine orator and would have been a great teacher, but Ed would likely never have the chance. It wasn't fair, she thought, but few things were. Ed was a dreamer who lived in the past, and Bessie believed in staying firmly rooted in the present.

A light appeared in the distance. They were home. "Teddy's up," she said, pulling into the lane.

Fearfully, Ed turned, catching Bessie's eye, and he wondered what was going to happen? He knew she didn't want him there, and wondered if this was her chance to evict him?

Bessie looked at Ed. "You'd better get a good night's sleep, Mooney will be here first thing and the eggs still need to be crated." She turned off the engine, and for a moment they both just sat there.

"Thank you," Ed finally replied.

Her kindness astonished him, but the pity in her eyes made him sick. There was nothing beneath him any longer—nothing to shore him up, to cling to, no private wells of strength to tap from. He was utterly beholden to others, and his fate was as uncertain as any wandering man. He got out of the car, stepped into the house, and without saying goodnight to the rest of the family, quietly retired to bed.

SIX

The Bright Red Tam

For several months, Bessie and the ladies from the Institute canvassed the county, collecting enough food and goods to fill a railway car. Tonight, all of them were to meet at the Knox United Church in Ayr for a presentation.

When Bessie, Charlie, Ed, and the children arrived, they were fortunate to get a spot, as the church parking lot was jammed. Nearly everyone had a car these days, but with gas being out of most people's reach, a number of farmers had come in driving horses and buggies.

Walking to the church, Teddy patted a nag on the head while Bette tried to get a look at the horse's teeth. "They're so yellow!" she yelled, then forgetting the horse's teeth, asked her mother if she had brought the cookies.

"Yes," Bessie replied, glancing around for Mr. Gillespie. Where was he? The church was the one his family attended, and he'd paid for the building of the new Fellowship Hall with its mission to help the growing need of the congregation. He'll be here, she thought. Looking across the parking area, Bessie saw several ladies from the Institute hurrying by carrying bags of food followed by husbands holding boxes of clothing.

45

Everyone was to contribute to a potluck meal held in the new Fellowship Hall following the meeting. "This is what it's all about," Bessie whispered to herself, thrilled by the size of the crowd.

At her side, Teddy, restless, was curious to see what Mr. Gillespie looked like. He'd promised Bill to tell him about the evening, as Wilton Gillespie was Bill's model farmer. Did you know he can tell to the pound how much a steer weighs just by looking at it, Bill had once exclaimed.

Almost reaching the Hall's entrance, Charlie led his family to the porch and opened the church doors. Ed, the last to pass, paused, telling Charlie he'd be right in. He just needed a breath of air.

Teddy was perched in one of the front pews with a bag of provisions on his lap as his mother walked across the plush maroon carpet with Mrs. Little. Mrs. Little reached the pulpit first. The minister had just finished introducing "Mrs. Charles Barnes and Mrs. Archibald Little—the women from the Scott's Corner's Women's Institute, who had organized the drive," and everyone clapped, a couple of lads even stomping their work boots on the balcony floor. Teddy looked up. A ten-year-old boy with white hair hung over the railing, waving at him. Beside the boy, a stout man with a shock of even brighter hair that stood straight on end, yanked the boy into his seat. The man wore a grey suit with a bright red tie, his wife, a navy overcoat with a fur trimmed collar. The two of them were flanked by five children ranging from ten to twenty-two years of age, three girls and two boys, all dressed in the finest clothing Teddy had ever seen.

The oldest boy reminded Teddy of Uncle Ed. He was probably a university student, too, he thought. The oldest girl was tiny with flaming red hair partly covered by a bonnet. The youngest boy, the one who had waved, looked just like his father. A blonde girl was poking at his ribs, and right beside her, sat the prettiest girl Teddy had ever seen, with dark auburn hair, wearing a bright red coat with a matching tam. She looked directly at him. Teddy looked away, but couldn't help himself from sneaking another peek. The beautiful girl smiled at him.

Checking her posture, Bessie quickly surveyed the room. Charlie was sitting up straight with Bette tucked into his side. She looked at Teddy, following his gaze up to the balcony. Of all the people to be gaping at, Teddy was staring at the Gillespie family.

"Bessie, is there anything you'd like to add?" Mrs. Little asked.

Bessie looked at the President, and her mind went horribly blank. She had forgotten what to say, not remembering why she was up there. The only thing alive in her mind was the look on Teddy's face. She quickly regained her composure and thanked everyone again for their kind aid with the drive. Still, Charlie knew Bessie had faltered, and it made him wonder why.

Bessie caught up with her son in the Fellowship Hall after the speech, threading her way through the crowd, bowing politely and smiling, not stopping to chat. "Dear, go to your father," she told her daughter. "I need to speak with your brother." Once Bette left, Bessie took Teddy's cake, set it on the table, and grabbed her son by the arm.

"Where are we going?" he asked as he was marched out the door.

"We need to get a little air."

Bessie was moving so fast that on the way past the coatroom she nearly collided into the pretty girl dressed in the red coat. Getting bundled up and ready to leave, the pretty girl dropped her red tam in the commotion, and as Teddy bent down to pick it up, the man with the white hair introduced himself.

"Mrs. Barnes, I'm Wilton Gillespie," he said, extending his hand, "and I'm very impressed with the work you ladies have been doing with the drive."

Teddy couldn't believe it. He was finally meeting Wilton Gillespie, the success story of the farming world.

"I certainly know who you are, Mr. Gillespie," Bessie replied, "but you're the one who's making this all possible. You arranged for transportation."

Teddy stood there with his mouth open. Wilton Gillespie was congratulating his mother! Maybe *she* was improving her lot in life—she always said she would.

While Mr. Gillespie congratulated his mother, Teddy was introduced to Mrs. Gillespie and the children. Jack was the eldest and was starting medical school. Anne was going to train to be a nurse. Teddy thought the whole setup was grand. If Jack Gillespie didn't have to farm, maybe Teddy could escape too?

He said hello to Janet, the tall blonde girl, little Joe, the white-haired boy, and finally, the pretty girl in red, Laura.

She smiled, and Teddy felt his stomach clench. "Can I have my hat back?" she asked.

Teddy stared down at his hand, the tam crushed in his palm.

When Bessie finally brought Teddy outside, the poor boy looked as if he'd been star struck. He would have followed the Gillespie's around all night, had his mother let him. "They're fine people," she told him, as the two of them sat, freezing, in the front seat of the Dodge. "But they're better than us," Bessie added, determined her son understood the weight of her words. "If a person," she explained, "tried to exceed their place in the order of things, they would very likely to be punished for the sin of pride. Your father is a very good man, and he does well by us, Teddy," she said, "but the Gillespie's are a cut above, and there will always be people like that in life. People to look up to and people who guide us. Always remember, son, we're not their equal, and shouldn't aspire to be."

"Like the Prime Minister?" Teddy asked.

More like King George, she thought, as she placed her hand on her son's shoulder. The child was shaking from the chill, but it was crucial he understood his reality. "You mustn't stare at them or make a nuisance of yourself," she said, "if you're spoken to, reply, but don't presume to treat any of those children like you would others of your own age."

His mother, busy monologuing about how a great deal of sorrow could be avoided if everyone knew where they stood on the tree of life, didn't notice Teddy looking out the window, vaguely listening, and completely enchanted by the perfect family parading by. Watching the Gillespie's get into their car, he wondered: What was wrong with improving your lot in life? His mother had always said a person should do so, improve his or her lot, so why a limit to what one could achieve if a person was willing to work hard enough?

His mother suddenly leaned over, "I'm glad we had our conversation," she said, giving her son a very rare kiss on the cheek.

"What was that for?" Teddy asked, completely surprised, as his mother never kissed him.

"Because I'm very proud of you," Bessie said. "Now let's go in with the rest. You're cold."

Walking through the snow back to the church, Teddy wondered if he had made any kind of impression on Laura Gillespie? Likely not, if what his mother said was true. It was like trying to speak to God, he thought, yet, Uncle Ed said according to history, anything was possible. Look at Hannibal and Alexander the Great, he had said. I'll pray to God, like I always do, and maybe He'll bring me closer to Laura Gillespie?

The Queen's Hotel had once been a stagecoach stop, and a series of hitching posts had been hammered into hard packed earth at the front. The Hotel reminded Ed of the watering holes of train robbers, cattle rustlers, and other dangerous men, a place where fallen men made wicked deals—a world Ed knew nothing about.

No one in his family had ever stepped inside such an establishment.

He played with the nickel at the bottom of his pocket, bouncing it around. His entire life, Ed Barnes had done pretty much everything he was told, and nothing had worked out as planned. Maybe solace resided here? Nobody would know, he thought.

Grabbing the worn brass handle, he opened the door and walked inside. He looked down as the crowd of men at the bar turned to see who'd just arrived. He needn't have bothered, because nobody knew him, and within seconds the men were back to their easy banter.

Well-worn wooden tables casually bracketed a small dance floor and piano. The air was sweet with liquor and smoke, and a woman not much older than Ed, hair twisted back, sat under a slightly dented lamp playing the piano.

A couple of men, Soakies to Charlie, were trying to sing along. Ed took a seat at the bar.

"What'll it be?" the barkeep asked.

"A cup of coffee, please."

"Coffee!" the man laughed. "This is a bar. What'll you drink?" he asked again.

"Give the man a shot of whiskey," the woman who had been playing the piano said. She stood and approached Ed. "Mind if I sit?"

"No," Ed replied, as the barkeep put down two shot glasses, filling them to the brim with a golden liquid.

For a moment Ed caught sight of himself in the mirror behind the bar. What was he doing there? He hadn't been raised this way. Many a time he and Charlie had sat at their father's knee listening to stormy warnings about liquor and loose women, about how your soul would be damned and your reputation lost if you became known as the kind of man who frequented saloons.

Looking around the dark room with light reflecting off the snowy windowpanes, and smoke curling up, rolling lazily around the rafters, Ed thought maybe his father was wrong, maybe they were all wrong—generation after generation of Protestant Scots, with absolutely no regard for human frailty.

Ed took a sip of his drink. The liquid burned like a swallowed ember as it traveled down striking his gut—it made him feel safe. He took another one, feeling his shoulders drop.

"First drink?" the woman asked, as she belted back the shot and lit a cigarette.

He'd seen women smoking in Toronto, but nobody back home.

"No," he replied.

He'd had the odd drink with his friends in Toronto, but never in a place like this. This was a series of firsts; first tavern; first gut rot; first time sitting at a bar with a country woman who smoked. He looked at her through the smoke that swirled around her face. Her brown eyes were large and playful, a streak of dark red outlining her lips. Something about the way she flicked her hair reminded him of Bessie, but this mannerism was the only trait they shared—Bessie would never enter a tavern.

"I'm May Billings," the woman said, extending her hand.

"Ed," he replied, throwing back the rest of the drink the way the woman had, the whiskey exploding through him as if he'd swallowed a firecracker.

"You want another one?"

"That's it for my budget," Ed replied, placing his nickel on the bar.

"Hit us again!" May called to the barkeep. "You can pay me back with a dance," she replied, pulling Ed to his feet.

The whiskey overcame his natural reticence. Why shouldn't he dance? Why shouldn't he have some fun?

One of the old timers started playing a slower song. Even though it was only a fox trot, Ed wasn't doing a very good job, the liquor throwing him off balance. "How did you end up here?" he asked.

"I'm the hostess," May replied. "My uncle owns the place. I left home to get a job in the city, but it didn't pan out," she replied, as Ed gave her a spin. "So here I am, slinging hooch, and playing the piano," she said. "Let's get another drink."

Ed followed her back to the bar where two whiskeys waited. He admired the gutsy way May accepted her fate. But what other choice did she have? he asked himself.

Helped by the setting force of the whiskey, the two of them fell into more of an easy conversation. I need it, he thought, remembering how, since meeting Bessie all those years ago, his dating skills had atrophied.

"Young men can ride the rails and look for adventure, but that's no place for a woman. I'm lucky my uncle took me in. If I didn't have a job, I'd be forced to taxi dance or even worse," May said, slowly crossing one leg over the other.

Ed liked the way the whiskey made him feel: soft, floaty, and alive. May was right about her predicament. Fen had written to him the city dance halls were full of desperate, decent girls, lining the walls, waiting for a man to pay them a dime for a dance. Homely girls stood there all night and weren't approached, he had said, while others had their dresses torn. And so many more of them, forced by circumstance, took the men up on their offers of money for sex, if they followed them into a rundown hotel, or into the backseats of cars.

"I always dreamed of being a secretary and having my own apartment. At least until I got married, and settled down," May said.

Another song began and everyone sang along.

"Why haven't I seen you before?" she asked, leaning into Ed's ear.

The heat of her breath made his neck flesh goose bump. "I'm just a shy farm boy."

"You don't look like a farm boy," May said, eyes twinkling. "And you don't look all that shy."

"I was going to be a professor, if it wasn't for the government and the greedy men who run the companies."

"We're all having our lives stolen out from beneath us," May replied, picking up the glass.

"That's the same for everyone," the barkeep said, as they both threw back their drinks.

May lit another cigarette while the crowd commiserated about the terrible luck of the times.

"You know, you don't just have to take it," Ed said, feeling the liquor generate a new sense of control.

"Take what?"

"There's a League that's forming in Toronto. A League that's meant to help the people—all the people, not just the cream on the top," Ed replied.

The other fellows leaned in to hear what Ed had to say.

"What's it called?" May asked.

"The League for Social Reconstruction."

One of the men harrumphed. "I heard about them. They're commies."

"They're not," Ed replied. "Besides, it's better than the robbers in Ottawa."

May nodded and the barkeep said he agreed. They were all a bunch of thieving scoundrels.

"You don't know anything about Reds, Fred," the barkeep said to the grumbling fellow asking Ed if he wanted another drink.

"Sure."

"Tell us about your league," another man said.

Ed couldn't believe he had an audience. A small one, he thought, but at least they're listening. "It's a third political party. One that will share the wealth," Ed replied.

"Where did you hear about this?" May asked.

"When I was at school. But then I couldn't get work and had to come back home."

"Where are you living?"

Oh, no! he thought, Bessie and Charlie—the church gossip. "What time is it?" he asked, looking at the clock.

It was after eight. The family would be wondering where he was. Jumping up, he grabbed his coat. "Thanks for the drinks, but I've got to go."

"Stay and tell us about that league," the barkeep said.

"And don't be a stranger," May called out, as Ed left.

When Ed returned to the church, the event was nearly over, and in the rush and excitement of leaving, nobody other than Teddy had noticed Ed's absence. Thankfully the boy had the good grace not to ask where he'd gone. The family, now back in the car was heading home, while Bessie proudly talked about the goods they'd collected.

"Oh Bessie, I think they'll likely ask you to drive the locomotive all the way to Regina, and then they'll give you a key to the city," Ed laughed.

Bette giggled, and Bessie turned around and glared.

Suddenly the Dodge fishtailed and Charlie played the wheel back and forth, trying to regain control. The car dipsy doodled, spun and danced, nearly sliding into the culvert, but Charlie pulled it back just in time, just not quickly enough to avoid wedging the front of the chassis on top of a huge snowdrift.

"Darn it," Charlie said.

Standing by the side of the car, Charlie, Ed, and Teddy looked at the mess they were in. "Do you think we'll need the chains?" Ed asked.

"Let's try and push first," Charlie said, as the snow flew.

Ed and Charlie pulled two pieces of barn board out of the trunk, fitting them under the rear wheels to provide added traction, while Teddy dug with a shovel he'd taken from the trunk.

"Okay, Bessie, when I yell, give it a bit of gas," Charlie called to her. "On the count of two, you boys push," he told his brother and son.

Charlie and Teddy were each on a bumper with Ed tight in the middle. They were all down low with their feet dug into the snow.

"One, two—gas it, Bess!" he yelled. Bessie expertly pressed down on the pedal, snow like confetti flying into their faces. The car didn't budge.

Charlie dug some more. "Okay, let's go again," he said, thrusting the shovel into a drift.

Ed put his shoulder low to the trunk so he could throw his entire weight against the car.

"Gas it Bessie!" Charlie yelled, as they pushed.

The Dodge rocked and then shot ahead up and out of the drift leaving Ed flat on his face. Teddy laughed. So did Ed. Charlie didn't say a word, not even extending his hand to help his brother as Ed struggled to his feet.

Charlie told his son, "Teddy, jump back in the car and tell your mother, Uncle Ed and I will walk."

Teddy ran ahead and hopped into the car. The snow was coming down harder, rising in drifts around their boots as Charlie and Ed watched the car disappear into swirls of white. The night was still, with only the sound of the wind, and snow falling. Charlie, looking down at his feet, turned and looked his brother directly in the eye. "Where were you tonight, Eddy?" he asked.

"At the church—" Ed automatically answered, not knowing what else to say.

"I can smell liquor on your breath," Charlie said, "and I won't have a man drinking around my wife and children. Not even my brother." He marched ahead, leaving Ed standing alone on the road in the snow.

It was a hot and late July day. Random hay bales filled the barn, and Charlie was scrubbing the spark plugs on the old Dodge for the umpteenth time, praying that a good cleaning would suffice. New plugs should have been purchased over a year ago, but every single penny counted these days and he couldn't afford new ones. It was true the family could survive from the land, but there were other things that required money: gasoline, sugar, coffee, sweets, and the odd movie for the kids Charlie couldn't bear not to provide. Bessie hadn't had a new dress in over four years, and the children didn't wear shoes from May to September. He carefully replaced the last spark plug, gave it some grease, and fired up the car that sprang instantly to life. He fondly patted the dashboard. "Good girl," he purred.

Charlie loved his car, his first and only one. He'd been planning on buying a new model years ago, but the kids had come along, and then the Depression had hit.

"You need a hand?" Ed asked.

He'd just come in from the wood lot carrying an axe. There were a couple of mature trees that needed felling for firewood for the coming winter.

"I've got it," Charlie replied, not looking at Ed. He turned off the engine and headed out of the barn without another word. Things were strained between the brothers for months now, ever since the night Charlie had caught Ed drinking.

Fed up, Ed tossed the axe down on the worktable, wanting to storm after his brother, but he had second thoughts. Charlie was stubborn, and talking usually made things worse, he reminded himself. He turned looking back at the hay. Charlie or no Charlie, the bales still needed to be stacked.

The boys were fishing in the creek that ran along the back of the Barnes property. To keep cool they stood in the chilly water up to their knees, soaking the bottoms of their dungarees.

"So, what are you going to be if you're not going to be a farmer?" Bill asked.

"I told you a million times, I'm going to teach history," Teddy replied.

"You can't teach history if there's nobody to study it anymore. You have to pick something real."

Teddy pulled his line out of the water. The worm was gone. There was one smart fish down there, he thought. I'll use half a worm rather than the whole deal, that way the fish will have no choice but to chomp down on the hook to get a good bite.

Sitting on the grassy bank, Teddy pulled another worm out of the old coffee can and broke it in half—what difference did it make to the fish?

"Come on, Teddy. What are you really going to do when you grow up?" Bill repeated, playing out a bit more of his fishing line.

The boys were using long switches of willow for poles with some of Bessie's heavy black thread. A couple of safety pins acted as hooks. Holding the worm between his thumb and middle finger, Teddy carefully threaded the worm on the pin. He considered the worm twisting on the metal. He'd always had a fascination with the mechanics of nature, and whether or not it was possible for people to be helped with the right mix of medicine and care. He'd always wanted to become a doctor but felt it beyond his reach—there would never be enough money, and besides, Dad needed him at the farm. Forever.

"If you won't be a farmer ..." Bill continued, checking his bait and recasting his line, "what about a locomotive engineer? Think of the adventures you'd have."

Bill was always up for any kind of adventure. One time, the two boys had fallen through a crevasse located in an old cave Bill insisted they investigate. Luckily, they hadn't broken any bones, but it was too high to climb out of and if his father hadn't come by after twilight with the torch and a rope, the boys would have spent the night in the cold, dank, pitch black. Bill boasted it had been his plan all along, but Teddy knew better than to believe him, as he remembered how Bill had started to cry when the sun was going down, and they couldn't find any way to climb out.

Teddy removed the worm from the hook and gently laid it on top of the loamy earth in the bait can when Bill let out a whoop—he'd had a strike. Running up and down, splashing through the creek in his bare feet, Bill played the fish as best he could. It was a fat, proud trout. Glossy and silvery fine, it flashed its beauty in the summer sun, breaking the surface of the water only to crash back down with an indignant splash. Bill tugged the line again. Laughing, and frantic, he ran into the water up to his waist, his arms over his head, following the fish.

Teddy leapt to his feet, running alongside his friend, yelling for him to, "Play it more. Reel him in. You've got it, Bill! You've got it!"

The trout soared into the air again, higher than Teddy had ever seen a fish jump, well over their heads, as if trying to leap into the tree branches. Suddenly, it whipped its head, snapping Bessie's thread, disappearing forever into the dark, swirling creek water.

"Did you see the size of that fish?" Bill exclaimed, "it would have fed a family of ten," he added, walking all squishy up the path in his wet pants.

Taking up the rear, Teddy followed with the bait can. "I've never seen anything like it."

"Either have I," Bill said. "I wish I landed it."

They'd harvested the winter wheat several weeks earlier, and Ed was in the barn tossing bales of hay in the loft. Dripping in sweat, he removed his shirt, dropping it over a rail. He grabbed another bale of hay, slinging it up into the loft. Nearly a year of steady farm work had toughened him up. He was still slim, but long muscles had grown snaking down his arms and legs and rippling across his chest. It made him look more like a man, and much less like the bookish student he'd been in a life that felt long behind him. He heard something behind him and turned as Bessie walked in through the big double barn doors. The sun was behind her and Ed could see the endless green fields beyond, cast out like a verdant wedding train. In that instant, he realised Bessie belonged to the land more than she could to any man.

Bessie's black hair, damp from the heat, hung loose, tumbling down, and rolling onto her shoulders. She stopped, surprised, thinking Ed was still out in the fields, and automatically began to twist her hair into a bun with one hand, while digging in her apron pockets with the other, searching for pins.

"Don't," Ed said, gazing at her. "It looks so lovely when its down."

Bessie stopped. "Is Charlie here?"

Ed shook his head, suddenly aware he wasn't wearing a shirt. He could feel the sweat trickling down his chest and couldn't think of a single thing to say.

"Tell him dinner's ready when you see him," Bessie said, quickly turning and walking back to the house.

Bessie hadn't expected to see Ed working in the barn half naked. That wasn't proper, she thought, flustered, nonetheless. Then, she considered the heat. Was it fair to expect him to swelter? No. She looked at the ground, seeing a couple of hens pecking for seeds in the gravel. Hannibal stood on the fence post and crowed. She leaned over and picked up a few kernels and walked over to him. "You're so beautiful," she said, remembering she didn't want Teddy to become boastful. But Bessie knew, the boy might win a ribbon for this rooster, Hannibal was that handsome. As the rooster pecked the corn from the palm of her hand, Bessie's mind drifted back to the slick of sweat covering Ed's chest, and the way the overalls hung from his shoulders. He was certainly filling out, she thought. When she'd first met him, Edward had been handsome, but not much more than a dancing stick with a book, but now, he looked like a man. She allowed herself to think more, of the muscles that roped across his chest. Charlie was hairy and much heavier, too many pies and potatoes had replaced his muscles.

Not Edward. His body had become perfect.

Bessie shook her head and fed Hannibal the final kernel of corn. What nonsense was she thinking? It was thanks to good hard work and home cooking Ed was filling out. Furthermore, if Ed was going to stay around, was it not time she—somebody—found him a wife? She felt a lump form in her throat. Who would want him, a man with no prospects, and stained by the rumour of politics that closes doors? No, Edward … Ed, would remain at home with them.

Bessie gave Hannibal a quick pat on the head and headed toward the house, reminding herself there was lots of work to do. There was laundry and baking, the upstairs beds to change, and the house needing a good airing out.

Ed hadn't returned to the tavern since Charlie had smelled the liquor on his breath, but seeing Bessie made him feel the need to put some distance between them. He leaned over the rain barrel and splashed cool water on his face and under his armpits, convincing himself work could wait until later. Slipping back into his shirt he poked his head into the paddock to see if Charlie was around. Seeing the place was empty, he entered the workshop. The axe still rested on the table. Quickly, Ed reached up to the shelf for the can that held screws and nails. Charlie kept a bit of private, emergency cash for oil and tools, his rationale being, Bessie didn't need to know about every penny. Glancing out the window, Ed took a dime, making a mental promise to replace it.

He hopped on Teddy's bicycle, pedaling fast across the yard, past Hannibal, through the scattering chickens, and down the long lane flanked by the alley of leafy maples. The sunlight slipped through the leaves, dappling the lane as Ed rode up the gravel. He didn't know how old the trees were, but he was certain they'd last a lot longer than he would. For a moment, he wondered what Bessie was doing, and then took a sharp left on the Concession Road, heading toward civilization, or at least, some form of it.

Charlie had slipped into the kitchen for a drink of lemonade when he caught sight of his brother through the window. Ed was on Teddy's bicycle, and more than halfway down the lane, much too far to call and ask where he was heading. The workday wasn't over yet, and Charlie wondered where on earth he was going? Maybe there was trouble at one of the neighboring farms. He could hear Bessie upstairs moving from room to room.

"Where's Ed off to?" he called.

Bessie didn't answer, and Charlie finished his lemonade. Kicking off his work boots, he climbed the stairs.

He knew his brother had been trying to make up for his failing that night at the church. Charlie wondered if he was being unfair while remembering the one thing his parents had firmly instilled in him, to never tolerate alcohol in one's life. But still, Ed was his brother, his family, and maybe the time had arrived for them to renew, to move on, for him to forgive and forget.

Charlie found Bessie in their room. Normally, she made each bed with fluffed pillows and precise nurse's corners, but this time, she seemed aloof, absentmindedly tossing the pillows on the head of the bed. In the flurry of making beds, Bessie's hair had come loose from its pins again. Charlie came up behind her and placed his hands on her hips. Bessie jumped, dropping the quilt she had picked from the floor. Charlie snatched it as it fell. "Didn't mean to scare you," he said, handing it back to her.

"I didn't hear you," Bessie replied, giving the quilt a good shake. "You shouldn't be sneaking up the stairs. Mrs. Moffatt told me that there have been men prowling around the country trying to steal food and money, if they can get it. Mr. Moffatt is in a terrible state about it. She told me he was keeping a loaded gun by the door."

Charlie sat down on the bench in front of Bessie's vanity and watched his wife finish making the bed. He loved to observe her fuss around the house, getting everything just so, in her own particular way, which was always perfect.

"Where's Ed off to?" Charlie asked.

"I don't know," she said, dusting the bureau, and trying to push Ed out of her mind. She didn't want to talk about him—no, she definitely did not want to *think* about him, out there in the barn without his shirt on. Had he put it back on to go wherever he was going?

Watching her methodically run the duster along the top of the windowsill, Charlie recalled the first moment he'd laid eyes on her at the Scott's Corners school house dance. Bessie had just returned from school, and they'd met that night. He couldn't have helped but stare at the raven-haired beauty handing out her homemade tarts, and in less than a year, the couple had married. Charlie often wondered how he had convinced her to be his bride. He'd even asked her whether or not she wanted to put that teacher's degree to work while she was still young. But Bessie Hunter had claimed she'd lost all interest in teaching and simply wanted to settle down and raise a family.

Stopping to look at the streak on the glass window, Bessie wondered about Edward, about the afternoon's encounter, about his leaving just now. Where had he gone to?

Charlie discreetly walked behind her and reached out to touch her hand. Bessie turned to him, absent from the moment and thinking more of Edward. And why was she thinking of Ed—still? Now. Charlie sat on the chair near the bed and he pulled Bessie onto his lap and kissed her. The kiss, slow but insisting, brought her back to their room, reminding her she was Charlie Barnes' wife.

Peddling down Northumberland Street with the wind on his face, Ed sped by the Knox United Church, taking a left on Main, heading toward the Queen's Tavern. He slammed on the brakes when he arrived at the tavern, the stolen coin in his overalls pocket. For a moment, he felt shame overcoming him, stealing from his brother. He quickly caught himself, rationalizing his thinking. The farm was half his birthright, after all. Surely, Mother and Father wouldn't have wanted their youngest son to have to beg for a dime?

Ed leaned the bicycle against the back wall, well out of sight. He'd been careful while riding, on the lookout for anyone they might know, but hadn't seen a soul.

I need this, he thought. I haven't left the farm in so long, and I need to get away from Bessie's ... pull—

Pushing open the oak door, the sweet smell of tobacco reached him. The fingers of his other hand lightly touching the dime. No, his parents would never have wanted him to beg, and as such, Ed refused to think about what they would have said about where he was spending the family's hard-earned money.

May was standing on tiptoe behind the bar, stretching high to polish a row of dusty liquor bottles and hadn't noticed Ed enter. Her cigarette lay in the ashtray, its burner long and red. They were the only people there. Ed picked up the cigarette.

"I'll be with you in a moment," May called over her shoulder. "Please take a seat." Ed examined the faint marks of dark red lipstick on the filter.

"Take your time," he replied, sliding onto a barstool.

At the sound of his voice, May turned, "I thought you'd forgotten all about me," she said, playfully shaking the duster, bits of loosened sediment gently floating through the air while Ed tentatively took a puff. Its strange smoke burned the back of his throat, but the idea of swallowing fire appealed to him. Ed imagined he was a dragon expelling long forks of flame. "How've you been?" he asked.

"Business is slow. When folks get their relief later this week there'll be some pickup. But you know the government. They're not even giving out enough money for food, so only the really determined drinkers will be coming in."

Ed pulled the dime from his pocket. "How much will this buy?" he asked, dropping it onto the bar.

"Plenty," she replied, pouring them both a glass. Raising the whiskey, she said, "Here's mud in your eye. Now tell me about your League."

Bette and Teddy were finishing their supper while Charlie watched the clock. It was after six and Ed still wasn't home. Where could his brother have gone without even finishing his chores? There were cows to milk and chickens to feed.

"Uncle Ed was supposed to help me with my homework," Bette complained.

Teddy didn't want his uncle getting into any trouble, so he kicked his sister under the table and said he'd help her.

"I don't want your help. I want Uncle Ed," Bette wailed, followed by, "you kicked me!"

"I did not," Teddy said, hoping there wasn't a bruise on her leg, in case Mother checked.

"Settle down this minute," Bessie said, placing a rice pudding in the center of the table. "Bette, if you don't finish your peas, you'll be getting no dessert."

The girl looked balefully at the peas, and then to her father for some support, but he wasn't paying attention. "After supper, I think I'll go over to the Moffatt's to use their phone," he said, scooping up a big portion of pudding and dropping it into his bowl.

The flat of Bessie's palm came down on the table. "You'll do no such thing."

She was terribly jealous of Mrs. Moffatt and some of the other ladies who had phones. Mrs. Moffatt called it a magnificent invention, almost better than the radio. Mr. Moffatt had stated his wife was keeping Mr. Bell in pocket change, as she spent much of her time perched on her corner chair, eavesdropping on the party line. Mrs. Moffatt insisted her husband exaggerated, but Bessie knew it to be true. There were as many as seven people on the Scott's Corners party line, and any time the phone rang, all you had to do was wait until the intended recipient picked it up, and then quietly lift your receiver to be transported to a private conversation, like a hearing voyeur.

Charlie leaned back in his chair and looked again at the clock. "I've waited long enough. I'm going to head over to the Moffatt place if Ed isn't home soon."

Ed twirled May around the small dance floor, the burn of alcohol coursing through his body. Four shots and the dime had been spent, just as the conversation around his politics had ended.

The music had stopped, but it didn't matter, Ed quietly sang, spinning May around the worn wooden planks. He took a drunken misstep and tread upon her foot. "You're heavier than you look," she squealed as Ed released her. "I don't want to stop," May added, pulling him back toward her. "I just want to slow things down." She tucked her head under his chin and began to rock back and forth. Unexpectedly, the room began to spin, and Ed held May tighter, closing his eyes, concentrating on the smell of her hair, wanting it to ground him. When he opened his eyes, she was staring up at him, mouth slightly open. Everything about May suddenly brought Bessie back to his mind, her lovely green eyes, lashes long and thick, skin white and soft to the touch.

As he gripped May's body, he traveled back to that night at The Normal School dance. If things had worked out differently, I would have pursued Bessie with everything I had, he thought. But she had left, and he had never been able to find her.

As May and Ed swayed, he looked at her, leaned down and kissed her.

"I don't think there's going to be any business tonight," May whispered, walking back to the entrance and locking the front door. Flicking off the lights, she led Ed upstairs.

There was no electricity on the second floor, and so May lit the oil lamp standing on an old bedside table. A tiny cone of yellow light ringed the corner of the ceiling. As Ed squinted into the darkness, May pulled him toward a single bed, gently pushing him down on his back. He stared at the ceiling while May pulled off his boots, the little cone of light slowly spinning around the room.

Sitting down beside him, May slipped off her blouse, revealing a flesh tone brassiere. Smiling, she asked if he'd like to take it off. He stretched his fingers to her back, instinctively knowing what to do, even though he'd never done it before.

May undid the buttons of Ed's shirt and slid the braces of his overalls down around his hips. As her fingers moved over his chest, and down his belly, Edward closed his eyes and moaned.

"Come here," she said, as she leaned over him and blew out the lamp. Hearing his overalls strike the floor, he felt May's smooth body descending upon him.

"What did you say?" May asked, her voice angry.

Ed mumbled and shook his head, not understanding. Where was he?

"Who did you call me?" she asked.

A match was struck, and the little cone of yellow light reappeared on the ceiling. A spidery crack ran across the plaster telling him he was still in May's room. He must have passed out, but he couldn't remember.

Ed heard a shuffle and saw May was up, tugging on her clothes. "I don't do this with just anyone," she said, snapping each breast back into the pointed brassiere. "I thought you were special, being a professor and all. But you're no better than the rest. Get dressed," she ordered, tucking her blouse into her skirt.

Ed looked down and saw he was naked. He had been intimate with this girl, and he didn't even remember. Thoroughly ashamed, he stood, pulled the sheet up around his waist, picked up his clothes and got dressed. "I'm sorry," he said, trying to piece together what had just happened. He remembered the whiskey, and the dancing, and not feeling very well. Then—May's fingers on his chest.

"What kind of a girl do you think I am?" May asked, hot anger beginning to wilt.

"A wonderful girl," Ed replied, fumbling with his shirt.

"Then who is Bessie?" May asked.

The look on Ed's face said everything.

"Get out!" May shouted, picking up one of his boots and heaving it at the door. "Get out right now!"

Charlie pulled on his boots just before midnight. He was going over to Adam's to call the police.

"Oh, for heaven's sake, Charlie," Bessie said, "Ed will be home. He's likely gone off with some friends and lost track of the time."

But Bessie was worried, too. Ed didn't seem to have friends to speak of, and he'd never been gone this long. Stacking the plates in the cupboard, she realized he had rarely been gone at all. When Ed had first returned from university, he went to the odd dance, saw some of his old friends, and even got all worked up about giving a grand speech on the Punic Wars at the Women's Institute.

Polishing her tea pot, Bessie thought she had to admit more was changing about Ed than his physique. What if Charlie was right? What if something terrible has happened? Stop worrying about it, she told herself, it never does anyone any good. I dealt with the damage following the Normal School dance, pulled up my boots, and got on with my life. All will be well now, too. Lost in her thoughts, Bessie shut the cupboard door as Charlie finished tying his boot. "I'll be back as soon as I can," Charlie said, pushing open the screen door.

"Wait a minute," Bessie said, grabbing Charlie's windbreaker from the hook on the wall, "you don't want to catch a chill."

It was much too warm for a coat, but to stop his wife from worrying, Charlie slipped on the jacket and kissed her on the cheek, before heading across the yard toward the Moffatt place.

Ed stumbled out of the back door of the Queen's Tavern into the night, nearly tumbling off the back stoop. Seeing double, he had to close one eye to see straight. Coming around the side of the building, he scanned for anyone passing by, but the streets were empty. The clock at the top of the Carnegie Library read just past midnight.

Ed's heart sank. How would he explain this? Wanting to look dignified, he retrieved the bicycle and weaved down the sidewalk. The night was bright, and Ed looked around again to see if anyone was watching.

May's angry, tear-stained face peered down from the second-floor window saw the bicycle slowly wobble, and then pick up steam, as Ed sped out of town.

He never saw her, the quiet of the village fooling him into thinking he was alone.

Eerie light flooded the countryside like the negative of a photograph held up to an enormous, accusatory moon as Ed crisscrossed the county, taking every back road he knew of. Anything to get there quickly, he thought. Maybe the family had all gone to bed and he would slip upstairs with nobody any the wiser.

If not for the strange light, Ed would have missed the break in the woodlot where they'd been logging that spring. The men had cut clear through to the dam. The bush road was rough, but if Ed followed the path the trucks had made, he could cut his trip in half.

It was darker in the woods than on the open road, the maples and oaks determined to trip him in their jagged trail of muddy ruts.

Charlie wouldn't be asleep, he knew. He'd be up waiting. They'd both be up. Nervous, he wondered—What was he going to say? His head filled with worry, he veered off the path, his bike sliding out beneath him, and he hit the ground hard.

Charlie walked up the cattle lane toward the Moffatt house thinking it would have been a lovely night for a stroll if he hadn't been so worried. Looking up at the moon he made God a promise, if Ed was found safe, he would ease up. Enough of the wrathful, unforgiving nature of the church-going folk, he thought, vowing to make things right once Ed returned home.

Adam Moffatt had done well by himself. Even in the depths of the Depression, he had an impressive operation, and still had managed to put a bit of money in the bank.

As Charlie approached, the chickens began clucking and he softly cooed, a sound the chickens liked, but then, another sound emerged—the quiet click of a rifle hammer being pulled back. Charlie's eyes shifted toward the coop. A shape moved in the doorway, and he saw the muzzle of a gun as the moonlight struck its barrel.

Before he could say, "Adam, it's Charlie," a bullet roared out of the rifle and blew him off his feet.

Approaching, Adam Moffatt said, "Charlie?" Falling to his knees, the rifle dropping to the dirt, he said, "Oh, damn." Charlie wasn't moving.

There was blood everywhere, the bullet having hit Charlie in the gut, with more blood seeping out of Charlie's back.

Mrs. Moffatt came rushing out of the house in her robe and slippers, her hair carefully twisted into curlers, calling, "What the Sam hill are you shooting at this hour, Adam Moff—what have you done?" she gasped.

Adam looked at his wife. "Call the doctor, and get him over here fast."

Bessie was pacing on the Moffatt's front porch.

"Would you like some tea?" Mrs. Moffatt asked, worried about Charlie, and nearly as worried about what people would say if word got out her husband had gone off half-cocked. She shuddered at the thought.

"No, thank you," Bessie said. She didn't want tea. She was so terrified, and doubted she could hang onto a cup. Doc Ramsey and Adam had picked Charlie up and gotten him into the house, but they couldn't stop the bleeding, and Charlie hadn't regained consciousness.

From where she stood, Bessie saw an outline made of blood—deep and dark—by the coop, but the sun, beginning to peer over the horizon, was turning the stain slightly pink. Or maybe Charlie's blood was disappearing, seeping into the earth like snow or rain?

What on earth was Adam thinking? she wondered, sinking down on the stoop, turning away from the sight of Charlie's blood. What would she do without him? As Bessie twisted the hem of her dress, she dismissed her fear. Nothing would happen to Charlie, she wouldn't let it. God wouldn't allow it—not her God.

"I'm so sorry, Bessie," Mrs. Moffatt said.

They'd never called one another by their first names. It just wasn't done … but neither was killing your neighbor.

Mrs. Moffatt sat beside Bessie and stared down at her own flowered slippers. A tiny hole was forming in the toe of the right foot, and escaping into the mundanity of a moment, she thought about how she needed to mend it. "We had some thieves through here the past while and Adam got it into his head he was going to catch them before they made off with any more livestock," Mrs. Moffatt said.

He was going to kill a man for a chicken? Bessie nearly asked, holding her tongue. It was a stupid question, of course Adam would kill a hobo over a chicken, and so would most farmers in the county. The farmers barely had enough for their own families. Besides, if word got around a particular farm was easy pickings, maybe the next time a whole group of wandering hobos would venture through and help themselves to all the chickens—or even worse, visit the family in the dead of night.

"Bessie?" Doc Ramsey called from inside the house.

Bessie and Mrs. Moffatt turned and stood as the doctor appeared at the open door.

Is he going to be all right?" Bessie asked, praying Charlie would materialize behind the doctor with a bandage around his midriff and a smile on his face.

"I finally got the bleeding to stop, but he's going to have to go to the hospital."

"And the bullet?" she asked, somewhat relieved.

"He's lucky, clear through. But we've got to watch for infection."

While Bessie and Mrs. Moffatt made the back seat of Doc Ramsey's car as comfortable as they could with blankets and pillows, Adam and the doctor carried Charlie out of the house and settled him into the back seat. Bessie didn't ask Doc Ramsey if he minded her coming along for the drive, and simply sat down in the front seat of the car.

Mrs. Moffatt asked again if there was anything she could do, but Bessie didn't hear her, trying to figure out where they were going to find the money to pay for a hospital stay.

"I'll send Adam into town to fetch you later," Mrs. Moffatt called, "and I'll give the children their breakfast."

Bessie, worried and tired, knew another hot, long day would be unfolding; for her; for Charlie—her family.

Ed's nose twitched as a mosquito took a nasty bite out of his nostril. He swatted it, smearing a streak of muddy blood across his cheek. He opened his eyes. Flat on his back, lying in the dirt, his head pounding, he rose to his hands and knees. Lifting his head, he saw Teddy's bicycle half submerged in the murky water, its fender badly dented.

"I crashed the bike," he said out loud, and then, he thought of May.

The bile rose and Ed vomited until there was nothing left, but the dry heaves kept coming. Whatever was rotting inside of him didn't want to leave. Exhausted and trembling, he finally made it to his feet. I have to get back home, he thought, Charlie must be crazy with worry. Picking up the broken bike, he started pushing it down the bush road, trying to come up with a plausible story.

Teddy pushed Mrs. Moffatt's eggs around on the plate. They weren't nearly as good as his mother's. Bette was crying as Mrs. Moffatt tried to get her to eat.

"She doesn't like them scrambled," Teddy said, as respectfully as he could. "Nobody, not even Mother, can make her eat scrambled eggs."

Hearing those words sent his sister off on another round of ear-splitting wails while Mrs. Moffatt rushed to the frying pan.

No matter how hard he tried, Teddy couldn't get Mrs. Moffatt to talk about what had happened. She kept repeating, Mr. Moffatt would bring their mother home soon and then everything would be fine. Teddy decided to try another tack. He'd noticed that when Dad wanted to get information, he didn't come right out and ask. Instead, he would circle around the topic of interest, and with each question, strike closer and closer to the truth—so different from Mother's direct way of dealing with things.

"How's your egg route faring?" Teddy asked.

"Oh Teddy, that's very kind of you to ask," Mrs. Moffatt replied, relieved to be in familiar conversational territory.

"You're welcome," Teddy replied, "I know times are hard."

"You're a wise child, Theodore," Mrs. Moffatt said, flipping the egg once over lightly, before setting the eggs in front of Bette.

"Where's my Daddy?" Bette wailed, shoving the plate of fried eggs off the table.

Teddy jumped as the dish bounced off the floor. His mother would have a fit if she saw Bette behaving this badly in front of Mrs. Moffatt, who, grabbing a dishrag, dropped to her knees and began mopping up the mess.

"She'll be home soon," Mrs. Moffatt cooed.

Uncle Ed burst through the back door, sweaty and covered in mud. "Where's Charlie?" he asked, looking around the kitchen. "Where's Bessie?"

"Oh Ed!" Mrs. Moffatt cried, rushing up to him, "there was an accident last night. Your brother's in the hospital and Mrs. Barnes is with him."

Bette sprang out of her chair and into Ed's arms. Teddy grabbed Ed around the waist and didn't even notice how bad his uncle smelled, relieved his parents hadn't killed themselves.

While Mrs. Moffatt drove the family to the hospital, Ed tried to talk himself out of a jam.

"Where were you?" Bette asked, "I was so scared."

"Don't worry about me," Ed answered, kissing the top of the girl's head, "and your hair needs a good brushing little girl."

Bette squirmed. "No, it doesn't."

Ed, tucked into the back seat of the car with the children, wrapping an arm around each of their shoulders.

"What happened to Teddy's bike?" Bette asked, noticing the banged-up fender.

Ed had hoped nobody would notice.

"It's okay," Teddy said, "I don't care about the bike. The main thing is you're home."

Ed smiled at the boy. He was such a considerate child, always putting other people's needs ahead of his own. For a moment, he wondered what kind of secret life Teddy had. On the surface he was always so calm and accommodating.

"I'd like to know what happened, too," Mrs. Moffatt said, staring into the rear-view mirror.

Ed could see Mrs. Moffatt wasn't going to give up this line of inquiry, and he knew it would worsen once having to answer to Bessie. He had to think fast. "I was attacked," Ed blurted out.

"What?" everyone cried simultaneously. The car swerved.

"Hoboes knocked me over the head and left me in the ditch."

"Oh Ed," Mrs. Moffatt said, shaking her head, "are you all right? Should we take you to see the doctor too?"

"That's a good idea," Bette exclaimed, "we're going to the hospital! There will be lots of doctors there."

Ed laughed and said he was fine, that there was no need to make a fuss. And as he did, he tickled his niece, wanting to alleviate the moment.

Mrs. Moffatt prattled away about the sad situation. Why, if young men couldn't ride their bicycles through the countryside without being jumped, it was too much to ponder. Yet, secretly she was somewhat relieved Ed had been attacked, since it made Adam's actions more understandable. If drifters were beating up people on bicycles, it didn't seem all that odd to be prowling around at night with a rifle protecting your property.

"Did they get anything?" Teddy asked.

"Just a dime," Ed replied, thinking of May and her room at the top of the Queen's tavern.

"That's a lot of money," Teddy said.

Ed nodded his head while watching a farmer in a big straw hat drive a team of horses down the road.

SEVEN

The Very Thought of You

Charlie was in bed with white gauze wrapped around his abdomen. Doc Ramsey had allowed Bessie, Ed, and the children in for a quick visit. While Bette sat on the chair staring at the bandages, and asking her father how much it hurt, Bessie quizzed Ed about his whereabouts.

Teddy looked around the room. Dad is in a ward with six beds, but there's only one other man in here, he noted. The other man, with broken legs suspended from a cable, was reading a newspaper. Teddy, curious about the man's cast, walked to the man's bed, determined to know more.

"The hobos got Uncle Ed!" Bette suddenly exclaimed, touching her father's bandage.

"Oh, for land's sake," Bessie muttered, "Teddy shouldn't be bothering that poor man. I'll be right back," she added, pulling her daughter off the chair, dragging her across the room.

"Are you all right?" Charlie asked Ed as soon as Bessie and the children were out of earshot.

"Don't you worry about me. You just focus on getting better," Ed replied, anxious to change the subject.

"Hear me out. I've been too hard on you lately," Charlie said, lowering his voice, "since that night in the winter … I know you're not a drinking man."

Ed tried to reply, but Charlie raised his hand to stop him. "That's all done and forgotten."

Ed could have dissolved. Here was Charlie apologizing, all shot up, while everything had been his fault. He wanted to confess about the whiskey and what had happened with May, but nobody, not even Charlie, would understand. He had entered fear country, a world stripped of grace, where his only hope lay in keeping everything secret. His only chance of redemption was to make this up to his family, somehow. But how?

Bessie and the children reappeared at the bedside. "Mr. Tilt fell out of a haymow and snapped his femur," Teddy said.

"Who's Mr. Tilt?" Charlie asked.

Teddy gestured at the man with the cast. "What's a femur?" he asked his father.

"I don't know. I guess you'll have to look it up," Charlie replied.

"He raises Bantam roosters," Teddy said, pointing in Mr. Tilt's direction, "and he gave me some tips on how to groom Hannibal."

"Don't point, Teddy, it's rude. You'd think with all this going on you'd have other things on your mind than that bird," Bessie said, leaning over to retrieve her purse from the wooden chair. "And it's late, we'd better be getting home."

Bette stared at Mr. Tilt. "Maybe he fell out of the haymow because he's on a tilt," she said.

Charlie started to laugh but grimaced from the pain.

"It's time we get a move on with all this silliness," Bessie said. She leaned down and gave Charlie a peck on the cheek.

"Be sure to do what the nurses tell you," Ed said, touching Charlie's shoulder. "I'll take care of the place, don't you worry."

"I know you will," said Charlie, and he watched his family leave.

The next morning, Ed beat Bessie out of bed, tip-toeing downstairs to put the coffee on. After the terrible night he had, and with what had happened to Charlie, he wanted to do something nice for Bessie and the children.

Creeping into the kitchen, he lifted the black iron lid and loaded the stove with wood and paper and lit the match. He removed the percolator from the shelf, filled it with water, and dumped in several tablespoons of coffee, placing it on the stovetop. The aroma of fresh coffee soon began to drift around the room as he proceeded to set the table.

The sun was finally up, an orange light slowly filling the kitchen, warning of the heat to come. Hannibal crowed from his post in the yard as Ed rooted through the icebox searching for breakfast food. There were plenty of eggs, but he couldn't see any bacon. Eventually, he found it in the keeper with the butter by a bowl full of cold potatoes.

"Something smells good," Bette called from the stairwell.

Ed was flipping eggs while bacon and sliced potatoes bubbled in another frying pan.

Bette plopped down in her chair, announcing men don't cook.

"Is that so?" Ed said, tossing a tea towel over his shoulder, removing the eggs from the stove.

"What are you doing in my kitchen?" Bessie said, standing in the doorway.

Ed grabbed her by the shoulders, steering her towards a chair. "Sit down, Bessie Barnes."

"We're eating man food!" Bette yelled, throwing her arms up into the air, a knife and fork in each hand.

Bessie poured the girl a glass of milk as Teddy came bounding down the stairs.

"I never knew a man who could find his way around a kitchen," Bessie said, pouring a cup of coffee but smiling just the same.

Doing up the dishes, Bessie watched Ed and Teddy head across the yard toward the barn. She had to admit Ed's breakfast had been tasty. The eggs were perfectly flipped and the bacon was nice and crispy. Sometimes, Bessie wondered, if Charlie even knew where the icebox was, never mind how to open it, and make something to eat.

It had been pleasant not having to cook that morning. She'd been up most of the night fretting about how they were going to pay for Charlie's hospital visit. With no money, she didn't know where they were going to find it.

For the first time in a very long time, Bessie felt afraid, threatened even. Putting dishes on the rack to dry, she thought, I could sit in here all day worrying and that wouldn't do any good, would it? I need to visit Charlie.

Seeing Charlie was fast asleep, Bessie quietly walked across the linoleum floor. She set her purse on the bedside table and removing her knitting needles and a ball of yarn, sat on the straight-backed chair. Crossing her ankles, hands in her lap, Bessie examined her husband. His color had improved, but he still looked chalky. She smiled. Charlie would often stare at the bald spot on his head, and comb hair over it. He had such a thick head of red hair when they'd married.

Watching Charlie's chest heave up and down, she wondered if she should wake him. Bessie caught Mr. Tilt's eye and nodded her head in greeting.

"He didn't sleep much last night," Mr. Tilt said, looking at Charlie.

Bessie brought her index finger to her lips, signaling for the man to be quiet. "You don't say," she whispered, rising from her seat and crossing the room.

"He was in a fair amount of pain," Mr. Tilt added as he tried to get his fingers down the top of his cast to scratch an itch he couldn't quite reach. "You ever broken anything?"

Bessie shook her head, no.

"The itching's worse than the break," he said, "and the only thing that's worse than the itching is paying for the doc."

"Let me see if I can help you," she said. "Where does it itch?"

"All over," he replied, "but especially the thigh."

Bessie handed him a knitting needle. "Try this."

Mr. Tilt slipped the needle down the top of the cast and began moving it back and forth. "That feels good," he murmured appreciatively. "Say, your husband got to talking a bit. He was asking the doc if he could go home. 'Course the doc said, no. Told your husband he has a gut wound, and he has to make sure it doesn't turn septic. Said he didn't save his life so he could go and do some fool thing like get it all ripped open again and risk infection."

Bessie smiled, but inwardly she sighed. If Charlie was worrying about money, he'd be out of the hospital as soon as he could stand. To heal, her Charlie had to stay put.

While Bessie was at the hospital, Mrs. Moffatt struck out for the Barnes' farm, balancing a raspberry pie and a round tin full of cookies. With Charlie laid up, Bessie wouldn't have much time for baking, and Ed and the children would need food—the comforting kind.

She decided to walk, it was a glorious day, and she needed the quiet to think. There had to be something else she could do. Her Adam had been the one to fire the gun, and it didn't seem fair the Barnes should suffer, especially that lovely boy with the gentle way.

Crickets hopped out of her path as Mrs. Moffatt pushed her way through the rows of young corn tickling her bare arms. The corn, it seemed, was already stretching up to the clouds. It was going to be a good year.

Crossing the property line, she thought about the years the two families had been neighbors. Such good neighbors they didn't even need a fence.

But now, the shooting might change everything.

She passed by the stream and decided to sit for a bit. The day was bound to be hot, and it was a pity not to appreciate the light breeze.

Cupping her hand, she leaned over the brook and took a sip of water. Her thirst gone, she opened the tin, lifted the waxed paper, and peeked at the peanut butter cookies. They wouldn't miss just one, she told herself, and taking a small bite, she leaned against the tree, congratulating herself on her baking. She closed her eyes, listening to the cicadas sing their summer song in the far distance, and for a brief moment, she forgot everything that needed forgetting.

"Toss up another one!" Teddy yelled down, as Ed swung another bale into the air.

"That's it," Ed called up.

"Does that mean we can play?" Bette asked, peering over the edge of the mow, looking down at her uncle.

Ed knew there was no time for play, but it was sweltering, and the children needed a break. "Come on. Let's go get some lemonade," he said, as the children quickly clambered down the ladder. "You did a really good job," and he patted Bette's back.

"Can we work on the radio while we have our lemonade?" Teddy asked.

"Maybe for a bit," Ed replied, "then we've got to get the eggs ready."

"I don't like Mooney Shantz," Bette complained, "he spits."

As a surprise, Ed had decided to set things up in the living room so Charlie could hear crop reports from all over the world, and Bessie could hear some different music. He twisted the dial again, receiving only static.

"What if I take it up on the roof?" Teddy asked. "I can tie it to the chimney."

While Teddy shinnied up the drainpipe and walked along the peak of the roof, Ed spun the dial. Unimpeded by trees, the radio signal traveled into the living room, and a voice began crackling out of the speaker. Teddy had reached the chimney and was holding the antenna up in the air.

"Ask him if he can get it any higher," Ed said.

"Higher!" Bette shouted out the window as Teddy leaned on the bricks and stretched up on his toes. A man's voice blasted loudly out of the speaker and Bette clapped with glee. "It's the King!" she cried.

"Quiet," Ed said, sitting down in front of the radio.

It wasn't King George. Graham Spry was reporting from Queen's Park in Toronto about the rallies that were occurring across the country. The threat of jail or being sent to Relief Camps was no longer enough to stop the gatherings, it seemed.

Mrs. Moffatt came through the gate with her cookies and pie, just in time to hear some man shouting in the Barnes living room. Why on earth was Bessie's daughter hanging out the window, and what was that man talking about? Thinking she had heard some mention of communism, and seeing Bessie's car was gone, she worried and thought, what was happening? As if that wasn't enough, looking up, she saw Teddy on top of the roof holding the antenna.

"Theodore!" she called.

Teddy turning, lost his balance, and feeling his right foot slipping on the peak, he let himself slide down the shingles, trying to grab the chimney to steady his fall. He missed the brick and the antenna slipped from of his

CATHI BOND

hand, skipping down the shingles as he followed it, rolling, skidding on the hot green roof, down toward the edge while a terrified Mrs. Moffatt watched. Another horrible event she in part had helped create, she thought, petrified. Dropping her baked goods, she ran toward the house. The antenna had snapped and was dangling several feet above the earth, saved by the short length of its wire. Teddy's right foot had slammed into the eavestrough, the metal bowed from the impact, threatening to snap, but holding.

Ed didn't even know what had transpired, too busy with the radio. The woman sat down to catch her wind. Teddy sat on the edge of the roof, examining the eaves trough. If his mother ever noticed, he could claim it must have been foul weather.

"What are you people doing?" Mrs. Moffatt asked, quite pale from the fright.

"We're hooking up a radio for my parents," Teddy replied. "When you feel better, would you mind tossing that antenna back up here?" he asked, his hand outstretched.

Bessie hung the sheets on the clothesline to dry. It had been over a week since the shooting, and she was no closer to a solution regarding the medical bill. A brisk wind clipped across the yard, and like the white sails of tiny ships, the bedding billowed and blew. They'll likely be dried by dinnertime, she hoped, smelling the roast beef cooking in the oven. Continuing to hang the sheets, she thought of Charlie, and of the conversation they had last night.

As expected, her husband wanted to recuperate at home. Luckily, Doc Ramsey had shown up on rounds, and told Charlie he needed another week of constant supervision in the hospital, and that was going to be that. Doc Ramsey even went so far as to say they could pay him over time, but that the hospital bill would need to be settled when Charlie was released. It was a matter of policy.

Bessie bit down on the wooden clothes peg between her teeth and moved the clothesline down. What good was a government if it couldn't give solid citizens a break at a time like this? There was an election coming in the fall and folks were talking about swinging back to the Liberals. Bessie doubted William Lyon Mackenzie King would do any better.

For the first time in her life, Bessie Barnes doubted the government. They kept talking about how they had to protect the Canadian economy and regular people, but she was starting to think they were simply protecting themselves. What person in their right mind would willingly go on the dole? They never gave you enough food. You had to beg for clothes, you'd likely lose your home, and if that happened, you'd either become a parasite on your relatives, or end up in the poorhouse.

She and Charlie paid their taxes, lived from the land and behaved like good Christians. Why, she and the ladies from the Institute had even sent all that food and clothing out to Saskatchewan. It looked as if the only salvation remaining was to mortgage the farm. How would they repay the debt? They barely made enough to keep food on the table, and the children didn't even have shoes for the spring and summer. How could they possibly make regular payments? And if they defaulted on the loan, the bank would foreclose.

Bessie dropped a sheet and watched it roll and blow across the dirt.

While Ed mucked out the horses' stalls, Teddy filled the water trough and pitched in fresh hay. Bette had tried to gather eggs, but was more of a liability than help since she broke one for every four she snatched.

Every afternoon, Bessie gathered the eggs herself, carefully stacking them into Mooney's crates. The family was going full tilt and Ed didn't know how much longer they could keep it up. Shoveling the last of the manure into the wheelbarrow, he took a breather, sitting on the rail of the stall, looking out at the land through the dusty window. Bessie was right, the wheat would be ready in less than a month. How were they going to get it in without Charlie there to help? There was no money to pay for a hired hand. Maybe if Bessie drove the tractor? The thought of Bessie in overalls and her straw hat driving the horses made him grin. Pushing his way out the door, Ed strode across the yard. "Hello Hannibal," he said, tossing some corn at the rooster. The bird crowed, pecking through the gravel as Ed hopped the fence, walking into the wheat field which nearly touched his chest.

Breaking off a head, he rubbed the hull between the palms of his hands, blowing away the chaff to taste the sweet seeds. Why was he thinking about Bessie? Since Charlie had been gone, he'd thought of her more and more. For years she'd lived in his dreams, but now he imagined smelling her scent while he was out mending fences or could see her face while taking the milk to town. Snapping the head off another stalk, Ed gazed up at the sky and began to shout, "We want a planned and socialized economy in which our natural resources and principal means of production and distribution are owned, controlled, and operated by the people!"

Every time he thought about Bessie, Ed concentrated on the League. He knew the doctrine by heart and as of late, he and Fen had been writing feverishly back and forth. When Bessie wanted to know where the letters came from, Ed simply responded it was a friend from school. It wasn't a lie, he just omitted to mention all the leaflets and articles that came with it as well.

Stuffed in with the latest news about the League, Fen had included an article about the Communist Party. Their leader, Tim Buck, had been unjustly jailed by Bennett for sedition, and shot in prison, but recently, back on the streets. The man who had tried to shoot him was never identified, and many claimed the government had attempted to assassinate Buck.

Ed pulled the letter out of his back pocket, and sitting down in a break in the rows of wheat, began to read:

"In the absence of any real leadership in this country, I think that it's time to give socialism very serious consideration as a political alternative for Canada."

Fen went on to say he was helping to organize a big rally in Toronto that autumn, and all the old gang would be there.

Ed folded the letter and slid it back into his pocket. The material was fascinating, and Ed would have loved to go, but his responsibilities lay first with Charlie and the family.

Bessie's work dress stuck to her back. She and Ed had been on their knees for hours, carefully picking ripe cucumbers from the long leafy trellises of vines. It could be a clever business venture, since Bette could sell them at the end of the lane to those passing by.

Physically demanding, the task was a loathsome one, especially in the red-hot heat. Ed slapped the back of his neck every once in a while, at the swarms of mosquitoes and black flies taking bites out of his exposed flesh.

A horn honked and Bessie looked up. Mrs. Little's bright blue sedan was rolling across the concession road toward town. Rising to her feet, and seeing Mrs. Moffatt seated in the car, Bessie waved. They're likely going for tea, she thought, dropping to her knees to resume picking cucumbers. Anger flooded her, why do they get to have tea while I'm down in the dirt? She looked at the green cucumbers placed in the basket. Long, fat, and firm, rightly priced, they could bring decent money to the farm. But what if these cucumbers barely paid for the seed? she thought, snapping another one from the vine. Beads of perspiration rolled down her back, and as they did, she acknowledged how tired she was—tired of fretting about money. Tired of endlessly skimping. On top of it all, Charlie was coming home tomorrow, and she would have to add nursemaid to her roster of duties.

Ed watched Bessie remove a floral handkerchief to wipe the sweat from her forehead. A light breeze blew across the patch, opening Bessie's blouse slightly, revealing her pale ivory skin lightly flecked with freckles. Absentmindedly, Bessie reached down and lightly patted her chest. Ed looked to the ground, his eyes searching for another cucumber. He wanted desperately to watch, but knew that if she caught him, she'd realize what she'd done and be embarrassed. He'd never seen her daydream before, with hands moving automatically across the vines. It was obvious, her mind was miles away. He watched Bessie's hands as they worked the patch together in a near perfect silence, and he wondered where she'd gone.

After another hour or so, a ball of dust appeared. "Looks like Mooney's here," Ed said.

Bessie looked in the direction of the barn. Sure enough, Mooney's old, slatted truck was pulling in by the chicken coop. She rose to her feet.

"I want to see what we fetched," she said.

"I'll keep picking," Ed replied, lifting the leaves, searching for more ripe vegetables.

"Why don't you come with me? I think it's high time I had a chat with Mooney," Bessie said. With hands on her hips and eyes clear, she walked down the well mulched patch toward the barn.

Mrs. Moffatt felt terrible seeing Bessie on her hands and knees exposed to the blazing sun. Work meant for men or older children, not the woman of the house. But Mrs. Moffatt knew the Barnes' couldn't afford hired help.

She smiled and nodded at Mrs. Little while having coffee at Rambel's, a small restaurant that provided fine cooking for good people. The establishment was a former stagecoach stop and was situated by the side of a dam. From there, one could see where the drivers used to tether the horses.

Mrs. Little dropped two sugar cubes into her coffee, and prattled on about how shameful it was to see Mrs. Barnes out in the field like a hired hand.

Mrs. Moffatt examined the cutlery, thinking. Folks knew Charlie was out of commission, but nobody knew Adam had shot him, as most thought infection was the culprit. It had been yet another kindness Mrs. Barnes had bestowed—to keep it to herself. Mrs. Moffatt wanted things back to the way they were before, with Mrs. Little chairing the Institute and Mrs. Barnes taking minutes as they continued to safeguard the moral fiber of the community, and make certain the children had nutritious meals.

"She hasn't been to a meeting in weeks," Mrs. Little said, setting her spoon down on the saucer with an air of finality. "How is she supposed to keep accurate minutes if she doesn't attend?"

"Mr. Barnes will be home soon, and things will get back to normal," Mrs. Moffatt said, adding, "I think it's the Christian thing for us to help carry the load."

Mrs. Little took a bite out of her cookie while staring at a bevy of swans in Watson's Dam. The largest one flapped its wings, spreading an impressive eddy, rocking the smaller birds. Mrs. Moffatt swallowed, not knowing what was to be done, but understanding she had to make things right with that family.

Mooney Shantz was rocking back and forth on his heels with his hands thrust deep into the pockets of his dirty overalls, staring at the chickens. "Well, I don't know, Bessie," he said.

"There is nothing wrong with those eggs Mooney Shantz, and you know that."

"Jim said about a dozen of them was cracked last time," Mooney drawled, expelling a long hork of spit that landed on the floor near Bette, who looked at Uncle Ed and grimaced.

"They were not cracked, and I want my money," Bessie said, moving an inch closer to Mooney.

"Aw Bessie, you know what Jim's like."

"Yes, I do and I know that it's not beneath you and Jim to occasionally pocket a bit of change for yourselves. Normally, I turn a blind eye, but not today. Today, I want my money," she added, stepping more toward Mooney.

Ed was surprised. Bessie generally didn't get this aggressive.

"Now Bessie," Mooney said, taking a step back.

"We've been one of your best suppliers for years and if you don't pay me for my eggs, and I mean every last egg that you take out of here, I'll go elsewhere. And I don't care if we have to take them into the market ourselves," she added.

"My brother's driving now," Bette piped up, "he can take them!"

Mooney looked at the floor and he looked at the window and he looked at the egg crates and he horked again. Clearing his throat, and after letting out the longest sigh ever heard from a miserly egg grader, he pulled some coins out of his pocket, and carefully counted out the exact amount. "Here," he said, as he handed Bessie the money.

Thanking him with a smile, Bessie proudly reminded herself nobody ever got an extra penny out of Mooney Shantz. Turning to Ed and Bette, she told them to get cleaned up, that she was going to fix her hair and change. "And tell Teddy to do the same," she added, "we're going to town."

"Can I have two scoops?" Bette asked, peering through the frosted glass front of the ice cream keeper. Bessie nodded to the owner of the Mercantile who dug the metal scoop deep into the chocolate bucket. Teddy was carefully licking his cone, creating perfect circles around its circumference with his tongue.

"What'll you have Ed?" Bessie asked, as the owner handed Bette her cone.

"Thank you, sir," Bette said politely, before she opened her mouth and dove face first into the ice cream.

"Elizabeth!" Bessie said, "take your time."

But Bette had already chomped off a chunk of chocolate and was merrily chewing away with her mouth open.

Bessie sighed.

"What would you like?" the owner asked Ed again.

"I'm fine," he replied, walking toward the window.

"Look," Bette said, pointing to a cut out of Wilton Gillespie standing in the middle of a pen of fat cattle recommending Shur Gain cattle feed. Good Enough for Gillespie? Good Enough For You.

They all looked at each other, and knowingly smiled.

"Two cones of maple walnut," Bessie said, shooing the children toward the screen door.

She paid the man, and taking the cones, Bessie approached Ed.

"Here," she said, handing him one.

"We don't have the money for this," he replied.

"We're not paupers," Bessie said, taking a bite out of hers. "Come on Ed, it's so tasty," she insisted.

Standing together in the store window, and watching an old married couple stroll slowly by, Ed took a lick. Bessie was right. It was delicious.

Adam Moffatt plopped down at the kitchen table without removing his boots while his wife silently fumed. Every day she asked him to take them off, and every meal in Adam stomped. "It's my house," Adam said, "and a man does what a man wants in his own home." He opened the newspaper and scanned the headlines, only looking up to his wife to ask what was for supper.

"Chili," she replied, stirring the pot on the stove. She hoped it would make him more amenable to what she had in mind. "Chili and fresh rolls," she added, appealing to her husband's appetite.

"When we gettin' it? Tomorrow?" he asked.

She lifted the pot from the stove. Adam had never been a sweet talker, she knew, but when he'd first courted her, she thought his gruff manner a cover for shyness. She'd been wrong. There was nothing sweet or shy about her Adam. Yet, the man was a successful farmer, a good provider, and as far as the rest of the community was concerned, the Moffatts were people of good standing.

Mrs. Moffatt had a seat on the board of the Women's Institute, and Adam was an elder at the church. Even with his spotty attendance. Nobody knew about the politics of their marriage, and so for years Mrs. Moffatt had toed the line and kept Adam's house clean, his belly full, and together they presented a unified front to the community. That night was the first time Mrs. Moffatt had dared even think of challenging his authority. But the matter was too important, for they just had to do the right thing by Charlie Barnes.

"How's the chili, dear?" she asked.

Her stomach was too knotted up to swallow so much as a bite.

Adam grunted, tore a roll in half, shoving it into the bowl, and turning the page. "The Prime Minister is making a tour of the country," he said, chewing on the roll. "Why is the government spending good money carting that bag of wind around?"

Mrs. Moffatt couldn't take it anymore. "Adam … I want us to pay Charlie Barnes' hospital bill."

Slowly the paper lowered as Adam stared at his wife in utter disbelief. "What did you just say?"

"I said we should pay Charlie Barnes' hospital bill."

Adam's fist came down so hard the dishes jumped. "There is no way in hell that I'm paying that bill!" he bellowed.

Mrs. Moffatt shook, but she was determined, and wouldn't back down. "Adam, we have the money. They don't. And after all … you shot him."

"Is it my fault if he comes creeping around my hen house in the middle of the night? I'm not going belly up for a family that can't save for a bit of foul weather. If you want to go to the poorhouse, Lily Moffatt, you'll be going by yourself. You're not going on my dime."

Mrs. Moffatt was raging inside, watching her husband leaning back in his chair, smirking and defiantly stuffing the roll in his mouth, and she had a sudden urge to dump the whole pot of chili over his head. Of course, that wouldn't do, though something else might, she thought.

Dinner was over, and Bessie, in a mood for entertainment, asked Ed to turn on the radio. "Would you?" she asked with a smile.

Ed removed himself from the kitchen table, walked over to the radio, and twisted the knobs. After a series of crackles and pops, strange voices swirled around the parlor like spirits from the netherworld. And then, all the way from Radio City Music Hall in New York City, a performance of, "The Very Thought of You", began.

"Would you care to dance?" Ed asked, bowing deeply.

"Don't be a goose, Ed," Bessie said, remembering his hand tucked into the small of her back as he had held her close so many years before.

"Come on," Ed replied, taking her hand, "don't you remember how?" he asked, pulling Bessie to her feet, sweeping her into the center of the room.

The music filled the parlor, and as it did, she decided to surrender, and it felt lovely to close her eyes and follow the rhythm—to follow him, again—if even only for a moment.

When the song ended Fred Astaire's "Cheek to Cheek" began.

"Are you tired?" Ed asked.

Bessie shook her head, no, she had become hooked—to the past? Or was it to the present? And so quickly, she caught herself thinking, surprised.

She felt as though she could dance as long as the music lasted, that she could dance all night just to put her troubles away: Dancing as a cure.

Ed grabbed her hand, and spinning her, folded her body back into his arms. That is where she belongs, he thought, in his arms, and while he felt her cheek next to his, he knew the moment to be a singular occurrence, that it would never—could never—happen again.

"Why did you change your name?" she whispered into his ear. "I liked Hannibal so much better," she sighed.

He looked at her and held her closer as they continued to sway.

So, Mother can dance, Teddy saw from the couch, and it seemed even stranger to see Uncle Ed waltz her around the parlor as if alone.

Bored, his sister had disappeared out to the barn to see how Ginger's kittens were faring, leaving Teddy on his own. It would be fun to listen to one of Uncle Ed's political broadcasts, he thought, the ones they listened to when Mother and Dad had gone to bed. Those folks really got whipped up, proclaiming how they were going to take the country back, and turn it into a place fair for everybody, not just the rich.

Teddy had become interested in hearing about Tim Buck and the League for Social Reconstruction. Ed had mentioned the LSR was organizing rallies all over the country. His good friend Fen was planning a huge gathering in Toronto in the fall, and it would coincide with the opening of the Royal Winter Fair.

To him, socialism seemed decent and was more likely the Christian thing to do and be, but Teddy didn't think the rich people would be all that willing to share. Just look at Mr. Moffatt, he thought. He and a handful of others in the county have more than enough to get by, but you never saw them helping people get out of the poorhouse. The more money you had, the fiercer you had to protect it, and if you had the ill fortune to land in the poorhouse, you either stayed there or you got yourself out. No, as nice as it sounded, there was something about communism and socialism that just didn't make a lot of sense to Teddy Barnes.

The music still playing, the boy observed his uncle twirl his mother again, the skirt of her dress blowing up. Funny, he thought, she has a strange, distant look on her face. To him, as with any other boy his age, she was simply his mother. Yet, that night, she had transformed into a beautiful woman, one dancing as if in a dream. Bill was wrong. Dancing wasn't stupid. If you learned how to do it properly it could take you somewhere magical—far away from the farm.

The music slowed and Ed released his grip, Bessie keeping hold of his hand. "Can we do one more?"

Ed nodded.

Teddy, go and find Bette," Bessie said, "it's getting late."

Teddy nodded, disappointed, as he wanted to watch his mother and Uncle Ed dance.

The moon was hanging low and one of the cows lowed. Mother was right, Teddy thought, it's getting late. They'd never been up past ten, other than New Year's Eve, and there was nothing special about this night.

"Hello!" Teddy called, entering the chicken house. "Where are you, Bette? It's time for bed!" he called again, not hearing an answer. "Come on!"

He walked farther into the coop and he finally saw her, curled up on a bale of hay with Ginger and her babies, fast asleep, oblivious to the world.

The lights in the parlor glowed as the strains of music drifted out of the speaker. Feeling light, Bessie moved in Ed's arms as if she'd always been there. When he turned, she followed. When he thrust forward, she drifted back. Ed dared to slightly nuzzle her hair, the smell of apple, and felt the warm heat of her body. Bessie closed her eyes, smiling. She felt happy, she felt light, and keeping her eyes closed, she rose her bosom, reciprocating the motion, answering what needed to be answered. Dancing more, they never heard the children enter the room.

"Mother," they said in tandem.

The couple separated as if oil and water, eyes askew.

The music ended, the concert over, and suddenly Bessie was herding the kids up the stairs.

Back in the kitchen, once the children were put to bed, they met again.

"I can't believe how the time flew by tonight," Bessie said, hitting the light switch. "And Ed," she added, sweeping by him through the dark on her way up the stairs, "thank you."

Ed, still feeling the heat of her body in his arms and thinking he hadn't wanted for any of it to stop, simply said, "goodnight."

Bessie slid between the bed sheets and gazed at the moon. She could see the outline of the Moffatt's silo in the distance and thought of dancing. She'd only known a feeling like that once in her life. Edward's arms still felt the same as when she was a girl. He even smelled the same, and moved the same, she thought. And then guilt began worming at the bottom of her stomach. She wasn't thinking of Charlie, instead, she was dreaming of dancing with his brother. Her husband was coming home the next day, and yet, she was having wicked thoughts about a way of life she was supposed to despise.

She leapt out of bed and opened the cedar blanket box. The metal box was at the bottom. She opened it—the tin was empty except for a long blue jewelry box, Charlie's pocket watch, their wedding certificate, and the deed for the farm. Bessie slid the deed in her purse, shut the blanket box, and crept back into bed. There would be no more thoughts of dreaming, and dancing, and pushing the inevitable away. Tomorrow, she and Charlie were going to have to mortgage the farm, and they would have to harvest the wheat.

She rolled away from the moon, wanting to sleep, feeling quieter. She had a plan, and she would stick with it, and it would yield.

Early the next morning, Teddy helped Bessie put the milk cans in the car. She was going to drop them off on her way to the hospital.

"Where's Uncle Ed?" she asked, looking across the yard. "He missed breakfast."

"He was up early," Teddy said, "I heard him get up before dawn."

"Then you keep an eye on Bette," Bessie said, sliding into the car, "she's spending way too much time with those kittens. Your Dad and I should be back before dinner."

Pulling out of the driveway, she carefully drove down the lane, wondering about the unfolding of her day.

Ed pounded a fence post into the earth and wrapped the old wire around it. A bit of the barb caught in his shirt, ripping some of it off. Furious, he hurled the mallet at the earth. He hadn't slept all night, and every time he had closed his eyes, Bessie had appeared. He would have read, but he didn't want the light to disturb his nephew, and besides, there wasn't a book in the world that could have stopped him thinking about her.

Picking up the mallet, Ed walked over to the next post, knowing it was loose as well. The whole line of fencing on the north side of the property needed work. I want to stay busy, he thought. And soon, he hoped, Charlie would be home and things would get back to normal. But what was normal? He brought the mallet down on the post with another angry bang. If he hadn't known it before, he knew it now, he was desperately in love with his brother's wife. Of course, he could never say it out loud, knowing the love was doomed. Besides, he could barely admit it to himself.

For the first time in weeks, Ed felt the need for a drink even though he'd sworn off the stuff following the incident with May. But right now, he thought, a drink would chase the images of Bessie from his mind. He brought the mallet down with another bang as Charlie came to mind, again. He loved his brother and would never hurt him. So how could he sit across the table from Bessie for the rest of his life? Confused, he swung the mallet harder, feeling the sun's rays beating down on him. And as he did, he asked himself: How could he not?

"Name please?" a nurse asked, leaning over the typewriter to reach a neat stack of pending invoices.

"Barnes, Charles," Bessie replied.

The woman's fingers quickly flipped through the papers as Bessie looked up at the clock. It was 9:15 a.m. If she got to the bank at ten, she could be back here and get Charlie home by noon.

"Mrs. Barnes?" the nurse asked.

"Yes," Bessie replied, forgetting where she was for a moment.

"There is no outstanding balance."

"I beg your pardon?"

"The bill's been paid," the nurse replied, carefully sliding the file back into its proper place.

"That doesn't make any sense," Bessie said, "who would pay my husband's hospital bill?"

"I'm sure I don't know," the nurse primly replied.

"Will you please look?" Bessie asked, setting her shoulders.

The nurse protectively set her hand on top of the files. "That would be against hospital policy."

"There must be a mistake," Bessie said. "Barnes, Mr. Charles Barnes."

"I'm sorry, Mrs. Barnes, as I told you before," the nurse curtly replied, "the bill has been settled. You should be grateful."

Frustrated, Bessie put her hands on her hips. "Can I take Charlie home?"

"Your husband is free to leave as soon as the doctor signs his release papers."

"Thank you," Bessie replied.

"Which won't be until this evening because Dr. Ramsey is away delivering a baby," the nurse added with not so much as a smile.

Bessie stared at the nurse for a moment, unimpressed, and tucked the deed back into her purse. Adjusting her hat, she couldn't stop wondering who had paid Charlie's bill. But she suspected, she knew where to look.

Bessie knocked briskly on the Moffatt's front door.

Nobody answered.

"Hello!" she called through the open window.

She knocked again—still nothing. Looking around, she put her hand on the doorknob, turned it, and stepped into the front hall. Walking beneath a small chandelier, she moved toward the dining room. A strange electrical purring was coming from the parlor, and it was getting louder.

"Hello!" Bessie called again, crossing the room.

Nervously, she opened the door.

Before her, Mrs. Moffatt was on hands and knees, reaching behind the sofa with what looked like the arm of a growling metallic octopus.

"What's that?" Bessie asked.

Mrs. Moffatt, startled, shrieked, and stood straight. "Oh, Bessie, it's you. I was about to make some tea. Would you like to join me?"

"Thank you, kindly," Bessie said, feeling shaky herself.

"Come dear, let's sit, just here." She pointed to the sitting area. Mrs. Moffat, hair tied back in a bright yellow bandana, fixed her apron and left the room wondering why Mrs. Barnes was standing in the middle of her house.

Bessie walked to her chair, and scanning the area, noted how lovely the parlor was, much of the furniture looked new. All of mine came from relatives, she thought to herself, suddenly feeling sad.

"Would you like some sugar in your tea?" Mrs. Moffatt asked, as she returned, bringing the teapot to the table.

Bessie nodded looking at the cup. It was a fussy one with a scalloped bright blue china plate. She allowed herself two lumps, noting Mrs. Moffatt even had silver tongs. "What is that contraption?" she asked, pointing at the metal octopus.

"It's a Westinghouse vacuum," Mrs. Moffatt replied. "It comes with all kinds of attachments so you can reach any kind of place."

Bessie nodded, looking suspiciously at the machine. She'd heard about vacuum cleaners, and was grudgingly interested, but scrunched her nose in silent disapproval. She decided it looked like something Adam had found at the fair. "Does it work?"

Mrs. Moffatt said yes, that surprisingly, while most would think it a gadget, it did work.

As Mrs. Moffatt didn't appear to want to converse, Bessie decided to come to the point. "Charlie's coming home today," she said.

Mrs. Moffatt, nodding, removed her bandana from her hair, untied her apron, and fixed her hair as she thought of the previous night when she'd taken money from Adam's cigar box. Fast asleep and snoring, he had rolled over and snorted, sending Mrs. Moffatt into a panic.

Bessie set the teacup down on the table and leaned forward, her fingers gently tracing the silver spoon. She looked at Mrs. Moffatt. "Somebody paid the hospital bill."

"Is that so?" Mrs. Moffatt asked, briskly stirring the sugar in her cup.

Bessie swallowed. "Was it Adam?" she finally asked.

"Oh my, no!" Mrs. Moffatt exclaimed, adding, "And he must never find out."

Thoughts of Adam riding his dirty horse into the house shaking the empty money box flashed through her mind. Would he dare bring a horse into her house in an act of revenge?

"Then how?" Bessie asked.

Mrs. Moffatt looked set to pitch a fit. Her normally placid neighbor looked positively wild. The woman didn't answer, imagining Adam parading the pigs through the parlor. There was no telling what he'd do if he discovered she'd stolen his money. Would he hit her? He hadn't so far, and they'd been together twenty years. Would he put her out of the house? Her heart thumped with fear, followed by a jolt of something even stronger—pure undiluted anger. How dare he put her out of her own house!

Bessie set her teacup down and stared quizzically at her.

Mrs. Moffatt hadn't stolen a thing. Yes, the farm had been Adam's, but I balance the books, barter with Mooney, and plant the vegetable garden that provide food and additional income. I've pulled more than my weight, she thought, while partnered to a bully who won't take his boots off before entering the house.

She looked at Bessie. "Don't you think that a woman's egg money is her own to spend as she sees fit?"

Bessie, not knowing what to say, simply nodded.

"I've worked my fingers to the bone in this house, and I think I should have some say, at least as far as my own egg money is concerned," she said, feeling a sudden swell of confidence replacing her ebbing fear. "He struts around here like a rooster that only knows how to crow."

"Did you pay the bill?" Bessie asked.

"I most certainly did."

Bessie couldn't believe it, and listening more, she brought the teacup to her lips.

"Your Charlie is in the hospital because of my Adam, Bessie."

"Thank you," Bessie said softly, understanding Mrs. Moffatt had done the unthinkable, broken with her husband to help a neighbor.

"Please Bessie. I don't want to hear another word about it."

Bessie could see there was no point in contesting it. Mrs. Moffatt had made up her mind, and whatever storm of fear had flashed through her, Mrs. Moffatt appeared to have retreated to a new and more comfortable place. Her face was now rosy, and there was a gleam in her eye, one Bessie had never seen before.

Mrs. Moffatt set her teacup on the end table. "Mrs. Barnes, would you like to try my vacuum cleaner?" Mrs. Moffatt asked, smiling, too.

Bessie nodded. Contraption or no, she was dying to find out if the machines worked better than giving a rug a good shake.

"But please," she said, "call me, Bessie."

"Only if you'll call me Lily."

Ed was in the shed cleaning the hay binder. The weatherman had promised sunny days for at least another week, and Ed was concerned about the sun's rays hitting Bessie's skin. Oiling the binder blades, he thought of Bessie commandeering the machine. No woman wanted color on her skin, as it meant the family couldn't afford hired help, and that they were poor. The sound of a car door slammed in the yard, momentarily catching his attention. It had to be Bessie home with Charlie, and he thought—the dancing was done. Continuing his work on the binder, he felt the tip of his finger catch the metal. He looked down and saw blood had dripped on the blade. When he looked back up, May was standing at the door.

Teddy heard the sound of crunching gravel as his mother pulled the Dodge into the yard. Where's Dad?" he called.

"He'll be released later today," his mother replied, slamming the car door. "Where's Bette?"

"Playing." Chucking Hannibal's wattle, the rooster tried to peck him, but Teddy was too fast.

"Whose car is this?" Bessie asked, peering inside of the sedan, where she saw a burgundy purse resting on the seat, the ashtray full of lipstick-stained cigarette butts.

"It's a lady. I think maybe she's Uncle Ed's sweetheart," Teddy replied with a giggle.

His mother wasn't laughing. She told Teddy to find his sister and to get in the house, and she began to walk toward the barn.

Before Ed could catch his breath, May was standing in front of him, asking him where he'd been? If he'd missed her?

"What are you doing here?"

"You certainly didn't make it easy, but I tracked you down," May replied. "I had to describe you to everyone I met, and eventually ... well somebody thought you lived out here and I borrowed my uncle's car."

Ed didn't answer and looked toward the barn door.

"I thought maybe you figured I was mad," she said with a flirtatious smile. "At first I was, but now I'm not."

As Ed tried to step back, May stepped forward. "Why didn't you come back to the tavern? I've missed you."

"What tavern?" Bessie asked.

Ed looked toward the barn door. "Bessie ..."

May looked behind her. "*You're* Bessie?"

"Please leave," Bessie said.

"I'm just here to speak to Ed," May added, "then I'll be going."

"You'll be going right now. My brother-in-law's got work to do."

"Your brother-in-law?" May asked, looking back at Ed.

Ed's eyes said everything, pleading with her to please just leave, and not make things any worse.

"Will you come and see me?" she asked.

He nodded.

"Okay," May replied, moving toward the door. Looking at Bessie, she added she didn't want to start any trouble, that she only had wanted to find a friend.

Bessie curtly nodded her head as May left. "Who was that?" Bessie asked Ed.

"I'm sorry," Ed whispered, his mouth dry.

"Why didn't you tell us?" Bessie asked again. "You're running around meeting women in taverns, and you don't say so much as a word?" Disgust emerged inside of her as images of dirty minded men and women reeling around filled her mind. A thought twisted her heart. "Did you dance with her?"

"No ..."

"Yes, you did!" Bessie answered, her voice raised. She knew he had held that girl the same way he had held her. And what else had they done? Still glaring at Ed, he stepped forward and seized her arms, and she wriggled, trying to pull free, but he wouldn't let go—and shoving her hard up against the wall, he pushed his mouth over hers. Startled, she pushed back, but then she heard his words telling her that he loved her, that he'd always had. She raised her hands, first tentatively, then furtively ran her fingers through his thick dark hair. Ed held her closer, kissing her and telling her how beautiful she was and how much he loved her, that he'd looked everywhere for her for over a year.

Bessie tilted her head, opened her lips more and kissed him back, forgetting she was Charlie Barnes's wife; forgetting she had children. And as they continued to whisper words each had been hungry to hear, a sound filled the room, prompting Bessie to open her eyes. When she did, she saw Teddy standing at the barn door, holding Hannibal in his hands.

"Let me go," Bessie hissed, but Ed held her fast. "Uncle Ed was just helping me," Bessie quickly added.

When Ed saw Teddy, his arms jerked back as if he'd been scalded.

"Why don't you go and get some dinner on," Bessie added. "There's soup on the stove. All you have to do is heat it up." A wave filled her with everything she didn't want to feel, and she thought, what have I done? I've shamed myself, my children, and my husband. And all because of Edward Barnes—again.

"I'm sorry, Bessie," Ed said, dropping his head, "but I do love you."

She didn't look at him. All was over; all had been over before it had even begun.

"Pack your things," she said. "I'll drive you to the station."

EIGHT

Building a Revolution

The train pulled into Union Station in a cloud of thick white steam as the sun fell behind the horizon. In a daze, Ed dragged his trunk down the platform and into the terminal, putting it in a locker. Feeling the heat of the day adding to his fatigue, he walked, his head hung low, unaware of the time; unaware of his destination. He felt lost, his bearings gone.

He'd never see Charlie or the children again, Bessie would see to that, and he'd never see her again ...

When they had stood on the railway platform to purchase Ed's ticket, she had avoided him, briskly paying the conductor and turning away. When she'd thrust the ticket into his hand, it was like he'd vanished, already nothing more than a nightmare she'd forgotten.

Ed pulled the ticket stub out of his pocket, the last thing Bessie had touched—a one-way, with no possibility for a return.

"Hey buddy, it can't be all that bad," a man said.

Ed turned and looked at a tall man in a shiny threadbare suit and worn-out shoes who stood in a doorway puffing on a cigarette. "You want a smoke?" the man asked, thrusting the pack toward Ed.

Ed nodded and slid one out.

"You new in town?" the man asked.

Ed nodded again.

"The name's Dutch," and he extended his hand.

Ed took it and gave it a shake.

"On account of my parents coming over here from Holland."

"Ed." Lightheaded from the tobacco, he leaned against the brick wall for support.

"Where you livin?" Dutch asked.

"Nowhere," Ed replied, realizing he didn't have a place to sleep.

"I've got a lean-to a couple of blocks up," Dutch said. "It's not much, but it's got enough room for two. You got any money at all?"

"Just a couple of bucks," Ed said, feeling the change at the bottom of his pocket. "That's enough for a bottle," Dutch replied with a grin. "Come on, I know a man who's got the best gut rot in town."

The hobo jungle was bigger than he remembered. The haphazard homes built from old loading crates, wires dangling everywhere, flapping tarps and straggly rope, all sprawling out from City Hall. Filthy people squatting on the sidewalk stared darkly up at him as he walked by. Afraid to glance at them for fear they'd descend upon him, he kept close to Dutch.

His new friend walked in a confident manner, knowing the rules of the place. Stepping over tumble-weeding garbage, Ed looked down at a woman and two little kids cooking soup over an open fire. The little girl, skinny and filthy, wore an old nightgown as a dress. It had to have been washed many times, he thought, the flowers on the nightgown barely visible. Where was the father? Ed asked himself, watching the mother stir a clear, meatless soup. It looked foul.

A toothless woman grinned at him and said hi to Dutch.

"That's Jenny. She's been out here for two years," Dutch said as they walked past more huts and tents. "She's like the mother we all miss," he added with a wry smile.

"And here's home," Dutch said, arriving in front of an efficiently assembled lean-to. Ed stared at the dwelling, its tin metal roof, clapboard sides, and a working door. "I got most of the stuff from one of the boondoggles the government was runnin'. They had us tearing down abandoned houses, and rather than see it all go to waste, I brought it home. With anything extra, I made the rounds and repaired other shacks."

Surprising, inside, it was spotless, filled with mismatched wooden floors and blankets rolled up in the corner. At the back, near the makeshift wall, was a can of Sterno for cooking, and a wash basin for cleaning up. Beside the basin, an old towel and face cloth were carefully folded over its side. Boards, supported on either side by several red clay bricks, created a bookcase that stood beneath a peaceful painting of a red canoe drifting in the middle of a lake. He reads, Ed thought. A lot.

His host opened the door in an effort to coax in the faint breeze. "Have a seat," Dutch said, patting the floor as he sat down. Pulling a bottle of whiskey from his breast pocket and uncorking it with his teeth, he said, "Here's mud in your eye," and took a long, hard slug.

Ed tried to match Dutch belt for belt, listening to his host regaling him with stories of political intrigue. The man was an avowed communist, he realized, one who'd taken the oath following the Regina riots. "Here," Dutch said, and he picked up several pamphlets on subjects of Trotskyism, Lenin, and Karl Marx. Ed leafed through them, glancing at the marked passages, intrigued by the ideas he encountered. He had heard of the riots, but knew little of the details, assuming a bunch of drifters had gotten out of control, prompting the police to gas them to maintain order.

Dutch roared and lit another cigarette. "There were 1,500 of us. 1,500 men without any hope, trekking across the country to protest being locked up in Bennett's relief work camps. We were heading to Regina so the P.M. could hear our grievances—righteous grievances, let me tell you."

Ed wondered if Dutch was right. He knew how he'd been treated at the university. He grabbed the bottle from Dutch and took another deep drink, listening intently to his new friend's stories.

"In a lot of places, folks came out and fed us. We slept under the stars. It was beautiful. We had purpose—a common purpose."

Ed wondered what it was like to have a real purpose, to believe in something that could never be taken away. He had put his faith in history, and he had loved Bessie. In the process, he had lost his future, his heart, and his home. No matter how hard he tried, nothing seemed to work. He was a failure.

Dutch continued talking about how he'd been radicalized by the Riots. He'd found the fight of his life, he said. Maybe that's what Ed needed? To join arms with like-minded people and try to change the world. With every sip of the whiskey, he felt the loss of the last years slide to the center of his belly and turn into a bright burning.

"Come," Dutch said, "let's sit on the front porch. It's too damned hot in here."

The moon hung over City Hall, but the heat remained, trapped by buildings and bodies while the concrete jungle broiled. "It all started because of the Relief Camps. Nowhere decent to sleep. Tents with holes with the rain running in, or windowless tin bunkies that slept ten men. There wasn't enough food to feed a child, never mind a fully grown man doing heavy labor. They set up humiliating jobs to keep us busy. Building roads that went nowhere. Finally, we started a newspaper, and then started a union. That's where Slim Evans figured in. He organized the march. We walked out of the camps, joined up in Vancouver, and trekked all the way to Regina. The plan was we'd have a face to face with Mr. R. B. Bennett. The chance to talk things through like men."

A couple of cats started to fight behind a trash can. Dutch lobbed a rock and a howl rang out. "All we wanted was a decent wage," Dutch continued, when three boys suddenly ran by, calling out the police were coming. People immediately disappeared into the shadows. "I'm not moving," Dutch grumbled. "We ain't doin' nothin' wrong." He took another chug and handed the last dregs to Ed, who tipped the bottle back and felt the courage of his friend. There was no point running away, he had nowhere left to go, and nothing left to lose.

Two cops with Billy clubs and tall black helmets came from around the corner. Ed swayed a bit, regaining his balance by leaning back on the palm of his hand.

"What have you got there?" the younger policeman asked, tapping the club in his hand. "Nothing," Ed said, defiantly draining the bottle dry.

"It's against the law to consume liquor in public," the other officer said.

Nobody ever challenged the local constabulary, and all knew of Chief Denny Draper, and what would happen if you got dragged downtown. They'd toss you in the hole until Draper would come by for a personal visit, sometimes wearing brass knuckles, other times, with a blood-stained club.

"Why there's no liquor here officer," Ed said, slurring slightly and getting up to wag the bottle back and forth. "In fact, it's empty," he laughed, the bottle dangling from his index finger as he began to dance a triumphant little jig.

Dutch got up and joined him, and the two new friends, arm-in-arm, gamboled about the lean-to. The older policeman moved nearer, examining Ed in the diminishing twilight. This boy didn't belong here,

111

his shoes were new and his clothes clean. "I think it's time for you to move along home," he said.

Ed stopped dancing. He felt his back go up. "I'm staying," he replied, brazenly sticking his chest out.

A couple of people nearby inched out from the dark, looking for a better view. The younger policeman looked, a gathering crowd in the jungle meant trouble. "This is none of your business!" he yelled into the blue evening, banging his club on a light standard to scare the bums away. "Get back to your dwellings."

The older policeman, sensing trouble, looked at his partner. "Come on Pete, let's go."

Dutch punched Ed playfully on the shoulder after the officers left. "You're a real fighter, aren't ya?"

"I don't know about that," Ed said, feeling somewhat pleased.

"Yes, you are," said a woman appearing out of the shadows. "Ain't nobody ever stands up to the coppers."

And now other homeless men and women came out of their shacks, wanting to congratulate Ed.

He smiled. For the first time in years, he felt like a hero.

Ed had spent the previous week repairing shacks and immersing himself in the reality of life as a homeless man, and had dismissed the thought of the others being dangerous. Life circumstances had done this, nothing else.

That night, Ed and Dutch were out for a walk, when they heard a voice, "What are you fellows up to?"

They looked up and saw the same policemen who had been there before. The older one was hard to read, Ed thought, but he felt certain, they'd come back to finish what they'd started. "Just taking a little night air," Ed replied.

"Is that against the law?" Dutch asked.

A man with no shoes took a couple of steps back.

"What's your name?" the older cop asked the retreating man.

"Go," Ed advised the hobo watching.

"Who are you, telling people what to do?" the younger policeman asked.

"This doesn't have anything to do with him," Ed replied.

The shoeless hobo looked at Ed and Dutch and backed away.

The older policeman looked at Ed. "I thought we told you to shove off," he said.

"I decided to stay," Ed replied.

The younger cop turned his attention to Dutch. "Mr. Van Drunen, my partner tells me that you're a rabble rouser."

Dutch stared at the policeman, curled up his lip and spat, the spittle missing the cop's boot. In his mind, he was drawing a line in the sand. The older policeman removed a shiny silver whistle from his breast pocket and blew it.

The younger policeman moved to the doorway of Dutch's lean-to and peered in. "I see you're still collecting seditious literature," he said.

Dutch stepped in front of the cop and pulled the door shut with a bang. "This is my place. It's private property."

"This is public property and you're squatting," the officer said. Pushing Dutch aside, he kicked the door off its hinges.

Dutch was up, and on the policeman's back, clawing at him, pulling him back out of the lean-to and yelling nobody could tell him what he could or could not read, that Canada wasn't a fascist state, at least not yet.

The older policeman brought his Billy club down on Dutch's back, sending him to the ground, crying in pain. A siren wailed and a searchlight swooped in the distance. Ed reached for a piece of wood lying on the ground. The policeman raised the club again, about to bring it down on Dutch's head when Ed smashed the wood over the cop's helmet. Stunned more than hurt, and with fury in his eyes, the policeman raised the club and swung it at Ed, who, seeing the blow coming, ducked. Ed, standing back up, threw a punch that landed on the older policeman's jaw, the officer dropping to the pavement as police lit up Dutch's lean-to. Ed looked the unconscious policeman lying at his feet.

"First timer, huh?" asked a fat clerk, when Ed arrived at the police station.

"Yes," Ed replied.

"Take a seat."

The clerk took Ed's hand and began to fingerprint him. Ed looked around. The room, with an absence of light, was gloomy. "I hope the policeman is all right," he said. "I never meant to hurt him." But he knew there had been no choice, the cop, about to hit Dutch, had to be stopped. We were only talking politics, he thought, and there's no crime in that, and if there was, the laws need to be changed.

Following the fingerprinting procedure, an officer ushered Ed down a long, cavernous hall leading to a green metal door. From there, they walked until Ed could see a thin woman standing behind a clunky black plate camera. A large flash rested on an enormous stand beside her. Ed entered the room with the officer behind him.

"Behind the line," the woman ordered, not looking at him.

Ed stood against a blank white wall behind a thick black line.

"Name?" the woman asked.

"Edward Barnes."

The woman chalked Ed's name and the date on a small blackboard. "Hold it," she said, handing it to Ed. "Chest height, and look straight ahead."

Ed stared into the lens as the light bulb flashed, strobing the room.

"Now to the side," she ordered.

The last time Ed's photo had been taken was the day he'd received his PhD. How ironic, he thought, rubbing his eyes, and as he did, something inside of him—like a trigger, clicked. When I get out of jail, he promised himself, I will find Fen and I will introduce Dutch and the hobos to the intellectuals. I will write treatises. I will distribute pamphlets. I will talk to everyone living in the hobo jungle, and bang on the door of every fine home in the city, and like Hannibal, I will build an army and change the world.

NINE

Hannibal

The first night following Ed's departure, Bessie slept in Teddy's room so Charlie could convalesce. Wanting to erase all traces of Edward, she had washed, starched, and ironed each sheet. Still, his smell lingered, unsteadying her.

"Mother?" Teddy whispered quietly into the darkness, listening to his mother toss and turn. There was no response. "What's wrong?" he asked.

"Just allergies, now go to sleep," Bessie murmured.

"Does it have anything to do with Uncle Ed?" he asked, hoping she would talk about the kiss.

Bessie sat up in bed and turned the bedside light on. Teddy stared at her, wondering what had happened to his mother? With hair wild and unruly, and eyes red and swollen, his mother looked like that crazy lady from town that had to be hospitalized.

"Don't ever mention that man's name again in my presence," she replied in a low warning voice.

Bringing the bedcover above his chest Teddy turned away from his mother. Believing she knew of Ed's whereabouts, he promised himself one day he'd find his uncle.

Several weeks later, Teddy sat at the kitchen table eating breakfast with his father. Something had changed, he had sensed it ever since Uncle Ed left, the day his dad returned from the hospital.

"Go get Hannibal," his father said, breaking into Teddy's thoughts.

"Where are we going?"

"We're going for a ride."

While driving, Charlie looked at his son holding the rooster's claw, his hair pushed back by the breeze. These kids growing up, he thought, in this damn Depression, seven years of it now, with nothing changing. And now, Ed had left. It wasn't fair to the boy. No matter what fault Ed had committed, Bessie had no right to ban his brother from their lives. And why had Bessie been absent from their bedroom—what had he done? He knew there was more to the story, more to it than Bessie was willing to share.

"What are you thinking about, Dad?" Teddy asked, noticing darkness clouding his father's face.

Charlie turned to him with a smile. "We need a good inch of rain. Well, here we are."

A tiny brick house with a small green barn and a huge chicken coop stood on top of the hill. The name on the mailbox read TILT.

"C'mon, son, bring Hannibal."

Slightly limping, his straw hat rammed down over his head hiding his eyebrows, Mr. Tilt walked over. "Let's see what you've got there," he said, reaching for Hannibal. Slipping his hands under Hannibal, he closely examined the bird. "Good color and symmetry. The feathering on the breast is perfect."

"And he's really well trained, too," Teddy said, unable to keep quiet, and slightly concerned Mr. Tilt might be handling Hannibal a bit too roughly. "You don't have to squeeze him, he'll stand on your hand."

Charlie frowned. "Teddy, Mr. Tilt has taken the time out of his day to help you."

"That's all right, Charlie," the breeder said, handing the bird back to Teddy. "Hannibal's a beauty. You want to sell him?"

"Oh no, sir! I just want to show him."

"That's a good idea, he might be a winner."

Teddy smiled, because of his father, he thought, this was a perfect day.

Bessie, washing the dishes, was hardly able to contain herself. How dare Charlie go ahead with his plan? He knew darned well how she felt about waste, and especially about Teddy getting a swollen head. Why, if he won, they'd likely have to invest in parading the darned bird around from fair to fair. Slamming a pot into the sink, she sent water to the floor, and didn't care—she was furious. Charlie had gone and spent their money entering Hannibal in the Royal Winter Fair. And there you have it, she thought. Turmoil. Too much of it.

Life had been nothing but a huge fuss since the day Charlie came home from the hospital. The night following his return home, she had tried as best she could to hide the truth. Charlie, stretched out on the bed, and feeling completely helpless, had questioned her about Ed's absence.

"He's gone," Bessie had replied. "Don't get yourself all worked up. You know what Doc Ramsey said."

"Gone where?"

"Didn't say. Just packed his trunk and left. Most likely Toronto," she said. "They'll live with that sort of thing there, but not here."

The thought of Ed touching May, kissing her, had constricted her heart.

"Did you ask him to leave?"

Upon hearing the question, Bessie gathered her determination, fluffed Charlie's extra pillow, and answered she wouldn't have that kind of influence around her children.

"He's my brother."

"There was drinking, and there was kissing with this woman, this whore that smoked and worked in a tavern—a public display of sin. Most of all, the thing that I just can't condone," she had said, pausing for effect.

"Teddy saw it."

Pouring Charlie a glass of iced tea, Bessie had remained silent.

"Has Teddy talked about it?" he had asked, worried.

"No. And I don't want him thinking about things like that."

She had left the bedroom, leaving Charlie to wonder about his brother behaving the way Bessie had described. He would know if his brother had a sweetheart, if he had fallen in love. They'd worked together, side-by-side, day-to-day, all day, every day. Turning on his side, wanting to reposition his aching body, their wedding photo, resting on the bedside table, caught his eyes. "I was happy that day," he had whispered to no one.

He knew Bessie was a spirited woman, and he let her have her way on most things, but this—she'd thrown his brother off the family home right in the middle of the Depression, and worse yet, without consulting him.

Sipping his cold tea, he thought about the night in the snow when he was certain he'd smelled liquor on Ed's breath, and of that other evening, too, when shot by Adam, Ed had disappeared. Where exactly had he gone to?

Turning the nightlight off and feeling conflicted, he felt doubt seep into his heart, pushing him to a conclusion he didn't want to consider. Maybe, I didn't know my brother as well as I thought?

Bessie moved methodically from nest to nest, gathering eggs, her mind still mulling over her conversation with her husband. Charlie wasn't finished with this yet, but as far as she was concerned, it was over—she never wanted to hear that man's name again.

Continuing to gather the eggs, the realization that Edward was gone for good settled upon her. That she'd never see him again. She felt woozy, and she thought about the day he had left, their exchange. While he was packing, she'd paced back and forth in the bedroom, hands on her hips, warning him she'd tell Charlie everything, how he had accosted her in the barn, how she was certain he was going to rape her.

"Is that what you think?" he had asked, staring at her in disbelief. She might as well have shot him.

She told herself she hadn't done anything wrong. She was a God-fearing farmer's wife with two little kids who had known where she stood in the order of things, but then, Ed had kissed her, and her world had crumbled. It was his fault, not hers, and tears rolled down her cheeks. She brushed them away thinking, Ed had held her like no one ever had before. He had looked at her as if seeing all of her, each time, as if she were a new sight. The feeling of being desired and wanted and needed—an aliveness, she knew she would never encounter again.

Leaving the chicken coop, egg basket in hand, she wondered how she was going to survive without all of it.

Without him.

After several weeks of convalescence, Charlie was deemed fit for farming and allowed to resume limited physical activities.

Bessie hadn't returned to their bedroom, still sleeping in the sewing room, finding it cozy and warm, like a sanctuary.

The agreement was a tacit one, one Charlie felt was right. Suspicious of the truth, he barely could look at her, never mind sharing a bed with her. Still, his heart was sick, having turned on his only kin out of fear of losing his wife, who had threatened to leave him and return to her mother, if pushed too much.

Who had she become, he kept wondering? Who was she really? And what about me? What had happened to the man who brought that beautiful, sassy bride home so many years ago?

Standing at the sink, Bessie was thinking of the money Charlie had spent for the entry fee. She tried to calm herself, realizing there was nothing she could do about it. The smart thing was to let him think he was the man of the house, and as long as he didn't go too far, gradually, things might get back to normal.

Caught in a daze, tranquility returning to her mind, she started to recite Granny Baxter's favorite saying, "Patience is a virtue, possess it if you can. Seldom found in woman, and never found in man." As she dried the dishes she prayed for patience, and for the persistent thoughts of Ed to vanish.

"What are you chanting?" a voice asked.

Bessie turned around. "Hello Lily," she said, suddenly feeling inspired, "would you like some tea?" She smiled. An idea, clever as much as guileful, sprouted from her mind, not her heart. What if there were no reminders left of Edward's passage in her life—anywhere? Not the house, not at the farm, and not even in town? Movements, all kinds, forever erased. And maybe then, she thought, these sad, and lost feelings would leave, and she'd find peace.

Mrs. Moffatt sat down at the kitchen table, habitually unfolding her napkin.

"Lily," Bessie asked. "I need your honest opinion on something."

"All right," Mrs. Moffatt said, as Bessie put on the kettle.

"Do you think if there is a bad influence in our midst, God wants us to ferret it out?"

Mrs. Moffatt rubbed the end of her nose and gave it serious thought. "I think it depends if it's good for the community or simply good for the individual," Mrs. Moffatt replied.

"I know of a woman'" Bessie said, "who is seducing young men."

Mrs. Moffatt's eyes widened. "You don't say … is that what happened to—"

Bessie raised her hand to silence her friend. "I don't want to drag our good name into it, but just know that a woman by the name of May is living on top of the tavern, plying our young men with liquor, and showing them the pleasures of her flesh." Bessie, aware of her doing, gauged the impact of her words while pouring their tea. "Do you think this is something we should bring up at the Institute?" she asked.

Mrs. Moffatt nodded her head in agreement. "I most certainly do."

Teddy was showing Bill some of Hannibal's new tricks, when a big grey Chrysler sedan pulled up, sending the chickens into a frenzy.

The boys stopped to stare as the door opened and a big farm boot planted itself on the earth. It was Wilton Gillespie.

"Hello, sir," Bill said, jumping to his feet, extending a hand. "Is there anything we can do to help?" he asked.

Mr. Gillespie shook Bill's hand, and looked past the boys to the barn. "Is your father about?"

"Dad's in the barn," Teddy said. "This is my friend Bill."

"Oh hello, Mr. Gillespie," Bessie said, walking out on the stoop in her apron. "We didn't know you were coming. What can we do for you?"

"I'd like to see the calves your husband has for sale," Mr. Gillespie replied.

"Charlie's in with the cattle," Bessie said. "Would you like anything, anything at all? Lemonade?"

"I'm fine, thank you. Would it be all right if my daughter played with the boys?" he asked.

"Why certainly," Bessie replied, giving Teddy a look filled with motherly warning.

Laura Gillespie emerged from the back of the car wearing a bright green dress dotted with tiny white flowers. Her wavy auburn hair was braided in a perfect plait that ran halfway down her back. Teddy looked at her eyes, mesmerized. Made of green and yellow and brown, he had never seen eyes like these before in his life. Hazel eyes.

"Pleased to meet you," Bill said, walking straight up to Laura, his hand thrust out before him. "I'm Bill MacMillan."

"Hello," Laura said, looking over at Teddy who had turned bright red. "Is that your bird?" she asked.

Teddy nodded.

"We met at the church," she added.

Teddy nodded again, still speechless.

"His name is Teddy," Bill said with a grin. "And he's scared of girls."

Teddy could have clocked his friend.

"Since your friend doesn't remember me, my name is Laura."

"This is Hannibal," Teddy said, showing her his bird.

"He's very pretty. Have you had him for long?"

"Teddy raised him since he was a chick," Bill said. "Do you want to see where he sleeps?"

Laura nodded following Bill into the barn with Teddy taking up the rear.

"You're right to show him," Laura said, inspecting Hannibal. "He's better than most."

"How do you know?" Teddy asked, feeling a bit more settled now that all the attention was on his rooster.

"We go to the Royal every year," she replied, stroking Hannibal's breast. "I always go to the poultry show. They have such beautiful feathers."

"We're going to show our lambs this fall," Bill said, breaking into the conversation. "Me and my sisters have got a couple of real showstoppers."

"Bill MacMillan, I think you're bragging," Laura said.

"My dad says a man has to know his worth and not hide his light under a bushel," Bill replied. "Let's go see Laddie," he added, jumping to his feet and tugging Laura by the hand. "We've got to clean out the pen anyway."

Teddy followed as Bill pulled Laura along.

Laura and Bill sat on the top rail of Laddie's pen kicking their heels against the lower planks watching Teddy shovel pig dung into a mound by the gate. Laddie was snuffling over the trough chewing on apple cores, lettuce, and corn, appearing to ignore the proceedings. The boar, purchased for breeding, was ill-tempered and known to fight with the other pigs brought into his pen.

"Why does your father even keep him?" Bill asked.

"My mother wants to sell him for slaughter," Teddy replied. "She says she'll get a better dollar next year."

Teddy hoisted up another heavy shovel full when Laddie, gobbling voraciously, lifted his head.

"You're not doing that right," Bill said.

Laddie snorted again, an apple core harpooned onto the end of one of his old yellow tusks.

"Let me show you something," Laura said, dropping into Laddie's pen, walking toward Teddy. "We tend hogs at home."

Unsettled, the boar backed up from the trough. Teddy caught the look in the old pig's eye and recognized the danger. "Run!" he yelled.

The smile fled from Laura's face as Laddie dug in and then sprang, galloping across the pen with a snorting fury. The girl turned, heading for the rails, but Bill knew she'd never make it and he jumped into the pen, grabbing a shovel he drove it down on the beast's back as the boar tried thrusting his tusks underneath Laura. With all his strength, Bill brought the shovel down on the animal's back again, and again, until Laddie shook his head and spun around, digging its hooves into the planks and charging. Bill dodged the hog, sending the animal crashing into the wall. The pig turned and charged again. Dropping the shovel, Bill ran for the railing and threw himself over the top as the beast's tusk slammed into the wood, pinning the hog to the plank. Teddy, with Laura in his arms, left the pen while Laddie roared with fury, determined to free himself.

The three sat beneath a maple tree, rattled but relieved.

"You are so brave," Laura said to Bill.

"It was nothing," Bill replied, trying to hide the swell of pride.

"You saved my life."

Mr. Gillespie, appearing from the paddock, called to Laura it was time to go.

"If you'd like, maybe I could come over to your house sometime," Bill said.

Laura lowered her eyes. "As long as your mother calls mine first."

Bill's face exploded into a brilliant smile. "I'll get her to call real soon," he said. "I promise."

"Thanks for the good time, Teddy," Laura said, turning to him. "And I won't say boo about Laddie."

The boys remained seated by the tree watching Laura run across the yard toward the big, grey sedan.

The moment the car was out of earshot Bessie called to Charlie who was crossing the yard.

"Did you sell them?" she asked.

"Every last one," he replied, dusting his hands off on his overalls. "Wilton Gillespie always pays a fair price for good cattle."

Bill glanced up at Teddy with a look Teddy had never seen before. "One day I'm going to marry that girl," he said, his eyes turning away to follow the grey sedan as it sped past the leafy maple trees down the dirt lane.

Teddy, too, followed the Gillespie's car as it took a left and headed down the Concession toward town. Saying nothing, Teddy stood and walked back to the house.

Rambel's Restaurant was nearly empty. "Hello Violet," May said. "Can I have my usual seat?" she asked, smiling at her friend.

Both Violet Rambel and May Billings had worked in the hospitality industry and known each other for a while. Many an afternoon, they'd commiserate over the dearth of customers, wondering when things would get better. A bond had developed, and a friendship formed.

"I'm sorry but we're full up," Violet said.

"No, you're not," May replied, with a bit of a laugh. "You haven't been busy in years," she added.

"I'm sorry," Violet said. "I've got reservations."

"Then I'll come back," May replied, feeling a bubble of panic: The few other diners in the restaurant had turned, starting to stare.

"We're booked up all day, May," Violet replied, turning anxiously away.

May turned and noticed Ed Barnes' sister-in-law sitting with a group of her female friends. She understood something was amiss when she saw Mrs. Barnes and her friends speaking in hushed, scandalous tones, side-glancing at her as if she were a curiosity meant to be avoided. When Violet passed by their table, Mrs. Little snatched her sleeve, yanking Violet down to whisper something into her ear.

Violet glanced over at May.

Confused and embarrassed, May took a step backward, her heel catching the carpet.

Violet instinctively moved to help her friend, but seeing the look on Mrs. Little's face, stopped. May lost her balance and fell to the floor. Nobody moved to help, and May scrambled to her feet and rushed out the door.

Walking away from the diner, May became aware her reputation was being tarnished, recalling the changes in behaviour of the men visiting the tavern. Drunken men trying to pull her to the dance floor, and pushing back against her refusals to oblige, their hands now insisting, their glances inciting, their eyes filled with spite as much as lust. Walking down the street, she had felt it—the stares and the whispers, all of it now made sense.

Bessie watched May hurrying away down Stanley Street.

Mrs. Little, adding a cube of sugar in her cup, said, "That hussy will be out of town by week's end," and she took a sip of tea.

Yes, Bessie thought, recalling all the afternoon tea sessions at the Institute where stories had been planted about a certain woman named May Billings, who lived on top of the Queen's Tavern. Stories about her seductive ways. Her laidback stance with men.

"Don't you think this has gone on long enough?" Bessie asked, secretly concerned about the fire she herself had set.

"There is truth in what Mrs. Barnes says," Mrs. Moffatt added. "The Billings girl is very young."

"Pshaw! If she was sidling up to your husbands, I imagine that you'd want her gone quick enough," Mrs. Little replied.

Bessie suddenly felt sick. Her seed was growing out of control. She had never intended to ruin May, having only wanted her to leave.

The Gillespie home was large with red brick, the barn emblazoned with bright white letters that read: Fairview. It stood on the top of a rise overlooking a vast acreage of pastureland that appeared grandiose, the antithesis of what Teddy knew farming to be.

At least 200 head of cattle ripped bits of hay from bales scattered around enormous pens. Teddy, in the back seat of the car, noticed the shadow of a tall silo that stretched over the yard casting a thick, dark line across an engine shop. A shirtless boy walked out of the shop pushing a lawnmower, he waved as the car drove up the long driveway. Teddy recognizing him as Laura's younger brother, Joe.

They stepped out of the car and walked to the house entrance, Teddy behind Bill, who knocked at the front door. They'd wanted to go around the back, but Mrs. MacMillan insisted they do things right. "Hired hands go through the back. You're invited guests," Mrs. MacMillan had said, reminding Bill to be polite as she started the car. "I'll be back in two hours," she added.

Bill knocked again, and getting no response, looked at Teddy. "What if nobody's is home?" Hearing some rustling from inside, Teddy leaned forward to peer in through the big, beveled glass windows, when the door suddenly opened. It was Laura's older sister, the nurse in training.

"I'm Anne," she said, holding the door open wide. "Laura's upstairs with Mom," she added. "You can wait in the sunroom."

Bill and Teddy carefully entered the front foyer of the big house, following Anne down the hall. The ceilings were high and the floors were a dark, highly polished wood. A wide oak staircase swept up from the center of the hallway, and a large round light fixture was suspended from the ceiling. Teddy had never seen a house like this. He looked at the partly wooden walls. "It's called wainscoting," the young woman said, amused. Teddy nodded, and tried not to blush.

"Dad bought some of your cattle," Anne said, leading them through a huge living room with a big piano and a fireplace large enough to walk into.

"Yes, I know," Teddy replied.

Huge chairs clustered around the hearth and a comfortable looking sofa rested beneath a painting of a large field. There were doilies and photos of the children covering all the end tables and crowding the mantelpiece. Petit point upholstered occasional chairs were tucked into little Secretary desks and a large brass box held a stack of wood. There were newspapers already in the fireplace. Clearly, the Gillespies spent a lot of time there, Teddy thought. His parents never lit theirs, telling him fireplaces were not made for show.

Anne pushed open two glass doors that led to a small sunroom that was mostly made out of glass. "He says your father's a good farmer," Anne added.

"Thank you," Teddy replied. "He works awful hard."

"Would you boys like some iced tea?" a woman asked.

Teddy and Bill stood as a corpulent woman wearing a blue dress with hair swept up into a careless bun entered the sunroom with Laura in tow.

"Mrs. Gillespie," the boys said in tandem.

"Laura, did you show them the kittens?"

"Oh, yes! we've got new kittens," Laura repeated.

"That's great," Bill said, "I love kittens."

Teddy looked at his friend, his eyebrow arched. Since when did Bill love kittens? He was always threatening Bette, saying that he'd put Ginger and her kittens in a bag and throw them in the river if she didn't leave them alone. Is that what it is to be in love—what it makes you do? Teddy wondered. Looking at Laura's piggy tails, he smiled, forgetting Bill's strange behaviour. She was pretty, so beautiful, even when wearing farmers' clothing. How was that possible?

"Time to eat, children," Mrs. Gillespie said, "you must all be hungry."

The kitchen was nearly as big as the living room. In its center stood a huge round table surrounded by ten chairs. Scanning the kitchen further, Teddy saw hints of wealth everywhere: a pump for the dishes, a modern fridge, and a stove twice the size of their own. Just like the stove in Hansel and Gretel, he thought. Hearing Bill sweet talk Mrs. Gillespie, he focused more on the oven thinking maybe he could put Bill in it and cook him.

"What is it Teddy" Laura asked.

"Nothing," Teddy said, surprised at being caught out. "I was just thinking what a big table you have."

"That's for all the hired hands," Laura said. "We have to feed them," she replied. "It's a lot of work."

"A job we're happy to do, because we have so many blessings. Isn't that right Laura Jean?" Mrs. Gillespie said, handing her youngest daughter the hamper.

"Yes, Mom," Laura replied quietly, taking the basket. "Thank you."

The three of them left to examine Laura's new kittens up in the haymow, a basket full of oatmeal cookies on hand.

"Do you really have to work?" Bill asked her.

"Of course, we have to work. Don't you?"

"Like a dog," Bill replied, letting out a howl.

"What about you?" Laura asked, turning to Teddy.

"Huh?" Teddy asked, unable to stop his entire face from flushing.

"What's wrong?" Laura asked.

"Nothing," Teddy replied, jumping to his feet and heading for the ladder.

"It's not like you're that lazy," Bill replied with a laugh. "You don't need to get all red in the face about it."

Teddy blushed again, muttering something about going to help Joe with the lawn, and hurried down the ladder. He brushed the hay off his good pants, striding in a fury across the yard. Teddy took a long deep breath and thought, there was no point being mad at Bill. He was his best friend and Bill was determined to make Laura his girl, and why shouldn't he? It wasn't as if Teddy ever said he was interested. He hadn't staked out any claim and he knew that's what you were supposed to do with girls. Teddy had learned the rules from the older boys at the community dances. If you liked a girl, you staked a claim and then you wooed her, and if another boy encroached on your claim it was acceptable grounds for a fist fight.

Teddy kicked a rock, sending it flying out of his path. Bill was the one who'd staked the claim. Sure, Teddy liked her, too, but he didn't even know he might be interested in staking a claim before Bill had gone and said he wanted to marry Laura. It all had happened too fast—one minute he was blushing and couldn't talk, and the next, his best pal was declaring Laura was going to be his future wife.

Teddy saw Joe out in the middle of the vast front yard. The boy was running out of steam, but still valiantly trying to shove the big mower. Teddy crossed the freshly cut grass wondering what Laura and Bill were doing up in the haymow. Were they still playing with the kittens or was Bill sweet talking? Where did Bill learn how to sweet talk? And how come he, Teddy Barnes, didn't know how? He felt like punching a tree.

"Hey Joe!" Teddy called across the yard.

The younger boy looked up.

"You want a hand?" he asked.

Joe smiled with relief as Teddy approached.

"Why don't I take a turn?" Teddy said, rolling up his sleeves and grabbing the mower by the handle.

Quickly and methodically, Teddy began pushing the mower up and down the lawn, leaving long ribbons of green grass in his wake. With each pass he felt his anger ebb. Mother was right, he thought, Laura was too high born for him. He hated the farm. She loved it. He wanted a life of the mind. She would never marry a history teacher. She'd be happier with Bill and a life full of kittens and white lambs.

Once Teddy finished mowing the Gillespie's vast lawn, he noticed Mrs. MacMillan returning with the car. Walking toward the porch he felt good, in control of his emotions.

Mrs. MacMillan honked the horn and Bill and Laura came bounding out of the barn as Mrs. Gillespie emerged from the house holding a tea towel.

"Thanks Teddy," she said, "for all your hard work."

He unrolled his sleeves and reached out to shake her hand. "Thank you for having me," he said. He turned to Laura, "I had a really nice time."

Laura gave him a strange look as he turned to walk toward the car. Teddy heard Bill say maybe they can do it again soon, but he never heard Laura's reply. His church shoes, the ones his mother had insisted he wear, had caught his attention—they were covered in grass and dew and looked as though they were stained. Mother wouldn't be happy.

It was starting to rain, but Ed didn't care, he and Dutch were busy handing out leaflets for a rally to be held the coming weekend. It would likely be small, but it was a good way to practice for the big November event.

A streetcar clattered by, heading toward the business district. Ed did his coat up. He didn't want to catch a chill—not now. He had learned to take better care of himself since he'd been living in the jungle. He knew how to spread food out so he wouldn't get too weak and run down, learning how to get by on next to nothing. He felt like he was feeding on the revolution.

Ever since he'd gotten out of jail, Ed had come to hold one purpose in his mind, to highlight the plight of the homeless victim of the Great Depression, and to show the country what real humanity looked like, and force the Prime Minister to help. Roosevelt was doing it down in the States with the New Deal—why not Canada? It would take a lot of work, he knew, but nothing was impossible. If the voters pushed hard, things were bound to get better.

Ed had moved in with Dutch and ate every meal with Jenny. She'd become almost like a mother to him. He told her about his adventures at school, and how he'd nearly taken to the bottle—even about May. But Ed had never said a word about Bessie. He missed her too much: her scent, the colour of her hair, the contours of her body, the way she kissed him, her mind, her pure sass.

Had it all been a lie?

When Ed asked Jenny about her past, she would shut down, and he'd long since stopped asking. Even still, a closeness between them had developed. His political platform now ready, Jenny helped him with speeches, and once mastered well enough, they'd practice in front of Dutch and the other drifters.

With time and dedication, Ed had become a charismatic orator, pulling the jungle's people in and keeping their attention until fatigue wore him out, or policemen stormed in, telling him and his audience to move along.

The day was cold, the wind even colder, blowing leaves across the path. Ed looked at the sky. It seemed to him as though winter was going to be a chilly one. Lost in his thought, he heard a familiar voice.

"Hey Ed!"

Ed looked behind him, it was Fen Hall.

A waitress carried two cups of coffee and a couple of tea biscuits back from the kitchen, setting them on the counter in front of Ed and Fen. Fen pulled some coins out of his pocket and dropped them on the scratched stainless steel. A dime rolled and Ed stopped it with his thumb. He took a big bite out of the biscuit. It was stale, but delicious. "Thanks," he mumbled.

Fen smiled. "You look good. Hungry and skinny, but good."

Yes, Ed thought, it was true, he did feel good. Ever since he'd started preparing for the rally, he felt as focused as the undergraduate he was the day he'd arrived in Toronto.

"But don't you think you're getting a little too close with these lefties?" Fen asked.

Ed laughed. Fen was as left as anyone he knew. "That's not the point," Ed explained, draining his cup of coffee.

Fen signaled the waitress for another cup and two more biscuits. "What is the point? Convince me."

"Well," Ed said, taking a bite, "we've got the League on one hand, and we've got the Communists. The drifters don't really have a party. Then, there are all the splinter groups. If we all came together under one umbrella, I think we could change the country."

Fen agreed it worked on paper, but how would one ever get all those different people to agree to the same philosophy?

"That's what the rally in November is all about," Ed said. "It's not about parties. It's about helping people. And I think if enough ordinary citizens see who we are and what we're proposing, a lot of them might vote with us."

More coffee arrived and Fen looked at his friend. The idea was sound and good, but what about the nature of men? Would the established order ruling the country ever let such ideas be heard? As Ed went on, Fen couldn't help but notice the waitress had set down the coffee pot, stopping to listen, as a number of the other diners had too. A middle-aged man in a blue fedora and woman in a blue striped dress and floppy hat leaned closer. The woman took a long thoughtful puff on her cigarette, her eyes squinting in their direction. These weren't homeless drifters or crazy radicals—no, these were regular Canadians having their lunch and interested in what Ed had to say.

There was a hard rapping at the Barnes' front door. Laundry hampers, stuffed with damp, recently wrung sheets, covered the kitchen table. Bessie, a yellow hamper glued to her hip, and another under an arm, wondered, who on earth would come calling on washing day? Moreover, nobody comes to the front door except on official business. Maybe, it was somebody from the church or the Institute.

Bessie's pace quickened. What if it was bad news? Granny Hunter had come down with a case of elephantiasis and had to have her swollen ankles taped so she could squeeze into her shoes, but surely nobody died of that. It was just ugly and unpleasant. Still, a knock at the front door on washing day didn't bode well. Her eyes swept through the front parlor. The room was spotless. Bette's sheet music, "I'll Be a Sunbeam for Jesus" was out on the piano. Had the girl practiced last night? she suddenly asked herself. It was so hard keeping on top of that child, especially now that she was not a little girl any longer. In that moment, thinking she would make certain her daughter did an hour that night, there was another hard rap on the door, only this time, whomever was banging was using the knocker.

Bessie reached the door and turned the handle.

May Billings was standing there in a dark skirt and white blouse. "I want to talk to you," she said.

Bessie took a long hard look at her and suddenly thought of May being in Edward's arms. "I don't have anything to say to the likes of you," Bessie replied.

They stood on the front porch, glaring at one another.

"If you don't let me in, I'll go and talk to Charlie," May said quietly, and she strode in and plunked her saucy behind right down on Bessie's best occasional chair. The woman crossed her legs, placed one hand in the other and got right down to business. "If you don't stop running me down, I'm going to tell your husband about you and his brother."

Bessie's heart skipped a beat. What did May know? Had she seen the kiss? "What about my brother?" Charlie asked.

May looked up and Bessie turned in her chair. Charlie was standing in the doorway by the piano. The grandmother clock rang noon, reminding Bessie the children would be home soon. She turned to her husband, then to May, then closed her eyes.

Teddy and Bette walked up the lane to the house, and seeing a car speeding toward them, jumped to the side of the road to avoid getting hit. Teddy, looking inside the vehicle, immediately recognized Uncle Ed's sweetheart seated behind the wheel. The woman, a cigarette between her manicured fingers, was crying. He followed the car with his eyes, saw the car take a hard right and tear out onto the concession road. What on earth is going on, he thought.

"Come on," he said, pulling his sister by the hand and hoping maybe his uncle had returned. Convinced he would see Ed, Teddy ran into the house, but instead, he found his parents in the middle of a rare argument.

"Teddy, make your sister a sandwich," his mother said.

"I can make my own," Bette insisted.

"Charlie, just hear me out," Bessie said as she chased her husband across the lawn and into the paddock. But Charlie, furious, entered the barn, letting the door swing shut in his wife's face.

"What's wrong with Mother?" Bette asked, now intrigued.

Teddy poured his sister a glass of milk and sat down beside her. The two children peered through the window, searching for something, or someone.

"What do you think they're fighting about?" she asked, nibbling at the crust of her sandwich.

"They're not fighting, Bette" Teddy lied, taking a big bite. "They're just talking."

Bessie walked across the barn, trying not to pace. "She was lying."

Ignoring her, Charlie stabbed his pitchfork into the bale, breaking it into smaller mounds to feed to the cattle. Bessie, wanting to tame her trembling, tried to pick up a full bucket of water from the ground, but her hands were too shaky and the water sloshed onto the ground. I have to hide the shaking from Charlie, she thought, shoving her hands into her dress pockets. She'd never seen Charlie so angry. May had told him Ed was in love with his wife. But Charlie hadn't wanted to listen, and raising his arm, he had told her to get out of his house.

May had shouldered on. "When we were together, me and Ed, he called me Bessie."

"Were you in love with him?" Charlie had asked her.

May nodded.

"Was he in love with you?"

Bessie, about to open her mouth, had looked at Charlie, and decided to remain silent.

"Why did he leave?" Charlie asked May.

"I don't know what happened between them, but she's the reason he left," May said "And now your wife is running around town ruining my good name."

Charlie had brought his fist down on the piano so hard the keys sang. "Your good name," he had growled.

May had taken a step back.

"You drove my brother off."

"But," May said, as Charlie took a step toward her, his fists clenched.

"I didn't," she tried to protest.

"Get off my property!"

Crying, May had run through the door and down the steps and toward her car. She had prayed Charlie Barnes would understand. Folks in town had said he was a fair man. She'd hoped he'd put a halt to Bessie's

138

vicious gossip and stop everyone from staring at her so hard they might as well have pointed and yelled, "Whore!"

Driving off in a fury, she had noticed two kids staring at her, their mouths opened. Ed's niece and nephew, she thought. Her heart dropped. There was no point staying in Ayr, she knew. Ed was gone. Bessie and the ladies from the Institute would drive her out and likely ruin what was left of her uncle's business if she didn't go. With tears rolling down her face, she felt the gravel kick out under the car's tires. As she squealed onto the concession, May Billings didn't know where she was going, but what she did know, was that her time in this village had been compromised enough, the humiliation too great. Her decision had been made. She was leaving Ayr, leaving this miserable place, forever.

Bessie's back was against the cattle pen. "What do you want me to say?" she finally asked.

Charlie looked at his wife. The Depression had etched a few lines around her eyes, but they still flashed with life, and some kind of maturity had infused her with confidence. In that moment, watching her, Charlie realized he hadn't truly seen Bessie in years. She had been with him, by his side, all along, through the years—a beautiful and loyal wife, and he'd taken her for granted. I am guilty of the sin of forgetting my wife, he thought, of forgetting to appreciate what the good Lord has bestowed upon me. He had never thought his brother was in love with her. What kind of a man did that? he asked himself. That was blasphemy, a sin of the highest order, and it sickened him. But what was he to do? Who was he to believe. That May woman was a liar, she had to be, he decided.

Ed wouldn't do that, he just couldn't.

And even if Bessie was the most upstanding citizen he knew, and Ed the finest brother a man could have, something still felt adrift. Nauseated by the thoughts running in his head, Charlie turned and wretched, vomiting into the cattle pen, prompting Bessie to run up to him and wrap her arms around his shoulders. He saw flashes of Bessie—his wife, her face etched with desire not meant for him. Resisting her presence as much as wanting it, and unable to fight the wrenching heaves, he surrendered, and let her hold him. All he had were theories, and a harlot's confession, he thought. Trying to hurl his suspicions away, he wretched again, a yellow bile spewing across the hay covered floor.

Bessie wiped her husband's mouth. "Come," she said, "we need to rest."

Together, they walked hand-in-hand back to the house.

Once inside the bedroom, Bessie walked to her closet and fetched her nightgown. Her best one. The one Charlie loved so much.

TEN

The Royal Winter Fair

Heading to the Royal Winter Fair they watched the sun disappear behind the horizon, the dark and blue sky slowly changing to black. Charlie was seated in front between the two adults, and Teddy rode in the backseat with the chickens, a brilliant white Leghorn with a recently cut comb and a red and black Bantam Sebring that was walking across the top of the driver's seat. There were two cages bearing a cantankerous Rhode Island Red and a Silver Laced Wyandotte that bounced along on either side of Teddy, as three enormous ducks waddled around on the floor, occasionally hopping up on the seat to see what was going on.

Teddy knew Mrs. Tilt was especially proud of her ducks, that she'd raised them since they were babies, and fed them special homegrown seed. He felt Mrs. Tilt was right to be proud, the ducks were beautiful.

Hannibal stood proudly on Teddy's wrist, as the boy listened to the adults chatting away.

"Are you sure you don't want to sell that bird?" Mr. Tilt asked Teddy, catching the boy's eye in the rear-view mirror.

"No, sir."

The car moved along Highway 2, next to Lake Ontario. Car and truck lights bounced off the tips of whitecaps that struck the rock break wall. An occasional train clattered by on their left, slowing down as it moved closer to the center of the city. More and more lights flickered on as they drove past small houses and apartment buildings. It was strange to Teddy to see the dark of an evening sky flooded with so much light. You could stay up all night, Teddy thought. How could a person ever sleep?

The duck honked as Teddy heard Mr. Tilt tell his father his son had a way with birds. Mrs. Tilt looked back and offered Teddy a cookie.

Teddy didn't care about the money, he simply wanted red, white, and blue ribbons like he'd seen hanging in the Gillespie hallway. The Best in Show is what I want, he told himself, even if vanity is a sin.

Charlie announced the fair grounds were up on the right and Teddy looked out the window, the Tilt's Studebaker passing beneath an enormous archway of white alabaster: the Princes' Gates. They drove past stock pens, farming families, and soon to be drunken hired hands who were on their way to paint the town. The Coliseum was a big Roman building, and it's where they held the livestock competition.

Mr. Tilt parked the car at the front. It was time to take their entry forms to the Culling Committee.

Teddy with Hannibal, stood in the long poultry line behind his father, the Tilts and all their birds, waiting to be seen. One of the judges, a lady wearing a fancy flowered hat, jumped back when a duck snapped, trying to bite one of her flowers.

"Breed?" she asked.

"Pekin, heavy class," Mrs. Tilt replied with a bit of a sniff. "Any judge worth her salt knows that," she whispered to Teddy.

Teddy nodded, but didn't want to make the judge mad, as she had the power to send Hannibal away. The Tilts explained the Culling Committee judges made sure nothing but show worthy livestock entered the fair, and that meant only good bloodlines, and animals with a clean bill of health.

One of the judges, a skinny man with a nose like a parrot, recognized Mr. Tilt. "Hello John!" he called.

"Fred," Mr. Tilt replied.

"I see you're showing again," Fred said, expertly running his hands over the Tilt's entries. His fingers paused on Hannibal. "Say, this is a nice bird."

"Not mine," Mr. Tilt said. "It belongs to this young fella."

"And who would you be?" Fred asked.

"Theodore Barnes," Teddy replied, rapidly thrusting forward his entry form. "His name is Hannibal and he's a purebred gold laced Sebring and he's all paid up. We sent in the money already."

The man took Teddy's entry form and examined it for the longest time, worrying Teddy. "Can you prove this bird's lineage?"

Teddy, unable to stop staring at the man's nose, knew they'd gotten the chick from an established breeder. He looked to his father for help.

"I'm just fooling ya!" Fred roared, poking Teddy in the stomach. "Mark all these birds as passed. Anything comes in with John Tilt's good enough for me."

And just like that, Teddy, Charlie, the Tilts, and their show birds were free to settle in for the night.

Most of the farmers slept in the Dormitory, a cavernous room on the second floor of the Coliseum. The space, filled with bunk beds, only had one bathroom with a dirty toilet, a grimy sink, and a cracked mirror. "Dad," Teddy whispered, "I don't want to sleep here. What if Hannibal gets scared down there all alone? The other birds could keep him up all night and if he doesn't get his sleep, how will he show?"

Mr. and Mrs. Tilt knew Charlie and Teddy weren't the first contestants to want to bunk in with their animals. Cattlemen who'd come to the fair with only a couple of steers nearly always slept with their livestock. If one had a potential winner, there was nothing stopping some jealous so-and-so from putting salt in the cattle feed so the animals would get diarrhea, or feed the cows beer so their bellies would swell.

Teddy and Charlie left the Tilts to get settled in at the Dormitory, and headed down to see Hannibal on the showroom floor.

The birds were to be judged the next day, giving farmers plenty of time to display their winners and give potential buyers enough time to purchase the prizewinning entry for their breeding stock. The Royal Winter Fair was a loss leader for most farmers, but it was the best advertisement money could buy. If, like the Tilts, you consistently had winners, poultry farmers from miles around that had come to the Fair would purchase your birds. Mr. and Mrs. Tilt had made a career out of doing the circuit.

"I think it's something you get in your blood," Charlie remarked as father and son ambled up an aisle full of cages.

A group of junior farmers were setting up cots against the far wall. Teddy had never seen so many colors before. Beautifully plump, vain birds of black, red, gold, ivory, green, blue, and orange pranced and scratched in their cages. Some were named, but most were arranged according to variety, breed, and class. Hannibal, a Golden Sebright, had his name proudly displayed on a card that also read "Barnes and Son." Charlie smiled down at his boy. This was their first farming adventure together, and he wouldn't have missed it for anything.

Hannibal tried to hop up on the boy's hand as soon as the cage door opened. "Sorry boy, not tonight. That's against the rules," Teddy said, stroking Hannibal and hand feeding him a few kernels of corn.

Charlie tugged their sleeping rolls out from beneath Hannibal's cage. There was barely enough room for them to sleep.

Ready to get to bed, Teddy closed Hannibal's cage and took off his jacket to use as a pillow. "This is exciting," he said, sliding into his sleeping roll. "Thanks for bringing me Dad."

A voice floated up from the end of the room, startling the boy. It was an inspector, standing in the distant doorway.

"Lights out!" he called.

A chorus of "good nights" and "good lucks" bounced through the air until the vast poultry room fell into darkness, leaving the nervous clucking of thousands of birds echoing around Teddy.

"Do you think Mother will make it in time?"

"I'm sure she will," Charlie replied. "Now get some sleep. Morning will be here before you know it."

The greasy spoon located on the other side of the Fairgrounds was full. Sitting down, not quite awake yet, they ordered their breakfast, none of which came close to Bessie's cooking. Charlie wasn't hungry, but Teddy, excited, chugged his orange juice in a single gulp. The front door opened, letting a blast of cold air in. Somebody shouted for them to close it when Teddy turned and saw Laura Gillespie, her brother Joe, and their father. Mr. Gillespie, wearing a long black duster, stood in the entrance. Walking forward, he wished Charlie the best of luck. They were here to show a carload lot of cattle.

Laura, wearing a pink checked shirt, overalls, and a windbreaker, said hello. They hadn't spent any time together since that day at the Gillespie's house.

"We'd better get going," Teddy said to his father.

Charlie was surprised the boy would be so disrespectful in front of Mr. Gillespie but chalked it up to the fair. "We've got a pretty excited farmer here," Charlie said, placing some money on the counter.

"Good luck, Teddy," Laura said. "I hope Hannibal wins."

Teddy looked back with a smile. "Thanks! The same to you!"

It was just a little before four o'clock and the judges were at the head of Teddy's aisle. Teddy was so excited he could barely stand still. Charlie, just as excited, was rocking back and forth, hands in his pockets. Hannibal had performed better than they had ever hoped. Mr. Tilt, agitated, paced back and forth in front of Hannibal's cage.

"Stay calm, Teddy," the old chicken breeder said. "This is the best advice I'll ever give ya."

Mr. Tilt borrowed a cigarette from a farmer passing by. "If the wife catches me smokin', I'll be the one who's burnin'," he said, striking a wooden match. "It's a good thing she's showing our birds at the Duck competition at the other end of the building."

Farmers were lining up to get a peek at Hannibal, one of the biggest stories circulating at the Fair. At nine that morning, Hannibal had placed first in his class, at noon, he had won best in his variety, at two, he had picked up best in breed.

Now, he was competing for Grand Champion.

Teddy bent down, sticking his fingers through the chicken wire to stroke his rooster. Colorful ribbons festooned Hannibal's cage making Teddy swell with pride.

"Have I got time to visit the Men's Room?" he quietly asked his father. He'd been too nervous to go all day, but now he felt he had to.

"Don't lollygag," Charlie said, as Teddy tore up the aisle, past the Jersey Giants, White Laced Cornishes, crested ducks, snowy mallards, and Toulouse geese.

He could see Mrs. Tilt a row over talking with the judges. Teddy waved at her as he sped out the door, almost crashing into Laura.

"I heard about Hannibal, Teddy," she said with a smile.

"He's in the third aisle, Laura. I'll be right back."

Laura nodded as Teddy dashed down the big hall toward the sign that read Men's.

Pulling his pants down, he collapsed on the seat, recalling his mother warning about sitting in public toilets. There's no time, no time, to lay tissues over the porcelain ring, he thought.

Teddy exhaled, and glancing up, he saw the back of the door was plastered with copies of a single leaflet, a demonstration that was to be held that night at Queen's Park. Everything else around him faded away as his eyes focused on one name, the main speaker: Ed Barnes.

"Uncle Ed is giving a speech," he whispered, as he pulled up his pants. Tearing a leaflet off the door he shoved it in his pocket, and he knew, finally, the time had arrived—he would see his uncle again. Soon.

Teddy could barely make his way through the crowd that had gathered around Hannibal's cage. Charlie was on tip toe looking for his son, but also keeping his eye out for Bessie. The train was in, and she should have arrived.

"Make way," Charlie called, seeing Teddy at the back of the crowd. "This is the boy who's showing the Bantam!" he added, yelling even louder.

The crowd parted as Teddy passed through, reaching for his rooster.

Once at the cage, the boy saw the judges examining Hannibal. Laura, standing by Mr. Tilt, gave Teddy a smile of encouragement. But Teddy, touching the leaflet in his pocket, was transported elsewhere, wondering how to get to Queen's Park. Just then, his dad grabbed him by the arm, pulling him up to the cage.

Fred, the man with the parrot nose, was looking at Hannibal's comb. "It's got a perfect cushion," he muttered, making a note.

The woman with the pretty hat inspected the rooster's legs and toes, while another judge, a large woman with a fur piece wrapped around her neck, was verifying Hannibal's general condition, and vigor.

The little rooster let out a hearty crow, as if on cue, and the judges put their heads together to go over their notes.

Laura leaned in and whispered in Teddy's ear, "You're going to win. I just know."

"I sure hope so," Teddy replied. Then, looking at her, he had a sudden thought. Maybe Laura could help him.

Charlie's heart was racing, this was the most thrilling time he had ever had at the Royal. Nearly as exciting as his wedding day. Maybe all this would shift Teddy's focus away from books, and towards farming, he hoped. How could it not?

The judges had finished examining Hannibal and were adding up their scores when Teddy leaned into Laura, "Can I talk to you in private?"

"I'll be at the train cars. But don't you want to know if you won?" she asked, puzzled.

Teddy saw three judges smiling at him. Of course, he had to stay. He shook his head in disbelief.

"Ladies and gentlemen, we have a winner!" Fred said, removing a red, white, and purple ribbon from his breast pocket.

The explosion of clapping and cheers were almost unheard by Teddy.

Charlie pulled Teddy into the center of the circle and the judges shook his hand and awarded him his prize, a sash emblazoned with swirling gold letters that read Royal Winter Fair - Grand Champion 1937. Cameras flashed, immortalizing the boy with his winning rooster high up on his shoulder. Charlie, soaking in the victory, thought his head would explode. A Barnes had never gone all the way to Grand Champion, and now, a color photo would feature Theodore Barnes on the front page of the Toronto Telegram the next day.

Teddy, unable to fully focus on what had just transpired, smiled, but barely, as Uncle Ed was too much on his mind.

His dad had gone to Union Station to try and find his mother leaving Teddy to stay with Hannibal. Dad was fairly certain that Mother had missed the train, but needed to be sure, while Teddy hoped that she had, as it would mean one less obstacle for him. The moment his father left, Teddy abandoned the rooster, and rushed over to see the Tilts. They'd won four ribbons, and Mr. Tilt was busy dealing with a couple of breeders. The Leghorn was attracting a fierce bidding war, and a poultry farmer seemed interested in taking the ducks off Mrs. Tilt's hands.

"What are you doing here, Teddy?" Mrs. Tilt asked.

Teddy pulled the leaflet out of his pocket. "I was just wondering if you knew where this was?" he asked, pointing at Queen's Park.

"Can't say I do," Mrs. Tilt replied.

Another man glanced at the leaflet and told Teddy it was behind the Parliament Buildings.

"Why do you want to know about a bunch of Commies?" the man asked. "I heard of this fella Ed Barnes. Meant to be a good talker."

Mr. Tilt leaned in, taking a closer look at the leaflet. "Any relation?" he asked.

Teddy quickly shoved the leaflet back in his pocket. "I should get back to Hannibal."

Mr. Tilt almost told the boy to stay put, but he had a buyer on the hook and didn't want to lose the deal.

Teddy, instead of returning to Hannibal's cage, ran over to the large livestock pens to find Laura.

"Do you know where the Parliament Buildings are?" he asked her.

Laura nodded. "You can get there by streetcar."

"Where's the streetcar?"

"Why do you have to go?" Laura asked.

"This is my uncle," he replied, pointing to Ed's name on the leaflet. "I've got to find him."

"Okay, c'mon, I'll show you."

Out front of the Fairgrounds, the sun setting, Laura and Teddy sat on a bench at a streetcar stop. A young couple holding hands told them they'd just missed one, frustrating Teddy, who was worried his parents would find out where he was going, and who he was going to see. He was worried, too, about Mr. Gillespie's reaction to him absconding his daughter to attend a communist rally. But there was no other choice, he thought, his mother would have said no. Teddy turned to Laura, suddenly grateful for her presence.

"What are you thinking, Teddy?" Still wearing her overalls and windbreaker, she had tied a pretty bandana over her hair, her eyes like beautiful sunbeams, he thought.

The sound of the streetcar clattering up the track in a whir of red and yellow made Teddy jump. When its doors opened, they hopped on with several others as the streetcar resumed rattling along.

"Five cents," the conductor said.

Teddy turned to Laura, embarrassed. "I don't have any money. We have to get off."

The conductor was saying something about not letting them off until the next stop when Laura pulled a dime out of the breast pocket of her overalls, and dropping it into the tin fare box, said, "Let's sit down."

They moved along Front Street, past Union Station, all ablaze with spotlights stretching far into the night. Unfolding before Teddy was a spectacle he'd never seen before: well-dressed men in dark suits and ladies in elegant dresses walking busy streets with storefronts all lit up. Lines of shiny cars.

The streetcar turned into the city's financial district, and Laura pointed to the Canadian Imperial Bank. "Dad regularly comes to Toronto to settle up his accounts," she said. Teddy was staring at her, watching her look out the window. She knew so much more about the world than he did, he realized. And then he thought, Hannibal had won Grand Champion, and he had found Uncle Ed.

"We must look like a couple of hayseeds," she suddenly said, looking ruefully down at her overalls. "This is the first time I've traveled dressed like this."

"Don't you like wearing overalls?" he asked. It was a stupid question, but he didn't know what else to say.

"Of course, I don't," Laura replied. She moved closer to him, her voice dropping just a bit. "If I tell you something, do you promise you won't hate me?"

Teddy nodded.

"You promise you won't tell?"

Teddy nodded again.

"Swear?"

"I swear," he said.

"I hate farming," she whispered.

"So do I," Teddy whispered back, happiness lifting his heart. "But you live in that great big house," Teddy said.

"Who do you think has to clean it, Teddy? You only see the big cars and the fancy house, but somebody must work to maintain it, women, that's who—me! My dad grew up poor, and while he now enjoys the finer things in life, he wants children to learn good hard work."

"But the boys?"

"They get to ride around on the tractor. At least that's more fun than washing floors."

"Don't they have to gather eggs?" Teddy asked.

"No," Laura replied, "we have to do that, too. And haul the water from the well," she said, adding with a long sigh, "in all seasons. And fill the troughs."

"And muck out the poop," Teddy added.

"And feeding all those hired hands," Laura said, "I hate that the most."

Teddy remained silent.

"We—the girls—get up at five to feed them at six. We barely get the dishes done and they're back for lunch. It never ends," she added, "it's nothing but hard work."

The streetcar chugged up Bay Street, past pedestrians, cars, horses, and buggies, Teddy and Laura continuing to share their secret plans and dreams. Laura was going to study Home Economics. Her mother had saved enough money for all the girls to attend university. "Mom says that an educated woman can't be turned into a slave. That's why I'm going to get an education."

Teddy, nodded approvingly, and he told her about his love of history, of how he was going to be a professor, just like his Uncle Ed.

"But isn't he a radical?" Laura said.

Teddy thought for a moment. "I think the Depression did it to him," Teddy said.

"Are you a radical, too?" Laura asked, "my father doesn't hold much truck with radicals."

Teddy didn't even have the chance to laugh, as Laura bound to her feet, "There it is!" and she pointed to a large set of red brick government buildings standing a block away to the west. The buildings looked like castles with turrets, Teddy thought, wondering if they had guns in there.

Laura pulled the bell. "We'll get out here, please," she called to the driver. "Come on, let's go," she said, pulling Teddy to his feet.

The trees, stripped of most of their leaves, welcomed them as Teddy and Laura made their way toward Queen's Park. Despite the night being chilly, people seemed everywhere, an obvious eagerness marking their steps.

Laura picked up her pace, but Teddy didn't mind.

"Pardon me, sir, is that where they're having the rally?" Teddy asked a stranger.

The man nodded. "It should be a big one," he replied. "I'd be going, but the wife doesn't like me to mix with commies. We're Conservatives. Aren't you kids kinda far from the farm?" he asked with a laugh.

"Yes, sir," Teddy replied, looking at their overalls and rubber farm boots. "Thank you for your help."

Catching up to Laura, he said, "See, city folks are friendly."

"It might not bother you, but I don't like being stared at," Laura said, quickening her pace.

She sure is fussy about her clothes, Teddy thought trailing after her. "Wait up!"

By the time they entered Queen's Park, a large crowd had gathered in front of an old band shell.

"Are all of them here to hear your uncle speak?" Laura asked. "I wonder why?"

"Yes, they are, and it's because he has something good to say."

They passed a picnic table, walking more toward the stage, overhearing a man saying this wasn't a legal rally because the Police Chief had denied permission to hold an outdoor meeting.

They continued walking through Queen's Park. The area, large, grassy, and tree covered, circled to the north of the Parliament Buildings. A wide roadway ran around it, and well-worn foot paths cut through the park, allowing easy access to the museum to the north, and the ivy-clad university buildings on either side.

"Look," Teddy said, "I can see my breath. Are you warm enough?"

"I'm fine," she replied, looking around. "There are more people coming."

Teddy looked at all the people streaming in from University Avenue when a voice came on over the loudspeakers: "Test, test, test."

"Come on," Teddy said, "I want to get closer."

They made their way through the crowd, a short man wearing thick glasses was standing on the stage thanking everyone for coming, saying history was being made that night and that they were about to hear the words of one man: A single Canadian with a clear vision and a plan—a unique plan to bring together the disenfranchised youth of the country, their families, and all the other Canadians who've felt trampled on by both the Conservative and Liberal parties during this period of extraordinary economic hardship.

The crowd cheered, as more and more people arrived, choking the front of the stage, clamoring to hear the speaker.

"Ladies and gentlemen," the short man started.

The crowd cheered again. Teddy looked at Laura.

"I'd like you to welcome the future of our country, Mr. Ed Barnes!"

Uncle Ed walked out from behind a curtain and the crowd cheered, whistled, and clapped. He bowed a bit sheepishly, but there he was, his uncle.

A whole lot skinnier than Teddy had ever seen him, Edward also seemed, somehow, fuller; of life; of fire.

"He has real presence," Laura whispered.

Teddy's skin prickled.

"Thank you so much for coming out on such a chilly night," Uncle Ed said.

The crowd cheered.

"I want to ask you all a question: How many of you don't have a place to sleep tonight?" he asked.

There was some hooting.

"Put up your hands," he continued.

More hands than Teddy thought possible shot up in the crowd.

The crowd murmured with dismay, scanning itself, the hands moving, stirring the air.

154

"And how many of you have gone hungry?" Uncle Ed asked again, this time louder, driving his fist down into his palm to make a point.

Even more hands shot up.

"Tell the truth," Ed said.

The people on either side of Teddy and Laura tentatively raised their arms as did most of the people at the front.

"It's not just the hobos who are hungry. We're all hungry, and I'm here to tell you that there's something that can be done about it. Something that's democratic. Something that's peaceful. And most importantly, something that's fair!" Ed called out.

"We don't just have to listen to William Lyon Mackenzie King telling us the youth of this country are lazy and that if the government helps them out, we'll breed a generation of indolent young people. We all know of a person who's lost, forever, the most valuable years of their lives. Not just because of this Depression, but because of the way both governments have dealt with them. They've been turned into vagrants and treated like criminals. Why can't we adopt a fairer way of doing business and a kinder, more decent way of treating people? Is it too much to ask?"

The crowd roared back, "No!"

"What I propose are policies that have to do with our very lives. Our Canadian society. Let's come together and create a party that will govern according to what's best for society and not just for the businessmen."

The crowd roared more, sending arms up in the air.

Ed beamed, taking in the applause. Looking at the crowd, he understood they heard him, and believed in what he had to say. He could see it in every face, remembering they'd started out here together, all of them marching toward change.

Ready to exit the stage, and wrapping his sweater around his shoulders, a movement, different because constant, caught his attention. He squinted, noting a boy's impatience to reach the stage. Squinting more, he held his breath. Teddy, his nephew, was there smiling and waving his arms at him.

They caught one another's gaze, and Teddy, feeling hot and thrilled, waved hello, relieved to have found his uncle. When Ed raised his hand to wave back, a series of sharp whistles blew, followed by the sound of explosions from behind the Parliament Buildings.

The stage shook and Ed lost his balance.

Scores of police, some on horseback, others on motorcycles with sidecars, burst from a long row of bushes and moved toward the crowd, rushing for the stage. Rows of spectators screamed, running for cover as the police charged into the melee wielding their black Billy clubs. Rubber hoses filled with lead ends whistled through the air cracking down onto onlookers as they stampeded over one another desperate for escape. People had abandoned the footpaths and were trampling shrubs and the autumn flowers. The police smashed loudspeakers as protestors leapt from the stage, sending the microphone stand to the ground from which a ghostly reverb howled through the air.

Teddy and Laura stood in the middle of the madness, holding hands, terrified. The boy suddenly turned as a cop on horseback was there, ready to bear down on them, a Billy club swinging over his head. Teddy threw his arms around Laura, expecting to feel the blows, when Uncle Ed barreled across the park.

"Teddy!" he shouted, "run!"

The horse whinnied as the mounted policeman sharply reined it in and turned toward Ed. The officer blew his whistle. A motorcycle cop near the stage saw Ed, and spinning the machine around, kicked up a high spray of mud. Both the horse and motorcycle were now bearing down on Ed.

Hiding beneath a picnic table, Teddy saw Ed run across the park and head for the steady traffic that hummed around Queen's Park Circle, but the mounted policeman and motorcycle cop caught up to him, flanking him on either side, and penned him in. When Ed ran to the left, the horse, waiting, reared up on its hind legs as the cop viciously brought the rubber hose down on Ed's back. Ed, unsteady, ran back through a grove of trees and stumbling on a ragged tree root, tripped and fell. When Teddy saw the motorcycle moving toward his uncle, he jumped out from under the table, ignoring Laura's plea to not go.

The cop in the sidecar leaped out and started kicking Ed, the mounted policeman jumping from his horse eager to join. "Get out of Canada, Commie!" he shouted as he swung his boots like pummeling pendulums.

When Ed cried out, Teddy yanked on the policemen's arms, imploring them to stop, yelling he was his uncle, that he wasn't a commie––they were wrong. The men tossed him into the dirt like a doll, sending the boy on his hands and knees. Lifting his head, horrified, Teddy saw Uncle Ed lost in a flurry of boots, hands over his face, struggling to protect himself while begging for them to stop. But they didn't stop, continuing to kick until Uncle Ed's body stilled in a pool of blood.

A paddy wagon wailed, and a line of triumphant policemen marched a string of bloodied protestors in handcuffs across the park.

"Get him up," a detective ordered.

The two motorcycle policemen bent down.

"He needs to go to the hospital!" Teddy cried.

"He's going to talk to the Chief," the detective said. "Get him out of here."

They hauled Uncle Ed to his feet and dragged his limp body across the grass leaving a trail of blood in its wake.

Teddy turned around. Where was Laura? Had something happened to her? Scanning the park, the passage of chaos imprinted on its land, he saw her standing under a tree with her father, and his own father next to him.

Teddy ran to them, yelling, "You've got to get him out of there! Please, Dad."

"Just be happy I got here on time," his father said to him, "and we're doing nothing, but getting out of this madness."

Mr. Gillespie had driven Charlie to Queen's Park on a tip from Mr. Tilt. All Mr. Tilt had to say was "Communist Rally" and "Ed Barnes" and Charlie had understood. When Wilton Gillespie had arrived at Hannibal's cage looking for Laura, they put it together immediately. They arrived by car just as the riot was ending.

Wilton Gillespie was furious, marching Laura across the park and into the car, but his anger was nothing compared to Charlie's.

"Dad, PLEASE!" Teddy pleaded harder, praying deeper than he ever had for anything in his life.

The paddy wagon was backing out of the park as the siren began to wail, Teddy stopping, fiercely yanking his arm free. "We've got to get Uncle Ed to a doctor," Teddy said. "If we don't, he's going to die."

"Teddy, no, not this time. I've done all I could do. Ed is on his own now."

That night, Teddy didn't sleep. Every time he closed his eyes, Uncle Ed was there, lying on the ground, looking at him, unable to stop the flying black boots from kicking him, over and over. Teddy tossed and turned, his stomach knotted by desperation. If only I could have done something to help. If only Dad had agreed. But more importantly, he thought, what if his mother hadn't driven Uncle Ed off the farm? Mother, he thought, sinking his teeth into his bottom lip, she is wicked.

Teddy turned his head to the window. The moon was fading, the black sky moving from indigo to red, the sun's yellow sunbeams rising and settling on Uncle Ed's old pillow.

From his bed, he heard wheels rolling up the driveway, a car door slamming shut, feet crunching on the gravel and up the wooden stairs and crossing the veranda. A rap on the door. He held his breath, praying for it to stop, to go away. It didn't. He put on his slippers and robe and walked down the stairs. Through the oak door with the glass oval, he could see Mrs. Moffatt standing on the veranda in her navy serge coat, hair still wrapped in pink curlers. Teddy opened the door.

"Oh, Teddy," she sighed, asking, "Are your parents up?"

"Is it Uncle Ed?" Teddy asked, seeing the sadness on her face.

Mrs. Moffatt nodded, gently placing a hand on his shoulder.

"Ed passed an hour ago. The nurse said it was head trauma. I'm so sorry."

Teddy stood there for a moment, trying to understand. "Thanks for letting me know," he said.

Walking past Mrs. Moffatt and down the stairs, Teddy continued on to the chicken coop. Stopping, standing still in the early morning light, he knew, something inside of him had died.

Standing in the hallway shadows, Bessie had heard everything. Ed was dead. Her Edward. How could that be possible? In her mind, she saw the way he walked. The way he danced. The way he laughed. His mind. And she whispered to the shadows, "You were beautiful, and you were brilliant, and you were my Edward, and you always will be."

Walking back to bed, sorrow breaking her heart, she said to him, "I'm sorry."

Teddy didn't cry, he just sat down quietly beside Hannibal and stared blankly at the ribbons on the rooster's cage. Why did Uncle Ed have to die? If only we could have gotten him to a doctor. If only ... and he stopped, tears coming, and he leaned his head back, and he yelled, "It was my parents, they killed you!"

He stood and retrieved the feed tin casting a handful of chicken feed down at Hannibal as the little rooster danced wildly searching for the yellow kernels. Blinded by his tears, Teddy thrust his hand deeper into the tin and threw feed to the chickens, and with each handful thrown, his rage increased, until he threw the feed tin across the room, yelling, "This is your fault, Mother! All your fault! And you, Dad! You could have helped him!"

The chickens clucked and pecked in a heightened frenzy as Teddy wildly kicked the feed tin around the coop. I am not going to be stuck on this dead-end farm as free labor, he suddenly thought, raging more. I will not be limited by *their* ideas of decorum and social ladders. And I won't be a guardian of history, either.

Exhausted, Teddy collapsed on a bale of hay, Hannibal strutting over, settling beside him.

"Teddy?" His father looked around, the coop was a mess. "Are you all right?" he asked, sitting down next to his son.

Teddy stared at him, wanting to ask why he hadn't stood up for his brother—defended him? Staring more, he realized his father had always bent to his mother's will, and for that, Uncle Ed had paid the price. He decided then, he would never allow his mother to dictate his choices and misguide his life. "Dad?"

"I'm right here."

"I want to go and see Mr. Tilt."

"Why?"

"I'm selling Hannibal. I want to start a savings account. I'm going to be a doctor."

The Ayr Cemetery was empty except for the undertaker's wagon, the minister's car, and the family Dodge. Bessie, Charlie, Teddy, and Bette stood next to the open grave, Ed's coffin resting in the deep, dark pit.

Teddy looked around, there was no one else, no one other than them to mark the end of Ed Barnes' life. If his friends in Toronto had known, they might have attended, but his father had decided against putting a notice in the paper. He felt the family had been through enough.

Teddy did not want to look at the wooden box containing the body of the most influential being he had ever known. Stifling a sob, he saw Bette cling to his father's leg, weeping.

"It's gonna be okay," he whispered to his sister.

As the ceremony ended, Bessie and Bette stepped forward and tossed a handful of earth each onto the coffin. Teddy clearing his throat, announced he had something to say. "I learned more from my Uncle Ed, than from anyone else. He taught me to want more from life than other people tell you is possible." He looked at his mother, and then, for the first time, he looked down at the coffin. "I know, because of my Uncle Ed, there is more to life than this." He closed his eyes and softly swallowed before opening them again. "I am going to recite a poem by John Donne that Uncle Ed taught me."

Charlie moved to stop him, but Bessie held him back.

Teddy began recanting carefully, the words he had committed to memory:

"Death be not proud, though some have called thee Mighty and dreadful, for thou art not so:
For those who think'st thou dost overthrown Die not, poor Death, nor yet canst thou kill me. From rest and sleep, which but thy pictures be.
Much pleasure: then from thee much more must flow, And soonest our best men with thee do go,
Rest of their bones, and soul's delivery.
Thou art slave to fate, chance, kings, and desperate men, And dost with poison, war, and sickness dwell,

And poppy or charms can make us sleep as well And better than any stroke;
why swell'st thou then? One short sleep past, we wake eternally
And death shall be no more; Death, thou shalt die."

Teddy leaned down and picked up a handful of earth. Stepping forward, he said goodbye to his uncle, and he let the earth fall.

ELEVEN

1944

"Slow down!" Teddy yelled, as Bill pushed the pedal to the floor.

Bill's souped-up, red Chevy coupe shot down the concession road as the raccoon tail attached to the antennae bounced wildly in the wind.

"I wish you'd take it easy. You're liable to kill us," Teddy said as the car hit a pothole, sending both their heads to the car ceiling.

They were men now, having turned twenty-two that year, and life was waiting for them.

Bill veered right, swinging into Gillespie's lane. He had promised to pick Laura up and drive her into the Ayr Community Centre. They were having an entertainment program that night, and Laura's brother Joe was going to be playing drums in a band. Bill laid on the horn, blasting it twice.

"Aren't you going to ring the bell?" Teddy asked, embarrassed.

Bill shrugged, straightening his hair in the rear-view mirror.

"We've been going steady for years. That's old hat," he replied, giving the horn another toot.

Teddy got out of the Chevy and crossed the parking pad, noticing Mr. Gillespie's car was parked by the cattle pen. Teddy had no desire to see him. Laura's father had been ignoring Teddy since the day Uncle Ed was killed. He and Laura had barely spoken at all.

Trotting up the steps, Teddy leaned on the doorbell and looked around at the yellow and orange mums and purple asters that filled the flower beds, and the trimmed deep, lush grass. A ladder and some paint cans were leaned up against the south wall, the veranda, trim, and eaves troughs had recently been painted a creamy white.

An alley of majestic spruces flanked the yard. Teddy had never seen such regal trees. The Barnes' maples looked puny in comparison. He rang the bell again.

A feminine voice from the inside called out, "Friend or foe?"

"Friend," Teddy answered with a smile.

Laura appeared dressed in a navy university frosh jacket, matching jumper, and saddle shoes. Her auburn hair was shorter. To Teddy, she looked more beautiful than ever.

"Theodore Barnes," she said, flashing her radiant smile. "I haven't seen you in ages. Where have you been keeping yourself?"

"Mostly school," Teddy replied, trying his best not to stare.

"It's nice to see that somebody has some manners?" she called across the yard. "We've got to go!" Bill called back. He hated being late for a program, especially since he was MC'ing the event.

"Can I catch a lift with you?" Joe called, shooting out of the house waving a pair of drumsticks. "Dad's not coming, and Mother is already there and I'm stuck," he added.

"Sure," Bill yelled back. "But get a move on."

The Chevy blew by a horse and buggy, and fields of golden cow corn. Teddy and Joe were wedged in the back of the coupe. Laura was in the front with Bill, his arm around her shoulder.

"I'm in Victoria College," Laura said, turning around to look at Teddy. "But everyone calls it Vic. I've already made friends. Where are you?"

"Medicine," he replied, "three years now."

"I know you're in the Faculty of Medicine. What college are you with?"

"University College," Teddy replied.

"Do you go to all the parties?" Laura asked.

"Not really. I don't have much time for that."

"He's way too busy studying. He's going to be the next Banting and Best and find a cure for cancer," Bill said.

And it was true. Theodore Barnes' grades were consistently at the top of his class, even prompting his anatomy professor to say he'd never seen a keener diagnostician. It seemed Uncle Ed's teachings had stayed with Teddy, following him everywhere. While the other students were anxious to simply diagnose a patient and move on, Teddy's focus was on methodically tracking the history of disease. He believed that if a doctor dedicated enough attention to any detailed diagnosis, he could anticipate disease and avoid serious problems.

"Really?" Laura asked, "cancer?"

"No," Teddy replied, "I want to get through school and set up a small practice."

"You spend all your time holed up with those books," Bill said. "It's getting to be old news. Bachelor Barnes who doesn't have any girlfriends and never goes to parties." Bill slowed the car as the Chevy swept down Piper Street and crossed over the old Nith River bridge. The Community Hall was on the right side by the river.

"A handsome man with no girl?" Laura teased. "That's a shame," she added, taking Bill's hand as the foursome entered the hall.

The United Church Women had decorated the hall with streamers of red and white bunting, unfurling from a big light in the centre of the ceiling to the four corners of the room. It looked like an enormous May Pole. Bill and Joe disappeared backstage.

"Do you want something to drink?" Laura asked.

Teddy nodded and she grabbed his hand, pulling him through the crowd.

"Hey Laura, good luck at school," a young woman said as they moved by a group nibbling on date squares and drinking coffee.

"Thanks," Laura replied. "I'll be home for Thanksgiving," she added. She turned to Teddy, "Do you come home a lot?"

"Not as often as my mother would like," he replied, thinking of what Mother had done to Uncle Ed.

"Do you remember what we talked about on the streetcar?" Laura asked.

Teddy nodded.

"I'll miss my family, but I'm leaving all the farm work behind," Laura said quietly, so no one would hear.

They slipped in the line for punch and cookies behind a couple of old farmers who were talking politics. "At least until you marry, Bill," Teddy said, with a wry smile.

"Bill says our life will be different, and I can focus on taking care of the family accounts. Besides," she said, slapping Teddy playfully on the arm, "who says we're getting married? I've got three years of university ahead of me first."

There was a sound coming from the stage and they looked up.

"Ladies and gentlemen, it's time to begin the evening's entertainment," Bill said, standing in the center of the wooden stage in front of a worn red velvet curtain and holding a microphone. "This is a fundraiser for our fellows overseas, so don't forget to open your wallets and your purses. We've got a puppet show, featuring the world-famous MacMillan sisters," as the crowd roared with laughter. "But first, Ayr's favorite band, "The Hayseeds." The crowd clapped as the curtain parted revealing Joe Gillespie on drums, and two others on base and rhythm guitar. Joe counted them down and they broke into song.

It was after ten, the talent shows were over, and the main attraction, a swing band from Galt, were just finishing tuning their instruments. The band struck up the opening chorus of "Lady Be Good" by Artie Shaw, sending the crowd quickly to the dance floor.

"Let's sit," Laura said to Bill, looking around for a seat.

"Just because I can't dance, that's no reason you shouldn't have fun," Bill said. "Do me a favour, Teddy, dance with my girl?"

"I don't know," Teddy said, "I'm not much better than you, you know."

That was a lie. For the last few years, every time he saved up enough money, he'd order another Arthur Murray class and secretly practiced with Bette. And now, the medical student could rhumba, fox trot, and even waltz.

"You're way better than me. Now get going. I'm going to clean out the icebox while everyone else is up there," Bill added, returning to the food table.

"Ready?" Teddy said to Laura.

She smiled and took his hand. "I love dancing."

One song dissolved into the next, and every time a song ended, and he asked Laura if she wanted to sit down, she shook her head, and away they went again. Occasionally Bill waved from the sideline, wandering around the hall visiting with the other farmers and their wives. As far as Teddy could tell, his friend was having a good time.

"What's your major?" he asked Laura.

"Home economics," she replied. "The science of food and how to properly care for a family. I hope I don't fail. It's going to be really hard."

"You're too smart for that," Teddy said, giving her a twirl.

"You're a very good dancer, where did you learn?"

"My uncle," Teddy quietly replied.

Laura looked at Teddy as the memory of that night returned, and said, "I'm so sorry."

"I'd much rather talk about school," Teddy replied. "What's your schedule like?"

"Classes every morning. Three labs a week in the afternoon. I'm even getting a credit for a skating course," Laura said laughing.

"You get to take skating and you're worried about failing?" Teddy laughed.

"Listen, Big Brains, not all of us can be doctors."

Teddy faltered. "I was only fooling."

"I know," Laura replied with a smile. "Don't be so sensitive." She looked over Teddy's shoulder. "Isn't that your little sister?"

Teddy looked and saw Bette dancing with Rusty Little. Rusty had been a nasty boy and was turning into a meaner man. "Would you mind if I had a dance with her?

"Of course, not," Laura replied. "I think it's cute. Go."

Teddy, releasing Laura, walked over to his sister and tapped Rusty on the shoulder. "Cutting in," Teddy said, twirling Bette out of Rusty's grasp.

"Hey," Bette said indignantly, "why did you do that?"

He looked at his sister. Tall and already curvy, with long flaming red hair. She had the makings of a first-rate tease.

"Rusty Little is much too old for you," Teddy said, "and you, miss, are only fourteen, and we all know he's trouble, don't we?"

"Says you," Bette replied, giving her brother a saucy face with a little bit of pout. "Hey Block Head!" a voice said.

"My turn to cut in," Rusty said, taking Bette's arm.

Teddy held her fast. "She's too young for you."

"I think that's up to the lady," Rusty replied.

"Come on," Teddy said, pulling his little sister by the arm.

Rusty stood in his way, some of the dancers, stopping to look.

"I don't want any trouble, Rusty."

"You never want any trouble, and that's the trouble with you," Rusty said, giving Teddy a bit of a shove.

"Leave him alone, Rusty," Bette said, pulling Teddy by the arm. "You know he won't fight."

Rusty held his ground and shoved Teddy again. "Lucky for you, you got the chicken pass and don't have to serve in the army," Rusty said with a sneer.

"I don't see you lining up for duty," Teddy replied. "And everyone knows you don't lift a finger around the farm."

Rusty shoved him again, and this time Teddy hit the ground. More people were stopping to watch as the band kept playing.

"Get up you coward," Rusty said.

"You know I won't fight."

Rusty was making a fist and pulling it back, when Bill appeared. Furious, he wrenched Rusty around, and twisting his arm behind his back, he shoved the young man through the throng of dancers, and out the back door.

"It's lucky for you Bill turned up," Bette said, watching Bill disappear into the alley with Rusty. "Isn't he brave?"

"Bravery's got nothing to do with fighting," Teddy said, remembering how his uncle died.

"C'mon, let's go watch," and Bette began to push her way through the dancers, Teddy remaining inside, refusing to watch.

When it was over, Bill walked up to Teddy, "You know, there's no shame in a man defending his honor."

"What if it gets you killed?" Teddy asked, thinking again about what happened to Uncle Ed.

Bill knew nothing more could be added, no one would ever win when Uncle Ed's death was concerned. "Let's get you and Laura home. Teddy. I need to tell you something, anyway."

The Chevy slowed down as Bill swung it into a vacant parking lot of an old church. He turned the engine off. "Let's get out."

Bill looked around and leaned up against the hood of the car and pulled out a cigarette and lit it.

"Smoke?"

Teddy shook his head. "When did you start?"

"First deck," Bill answered. "I figured I'd better get used to them with where I'm going."

Teddy dove his hands into the pockets of his pleated trousers and looked up at the old stones of the church. It was a small church, built nearly a century ago by the local settlers. "Which is where?"

"I signed up for the army."

Teddy's heart rate accelerated.

"I'm on the train in Galt tomorrow to Camp Borden for basic training, then they'll ship me overseas." Bill took another drag, exhaling slowly, and waited for Teddy to speak, half expecting a sermon of some sort. "I know you don't approve of the killing, but I want to help."

"You're exempt," Teddy said. "You're needed at home to grow food, Bill, and that's just as important as fighting."

"Oh heck, Ted, you know Dad can do just fine without me. It's not right all of us farm boys sitting on our keesters while the Allies are getting shot. Look at Rusty picking fights. He should be over the pond, not here shoving you."

"Does Laura know?"

"I told her yesterday. She wasn't happy, but she understands why. She's got a brother over there in the medical corps. Jack."

"Your folks?"

"Uh, you know, Pops, he'd have lock me up in the chop box and not let me out until the war was over."

"Not a bad idea," Teddy replied.

"I'm catching the early morning train. I'll leave them a letter. By the time they read it, I'll be long gone."

Teddy remained quiet, his new default mode of being, understanding there was nothing he could do or say.

"I was wondering," Bill added, "if you'd do me a favour?"

"If I can," Teddy replied, intrigued.

"Will you take care of my girl? She's going to be new in the big city and I'd like my best friend to watch out for wolves."

A fox running across the field caught Teddy's attention. Turning to Bill, he said, "Of course, it'll be an honor for me to watch over Laura."

Teddy tossed and turned in his bed that night, and every time he drifted off he saw his uncle lying unconscious, bleeding in the dirt. Only it wasn't Ed's face he saw, it was Bill's. He looked out the window, and he thought about the war. What good, he thought, was caused by bloodshed? He had consulted with Doc Ramsey and the College Chaplain at University College, wanting to understand the ethics behind the killing of men. God taught us, they had said, "An eye for an eye and a tooth for a tooth," but he had never taken the Bible literally. Privately, he often wondered if men of power had secretly put words into God's mouth to sanction their own evil. He'd grown up with the gospels of Jesus, and he believed in them as much as he believed the sun rose and set, and as such, he believed Jesus didn't want him wearing a uniform and traveling to Europe to kill Germans. Maybe God whispered in my ear while I was sleeping, he suddenly thought, telling me to abandon history and learn how to heal instead. He pushed me into medicine knowing the government wouldn't conscript medical students. He saved me.

Teddy waited for the sun to rise. When it finally did, he slid his white shirt, tie, and dark trousers on and walked down the stairs, Bill still on his mind.

"What's with the getup?" Bill asked, waiting in the car. "Aren't you doing chores later?"

"This is the look of a young professional," Teddy replied, as he slid on the passenger seat. "And you'd better get used to it."

"Whatever you say," Bill said, "let's hurry up. We need to get Laura."

In silence, Bill sped the Chevy to the Gillespie's, wondering what the day had in store for him. He watched Laura walk to the car, and he wondered if he was doing the right thing? But he knew he was. It's what he had to do. For himself. For the country.

"So, you've heard the gruesome news," Laura said, as Teddy moved to the back seat. She was wearing a white dress with lips that matched the bright red polka dots of the dress's fabric, and Teddy could see she had been crying.

"There's nothing either of you can do to talk me out of it," Bill said, backing up by the barn. "I belong to the army now."

"Do we have time for a coffee before you go?" Laura asked.

Bill put his arm around her shoulder. "No honey," he said, looking at his watch. "The train leaves in a half hour."

Nobody spoke as the coupe flew by the yellow bean fields, leaving Teddy to look at Laura's profile. He watched her turn to Bill—she wasn't smiling. "Can I come and visit at Camp Borden?"

"I could drive her," Teddy said.

Bill shook his head and turned the radio, saying no civilians were allowed. "They don't want us getting distracted from the job we have to do."

The sound of Billie Holiday's "Lover Man" filled the car, prompting Laura to turn the radio off. Nothing but the purr of the Chevy, nothing but the weight of a misunderstood moment, Laura gazing out the window.

Bill finally broke the silence. "I'll be home before you know it. Churchill says they've got Hitler on the run."

Laura turned, teary eyed. "You don't have to go. You've chosen to."

"That's right, and I think it's what a man ought to do," he said, then quickly looked at Teddy. "You've got to learn how to stitch up bodies and make folks better. Me, I'm not doing any good hanging around the farm bringing in crops. Dad's got more than enough help and the girls can pitch in. They're as strong as a team of men, anyhow."

"My brother told me what's happening over there," Laura said. "Boys are getting their arms and legs blown off. Some are so emotionally damaged they'll never be normal again."

Bill turned his attention to the road and said nothing.

"If your father knew what you were doing, he would stop you," Laura said.

Bill knew exactly what direction Laura was traveling to. "If you dare tell him, I'll never forgive you," Bill said, turning to look her straight in the eye. "I mean it."

"Fine," Laura replied. "Just go over there and get yourself killed. See if I care."

Teddy leaned forward, touching Laura's shoulder. "Bill will be back before we know it, and there will be no shutting him up."

Laura smiled slightly.

Bill looked back at Teddy. "You know it, buddy."

They arrived in Galt and turned down Water Street toward the wide river. The stately grey stone Knox Presbyterian Church stood on the right, and St. Andrew's stern brick Presbyterian flanked it on the left. As the Chevy bounced along the cobble stones covering the bridge, Teddy saw a group of teenagers fishing for bass in the Grand River. All those summers with Bill taken for granted, he thought, staring at the back of his friend's head.

The Chevy sped up Hespeler Road, past the vast Galt Collegiate Institute where he and Bill had attended high school. Bill playing football while Teddy took notes. Bill learning how to court while Teddy read books.

Reaching the parking lot, Bill cut the engine, and as he did, Teddy saw Laura take Bill's hand.

"All right," Bill said, "let's do this."

From the car window, they scanned the area. It was jammed with cars and pickup trucks, the Grand River churning through the deep valley below, enlisted men and their girlfriends smoking and chatting, a neatly attired conductor strutting, calling out the next train for Toronto, Kingston, and Montreal.

Seeing a young woman struggle with her trunk, Teddy hopped out of the car. "Let me help you."

"I'm on my way to Kingston to attend university, and I've got my whole life in there," she said.

The whistle finally blew, sounding from the west. Teddy swung the woman's trunk down the platform, and wishing her well, returned to Laura and Bill standing near the back by the ticket counter. How I can see their sadness, he thought, noticing Bill's arms wrapped around her shoulders. Laura brushed the hair out of his eyes as Bill leaned down to kiss her, Teddy looking away.

The whistle sounded again, another reminder, and the couple walked through the crowd toward the inevitable.

"You'll write?" Teddy asked, clapping Bill on the shoulder.

Bill nodded.

"You better," Laura replied, trying to keep her mind focused, and trying even harder not to cry.

Bill looked at Teddy. "And you'll take good care of my girl?" he asked.

Teddy nodded. "I promise."

The whistle blew a final time, and the conductor called, "All aboard!"

"I guess this is it," Bill said, shouldering his rucksack.

"I guess it is, Bill," Laura replied.

Bill stuck out his hand to Teddy. "Don't worry about me." They shook hands and Bill looked at Laura. "And you," he said, letting go of Teddy's hand, "Oh heck, honey, you just take care of yourself. I'll be home before you know it."

As the train began pulling out of the platform, Laura threw her arms around Bill's neck and placed a quick kiss on his cheek. "I gotta go," he whispered to her, and he hopped on the moving train. Standing on the train stairs as Laura called to him, "Don't do anything stupid or too dangerous! I mean it, Bill MacMillan. I want you home in one piece."

Bill nodded, gave a goodbye salute and disappeared into the car.

They watched the train pull out of the station, and was halfway over the Grand River trestle, when Laura turned to Teddy. "I'll miss him," and she fell into his arms, dissolving into tears.

TWELVE

Psi Upsilon

Buffeted by the brisk late October wind, a lone red maple leaf released its grasp on the tree that had anchored it its entire life. Teddy took it in, drawing his coat collar up against his neck. He stamped and looked at his watch, it was 2:10 p.m. Laura was late, and her class had been out for ten minutes. He closed his eyes for a moment, tired, having studied late for a biology exam.

The tall oak doors of Victoria College swung open and a group of young men wearing blue and white Varsity Blues jerseys came running down the steps. A football game was being played later that day, the University of Western Ontario Mustangs, and Teddy was there to escort Laura.

Recognizing their voices, Teddy opened his eyes, it was Laura and two of her friends, Ruth and Agnes, standing in front of him, clasping textbooks to their chests. "I think you should be on time when your escort is freezing to death," Teddy said, smiling.

Agnes wasn't as attractive as Laura, but she had a great sense of humour and a winning smile that was loaded with good intention.

"I think you should have worn a scarf," Laura said in return, taking his arm. "Where are we going for cocoa?"

Ruth took Teddy's other arm. "Is the gentleman treating?" she asked. "I'm positively parched."

"You don't have to treat," Laura said to Teddy. "We've got pocket money."

"I can't have three ladies dehydrating," Teddy replied.

Seated at the counter, Teddy pulled fifteen cents from the pocket of his trousers and paid the cashier.

"Thank you," Laura said, as she and her friends carried steaming cups of cocoa back to one of the long wooden tables that flanked the enormous student dining hall.

"Nothing for you?" the cashier asked.

"I'll have water," Teddy replied, filling a glass from the pitcher that stood at the end of the counter.

Following the girls, he walked through the hall, oblivious to the noise. The space rocked with the riotous sounds of clashing dishes, cutlery, and conversation. With the cool autumn sunlight pouring in through the tall gothic window and its majestic vaults, the room had an ethereal feel to it. Everyone seemed to be carrying a varsity flag or wore the blue and white colours of the university.

"It's a big game today, cup game," said a young man Teddy had never meant before. "I'm Ross, by the way, Agnes's boyfriend."

"Right. You're a med student at Western and you're playing today," Ted replied, half-interested in the lumbering brute before him.

"A lineman," Ross added.

"You can't wear the purple *and* white," Laura said, turning to Agnes, fretting about how she could be true to Ross and her alma mater at the same time.

"Well then, maybe I just won't go," Agnes said.

"Of course, you'll go," Ruth replied, taking a sip of cocoa.

There goes my supper allowance, Teddy thought, looking at the ladies drinking their cups. I sure hope they taste as good as it smells.

His mother and dad paid his tuition, books, and board, but there were other expenses that needed to be incurred. Mother said girls today could buy their own, and that Teddy needn't offer. But he believed no gentleman would dare suggest a lady pay her own way. The main issue was, how to maintain appearances with this new class of friends on his budget? Looking at the cuffs on his overcoat, threadbare and flayed, Teddy felt the full burden of being a student. "So how was lab?" he asked Laura.

"Laura burnt her hand," Ruth said.

Teddy, concerned, turned to Laura.

"Oh, it's nothing," she said. She looked at Ruth. "I told you to keep it to yourself." She looked back at Teddy. "I managed to turn the Bunsen burner on myself. It was stupid. We'd better get you a scarf," she added, "or you're going to freeze at the game."

"I'll be fine," he replied. "Let's have a look at your hand."

Laura reluctantly stretched her arm out, letting Teddy gently turn her palm toward the light. "The skin is slightly burned and there's a bit of inflammation, but it's going to be okay. You'll get some blistering, some peeling, that's all." He continued to examine the wound, stoking the skin near the burn with his index finger. And for a moment, the young medical student got lost in Laura's skin, its softness.

Her eyes settled on him. "Funny, Teddy, I never noticed your hands before. They're nice …"

Teddy let go of her wrist, as if he'd been burned himself, and regrouping, told her he'd like to get some salve on the burn, to avoid an infection.

"I don't want to miss the game," Laura replied.

"I'll dress the wound myself, then. I have bandages and salves in my room."

"All right Dr. Theodore Barnes," Laura quickly agreed, as she got ready to leave for his room. "We'd better get you a scarf," she added. And maybe a sweater, too."

"Do you frequently have women in your room?" Laura asked as they quietly climbed the stairs of the boarding house on Huron Street.

Teddy brought his index finger up to his lips. "Shhh. You'll get me evicted," he whispered, only half in jest.

Once on the third floor landing, Teddy pointed to the door at the end of the hall. Laura nodded, following him down the drafty hallway.

"Here we are," he said, unlocking the door.

Laura stepped in and looked around, curious to see where Teddy lived.

The room was small with a tiny gabled window at the back. The bed was made, and his clothes were put away, but the card table, acting as a desk, and floors were covered with sheets of balled up paper, pens, pencils, stacks of foolscap, and textbooks. A new medical bag rested on the windowsill. A Christmas gift from his parents.

Teddy flicked on the desk lamp and asked Laura if she would please take a seat so he could dress the wound.

"So, this is life outside of residence," Laura said, looking around. "Can you really stay out as late as you like?" she asked, sitting down.

Teddy nodded, opening the medical bag.

"I hate having to report in by midnight, or risk being removed. Do you eat here?" she asked.

Teddy shook his head. "Just room. No board," he replied. "Let's see your hand again."

"I do appreciate this," she said, catching his eye. "It actually stings quite a bit."

Teddy cleaned the wound with hydrogen peroxide and cotton batten, and then took a swipe of white salve out of a jar with a wooden tongue depressor, carefully applying it to the burn. He placed a sterile gauze swab over the burn and gently wrapped her hand.

"Have you heard from Bill?" she asked.

Teddy glanced up, Laura's hand still resting in his. She was looking at a picture of Bill and Teddy that rested on a tall wooden chest of drawers.

"Not much, no. I'm concerned. He writes, but he doesn't say anything. It's as if he's not even there. He talks about the fall harvest and wonders if it's a good idea to plant wheat this year, or not," she said.

"I suspect he's just trying to keep his hand in," Teddy replied.

"That's what I thought at first, but it's more than that. It's odd. The other boys talk to their girls about what's going on, but not Bill. I haven't had the nerve to ask his mother, but I'm worried."

"You might want to ask your brother, Jack, since he's a medic on the front," Teddy replied. "He's been in Normandy for a while already."

"Or maybe I could ask Jack's wife, Sue," Laura proposed.

Teddy looked at Laura's bandaged hand, still resting in his. He gave it a gentle squeeze and a light tap. "You're all fixed up. Let's go to the game."

Laura looked at her hand. "You're going to be a good doctor, Teddy. I can tell."

As they left his room and heard the door close behind them, she knew it to be true, Theodore Barnes had been born for this—to make the world a better place.

Crammed into a restaurant located on the main floor of the Park Plaza hotel, the whole gang was there, happy—their team had won, they had beaten the Mustangs.

An established watering hole for the university crowd, Murray's was a large square space with a small counter lined with stools and small tables.

"What'll it be?" the waitress asked, setting the tray on the table, and dealing the coffee cups like a deck of cards.

A couple of kids asked for coffee. Ruth wanted tea.

"Put on another pot, Alma!" she called to the woman behind the counter.

Teddy loved the place, its novelty. Waitresses dressed in starched white uniforms complete with matching aprons, shoes and caps, looking more like nurses, or admirals on a ship. Back home, the waitresses only wore an apron and maybe a hairnet.

The waitress turned to Teddy. "What'll it be, Ted?"

"Just a glass of water today, no eggs or ham on the house, Clara. Thanks," Teddy replied with a wink. "No upsetting Murray … "

"Still waiting on the letter from home?" she asked with a knowing smile.

Teddy squirmed. He'd confessed to Clara his parents sent him room and board money every couple of weeks, but he didn't want her disclosing his finances in front of the rest. Laura, listening, didn't say a word.

"I'll have water, too," Laura said, after Agnes asked for coffee. "Besides, if I have another drop of caffeine, I'll be up all night," she added, removing her tam.

Teddy watched Laura fix her hair. It's true, he thought, remembering her and Bill seeing the movie "Laura" before he'd headed overseas, she does look like Gene Turney.

Ruth pulled a cigarette out of a sterling silver cigarette case, catching Teddy's attention. Here he said, leaning forward and offering her a light. Just then, the front door of the restaurant opened, and a group of Mustangs walked into the restaurant with Ross in the middle.

"Over here!" Agnes called as Ross and his pals made their way through the restaurant, stopping only to engage in a bit of banter with Varsity fans.

Ross gave Agnes a smooch on the cheek and pulled up a chair. "Say, where's your scarf?" he asked.

Agnes turned to Laura, "See? I told you! You're not really mad, are you?" she asked Ross.

"Nah, are you going to the party at Psi house this Saturday?' he asked Laura.

Laura shook her head, no.

"What?" Ross responded, turning to Teddy. "What kind of escort are you?"

Before Teddy could answer, Clara arrived with another pot of coffee.

"Hey beautiful," Ross said, grabbing Clara by the apron strings as she swung by. "Can I have a cup of that?"

"We don't serve the enemy," Clara replied with an elegant pirouette, spinning out of Ross's orbit with a sniff.

"Come on, Clara," Agnes said, with a laugh, "he's my boyfriend."

Clara poured a fresh cup, as Ross turned to Teddy. "You've got to escort Laura to the party tomorrow night. It's going to be filled to the rafters."

Teddy had been rushed for the fraternities before, but he'd always declined. Until Laura arrived at school, Teddy had spent all his extra time studying.

"Don't you have to be a member?" he asked.

"No," Ross replied. "Anyone can attend the parties. At the fraternities, like mine, at Psi Upsilon, that's how we make our money."

Teddy looked at Laura. "What do you think?"

She shrugged. "It might be fun … I think …?"

Teddy nodded and agreed.

Walking back to his room that night, he heard students talk about the upcoming Christmas exams. Feeling frustrated, he kicked a fallen horse chestnut out of his way, putting it across the pavement and into an open gutter.

Laura, preparing for the evening, held a pale green dress up to her ivory satin slip and looked in the full-length mirror. "What do you think?" she asked, twirling around so Agnes could see.

"I think you'd better get dressed. The boys will be here any moment."

Laura unzipped the back of the dress and carefully stepped into the gown. "Will you do me up?" she asked, throwing back her hair and giving it a shake.

"I love your choice. Very elegant," Agnes said as she zipped the dress up.

Laura looked at Agnes's reflection in the mirror. "What should I expect?" she asked, worried.

Pulling a brush through her short blonde bob, the stocky girl looked back to the mirror. "What do you mean?"

"I've never been to a frat party, and I've heard they can get a bit wild."

Agnes shrugged. "It really only gets as wild as you want it to. There are kids who drink, but lots who don't, and only show up for the dancing."

Laura, carefully applying her lipstick, mused over her friend's comment. She'd never been to a party where people drank—ever. She knew her parents wouldn't approve, but they didn't approve of anything, did they? Her choice of hairstyles had been frowned upon, the posters of Van Johnson tacked over her bed, too.

Blotting rouge that had mis-landed around her mouth, she thought more of Bill, of Teddy, of how, while the two boys came from similar backgrounds, Bill loved the land and Teddy the city. An oddity, she thought to herself.

Laura gave her hair a final brush, as one of the girls called up from downstairs, "Laura, your date is here!"

She smoothed out her skirt, smiled at herself in the mirror, and walking toward the door, thought of the party, a real one—one she could have fun at.

Teddy was sitting in a wing chair balancing a cup of tea in one hand, holding his fedora in the other. Around him, everything felt luxurious, the curtains falling to the floor into carefully choreographed pools of fabric, the furniture, a mix of both antique and modern, the walls, covered with vivid oil paintings featuring scenes of city and country life, compelling the eye. I don't know much about art, Teddy thought, looking at one, but I bet they are originals.

"Don't you look handsome," Laura said, as she swept into the room. Teddy leapt up so fast, he nearly spilled his tea.

"So do you," he replied. "I mean, you look very pretty," he added, feeling clumsy.

"Thank you," Laura replied, walking over to the window and looking out. "Now if only Ross would arrive."

Just then the doorbell rang, sending Agnes to barrel across the foyer in a remarkably unladylike manner.

"Let's go," Laura said, "we're almost late."

Psi Upsilon House reminded Teddy of the Parliament Building with its tall redbrick walls and rounded glass windows. This was a smaller version, but when he stepped under the arch, he felt as if he'd passed into a medieval castle. Dark wood. Noble statues.

"Look," Ross proudly said, pointing to the huge stairwell in the center, "up there we have eight bedrooms. The frat house can sleep sixteen students at a time. When a brother's in from out of town, he always has a bed."

All three stared at the huge stairwell, and slowly walking across the grandest room of the mansion and seeing beverage stains on the Persian rug, understood they had landed in a mansion meant for half-grown men.

Teddy looked around for a bartender.

"Where do you pay, Ross?"

"It's an honour system," Ross replied, as they reached the front of the line.

An honor system, Teddy wondered. I'm sure I'm not the only man in this crowd low on cash. Dad always said to get the money at the door.

He leaned over, grabbed the pot of hot coffee, and after pouring two cups, dropped a dime on the plate, his rent having arrived earlier that day.

With their liquids in hand, Teddy and Ross navigated their way through the crowd, to where Laura and Agnes were waiting by the fireplace.

"Hey," the girls said in tandem.

"Not bad, right?" Ross replied, pointing to a group of dancers.

Just then, the soft music coming from the hi-fi stopped. A tall willowy girl dressed in a tweed dress flipped a record, bouncing the system's needle to Bing Crosby's "The Very Thought of You."

Ross placed his coffee on top of the mantle and offered Agnes his arm.

"I thought you'd never ask," she said, as they moved into the crowd.

Teddy set down the coffee as well and offered Laura his hand. She took it, half expectantly, and following him onto the living room floor, smiled a little more.

With Laura inside his arms, Teddy thought back to that evening when Uncle Ed and his mother had danced to the same song. Mother had seemed so light, he thought, so different, with Uncle Ed sweeping her around the room. He would never forget the magic he had witnessed that night. The clarinet crooning into the falling night as two people moved completely as one.

"Are you okay, Teddy," Laura asked, seeing his eyes staring through her.

Teddy nodded, and coming back, tucked his hand into the small of Laura's back. The pace of the music accelerated, and he nearly lifted her off her feet as he effortlessly spun her around.

"You are an excellent dancer," Laura said, her arm resting comfortably on his shoulder as the song changed.

"Who taught you?" Teddy asked.

"Jack," she replied laughing, "and as you very well know, Bill couldn't dance if his life depended on it." She glanced around the room, remarking on how the Psi House was easily as nice as her residence. "You should think about living here," she remarked. "You'd make a lot of good connections."

Ross tapped Teddy's shoulder.

"I'm cutting in," he said, taking Laura's hand.

"Watch out for her, she'll wear you out," Teddy warned, heading over to the fireplace to retrieve his cold cup of coffee.

Near his table, a couple of medical students were loudly chatting, chasing away his thoughts about the way Mother and Uncle Ed had danced. A year ahead of Teddy, the students were talking about some professors he currently had. One of the students, sipping his beer, turned and looked at Teddy. "We're members of Psi Upsilon."

"You are?" he replied, realizing Laura was right, maybe this was the perfect place for him, if he wanted to advance his life.

"My feet are so sore," Agnes said, as the four of them hurried along Bloor Street on their way back to the women's residence.

"Say, Ted," Ross said, "what would you think if I was to recommend you for the fraternity?"

"I can't afford it," Teddy replied, thinking they were out of his league.

"It's the same as room and board," Laura said.

"What do you mean?"

"Your folks send you the money and you pay us. It's once a month. Just like room and board," Ross replied. "I'll recommend you and you can move right in. That is if you're interested."

"Interested?" Teddy almost shouted, feeling suddenly breezy. "Where do I sign?"

"You'll have to settle all that later," Laura replied, as they arrived in front of the girl's residence. "Agnes and I should disappear before we turn into pumpkins." She looked at Teddy. "Good night and thank you." She placed a hand on his shoulder. "I had a wonderful time."

Teddy watched Ross escort the two ladies up the stairs and into the house.

"And don't be a stranger," Laura called back as she disappeared behind the closing door.

Walking down Huron Street with his trunk on one shoulder and his medical bag on the other, Teddy considered the proposition. It would cost more than the boarding house, but it was worth the expense, as it was more like an investment in his future. Of course, he'd need to economize in other areas, he just wasn't sure where?

Laura's right, he thought, beyond studies, there is connecting with people, on other levels. She often cited her father's ability to converse with any man about any matter, having contributed to his success. "Dad never has to sign any papers at the bank. All he does is tell people his name and his handshake is enough."

Teddy wondered what it would be like to get anything you wanted on the strength of a handshake. He knew Wilton Gillespie didn't think too much of him, not since the time Teddy had exposed Laura to what her father called, 'the communist' threat."

In his letters, as of late, Bill wrote about how communism was growing in certain parts of Europe, most likely as a backlash against all the Fascism spewing across the continent. Bill's letters were strange. He never talked about the actual war, alluding instead to the beauty and demeanor of French girls. That and other topics.

Maybe Laura was right. Maybe they should be concerned. He walked on, trying to push Bill from his mind.

Ross and Agnes were waiting, sitting on the front steps of the Psi Upsilon House when Teddy arrived.

Agnes leapt to her feet, ordering Ross to help Teddy with his trunk. "That thing must be heavy," she said. "Hurry up," she told Ross who slowly rose and ambled down the sidewalk.

Teddy smiled, he had never seen Ross actually run. Even when he played football, Ross simply stood there waiting to throw his weight at whatever was coming his way.

Ross snatched the trunk from Teddy's shoulder and onto his own, muscling it up the stone stairs and through the front door with Teddy and Agnes is tow.

"They've got a house meeting tonight," Ross said. "As a brother you're required to show up in a shirt and a tie and say something intelligent."

"Hum," Teddy said, his voice ironic and amused, "you think it's possible?"

Ross, laughing, walked down the hall, Teddy following.

The Psi Upsilon house, built for the brotherhood just after the First World War, had a mission all chapters had to adhere to: To seek a moral, intellectual, and social excellence for themselves, and inspire the same values in society.

It was made for the likes of Teddy Barnes.

"You're here," Ross said, pointing above the room's door where an owl flanked by two gryphons proudly hung. "Our crest. It's on every door."

While Ross was telling Teddy how the Mustangs were going to trounce the Blues next time, Teddy wandered the space. It was bigger than the Barnes' family parlor, and had large leaded casement windows that opened onto a magnificent view of the university and the distant lake.

"No one with me?" Teddy asked, pointing to the empty bed opposite his.

"For the time being you've got the room to yourself. It's hard with the war on. Not many boys," Ross said, looking at his watch. "I've got to catch the 5:10."

"All right," Teddy said, opening one of the two large closets. "I guess I'll see you around. And thanks for everything."

"Of course. And hey, don't forget the meeting. I hope you've got some bright ideas about how to raise money because," Ross leaned forward, whispering, "we're broke, and that ain't funny."

After Ross left, Teddy sat down and removed the stethoscope from the bag. Hanging it around his neck, he leaned back on the chair, feet up. Before him, Lake Ontario glistened, and in the distance, a large red and yellow merchant vessel was throwing up a cloud of steam as it moved through the waves.

How my luck has turned, he thought. Yesterday, I was stuck in that dreadful rooming house, and now I have a home fit for a king. What would Mother and Dad think of this arrangement? This form of luxury? After all, they were sacrificing so he could advance himself, expecting a minimum of hardship to help carve out his character.

As the familiar feeling of guilt made its way to his stomach, the newest fraternity member quickly rose to his feet and began stowing away his gear. He'd kept all his correspondence, storing the letters in his bedside table, re-reading them when he felt lonely. Letters from his parents, and his sister. Bill's, too, of course. Which were scant.

Stacking them into the drawer, Teddy randomly removed one of the last letters his mother had written him. He remembered how, at first, he had refused to read her words. The pain and turmoil she had caused, that he was still carrying with him, dark tentacles made of shadows.

Following his second year of medicine, he had started to miss Mother, and after reluctantly glancing through the letters, he had discovered a part of her he never knew existed. She wrote well, filling her letters with colorful anecdotes, telling stories about their life at the farm, about Bette and her scandalizing behavior, which he loved to read best, for it served his mother right, to have a child she couldn't control, and didn't fear her, at all.

How to tell his parents he'd moved? he wondered. It would be easy, they never came to Toronto to visit him, and all he'd have to say was he'd found other accommodation, a sensical solution, really. He'd tell his mother he'd found a place where they served decent food, and then quietly mention getting properly fed justified an increase in living expenses. It's not a real lie, Teddy said to himself, and it might work.

THIRTEEN

Boys and Girls

"Bette! Get down here this instant!" Bessie called, whisking scrambled eggs in her mother's old enamel bowl. "You're going to be late."

"Don't be such an old growler," Bette called back, purposely stomping her way down the stairs.

"That dress is too tight," Bessie complained as she poured the eggs into the skittle. "We can practically see your business."

Bette glanced down at her chest, thrilled she was starting to show. She flicked her red hair, ribbons and all, sending it tumbling around her shoulders.

"What do you think, Daddy?"

Charlie had just come in from mucking out the cow stalls. "About what?" he asked, swinging his leg over the chair.

"My dress," Bette replied, with a curtsy.

"It's nice," Charlie said, swallowing a spoonful of porridge.

Bessie rapped the spatula on the counter. "Honestly, Charlie, if you think it's appropriate a fourteen-year-old—"

"Fifteen!" Bette interjected. "I'm fifteen. And soon, I'll be sixteen."

"Fine, fifteen," Bessie added. "If you want your daughter running all over the township looking like that, Charlie, you're not the man I thought you were."

Charlie sighed, and for a moment missed Teddy's easy company—another man in the house might help stop all the bickering. "Bessie, I think the dress is fine," he said, as Bessie fumed, scrambling the eggs in an escalating huff. "But your mother is right, it's a bit snug. How about when you get back from school you let it out a bit?"

"Breakfast is served," Bessie said, scraping the eggs out of the pan and onto their plate. "And stop your pouting, Bette Barnes, it is not becoming of a young lady."

"All of the other kids are wearing their clothes like this," Bette said, playing with her food. "And you know I hate scrambled eggs," she added, pushing the plate away.

Charlie quickly finished his oatmeal. "If you're not going to eat your breakfast you can go hungry. Now shake a leg. I'll give you a ride to school."

Bette shoved her chair back, dramatically grabbed her books and walked out the door.

"You come straight home, we've got sewing to do," Bessie called, looking at Charlie as if to say you deal with it, she's your daughter as much as mine. Bessie turned to the sink, tightening her apron around her waist.

Bette, seated on the passenger side, looked at the back of the Dodge carefully wedged full of milk cans.

"I don't want to hear you talking to your mother like that," her father said.

"She's the one who's always picking on me. Ever since Teddy left, it's like I'm all she thinks about."

"You need to show her a little more respect."

Bette looked at her father, his red hair nearly all gone at the top, the crown wrapping around his head, silvery white. Examining him further, she thought of how he seemed more tired than usual, of how managing the farm alone, without help, was taking a toll. Or was it just normal aging?

"The motor sounds funny," she said, wanting to pull the discussion away from her. "Maybe I could help you with it tonight?"

"I know you like to help, but it's too big a job for us," her father said.

The family needed a new car. They all agreed the Dodge had done its time, but where would the money come from? Charlie couldn't understand why Teddy couldn't budget better, why he had asked for a bigger allowance? While discussing the issue with Bessie, she had shushed him, saying Teddy would never ask for anything he didn't need. And humming some tune she'd heard at one of the dances, Bette had left for somewhere else in her mind, her fingers absentmindedly tapping the melody out on her book.

Charlie smiled, his hand loosening the grip on the wheel. His daughter had a lovely voice, too. And so, yes, Bette was strong willed, but she was also smart, resourceful, and blossoming into a very beautiful young woman. Why Bessie placed all her faith in Teddy, he didn't understand. I guess they're just too much alike, Charlie thought to himself. And surely, soon enough, they'll get on better once Bette is older.

Bette walked across the football field of Galt Collegiate, books swinging on her hip. There was enough nip in the air to remind her of the coming winter. Mother had finally finished the canning, and Dad was planting the winter wheat. The fields would soon be covered with snow, and then she would get her skis out, and fly down Baden Hill, a hill most of the kids wouldn't dream of skiing down.

A group of boys were playing football, among them, the tall, good-looking Jimmy Clyde, who stood waving at her. She smiled a half a smile, not returning his wave. Bette had learned from sitting quietly in washroom cubicles, listening to the older girls talk, you shouldn't look too eager with boys, they liked you a lot better if you acted standoffish.

The players started clowning around trying to get Bette's attention, but she had already turned away, listening to the sound of the distant river in the valley, and thinking of Uncle Ed. She missed him, and still did not fully understand the circumstances surrounding his departure, or his death. So much of him had disappeared, as if someone had brushed over his passage. His radio, his books, his trunk were all gone. You vanished like a shadow at high noon, Uncle Ed. Why? Asking the wind if Uncle Ed was still out there somewhere, she wanted him to be like Bill, on the verge of an eventual return, even though she knew it was impossible.

"Miss Barnes, can I carry your books to class?" Jimmy Clyde asked, shaking her out of her thoughts.

Running across the field, stocky Bobby Riddell appeared. "Hi," the boy gasped, catching his wind.

The rest of the team had clumped together beneath a goal post to watch. Clearly, the two boys had been racing to see which one would reach her first. Bette looked at Jimmy as beads of sweat covered his brow.

"No," she replied. "Your hands are dirty," she added with the tiniest hint of a smile.

"Mine aren't," Bobby said, placing his palms in front of her for inspection. Bette moved closer to him, taking his hands, palms up, in hers.

"Clean as a whistle," he said proudly.

Jimmy glowered at his friend as the rest of the boys watched.

Playing to the crowd, Bette slowly considered the offer. "I don't think so," she finally replied, dropping Bobby's hands.

Bette turned back toward the school, hips swinging side-to-side the way she'd seen women walk in the movies. Bobby stood there, hands still in the air. "See you boys in class," she called back over her shoulder.

"I think Jimmy Clyde has a crush on you," Tina said, approaching Bette as she neared the front of the school.

Tina, shorter than Bette, had long, light blonde hair, big brown eyes, a nice figure, and a bright white smile that bedazzled. She had a locker next to Bette's, and since they'd started high school, Tina had become Bette's best friend.

The first time Tina had smiled at her, Bette had felt a lump form in her throat, having to swallow it down while smiling back. It intrigued her, this feeling, new, as much as enticing, enticing because new. In the autumn, they'd started regular sleep overs at Tina's house. Wearing flannel nightgowns, they snuggled in Tina's wood spindled bed, talking, and dreaming out loud, about girls, about boys, about school.

Walking together across the field with Tina, Bette recalled how, lately, the girls had discovered tickling, a new game, one that released a contagious laughter.

What followed these sessions for Bette was some kind of strangeness that was almost recognized, and kept her awake and aware of her friend's breathing, of the smell of her breath, even. And wondering more, about the feel of Tina's body, about the scent of her hair. Bette, slowly, had allowed herself to question, why did she feel this way? And as their fingers moved more and more over each other's skin seeking to make each other laugh, each sleepover seemed more and more like a conduit, until one night, Bette had slowly inched her body across the mattress, wanting to get closer, wanting to look at Tina. Her face and her lips.

"I really do think he does!" Tina said, interrupting Bette's thought, resetting her mind.

"Don't be silly," Bette replied, feigning disagreement, and remembering how once Jimmy had asked to walk her to the school bus stop, how he'd wait for her at the water fountain leaning against the wall. Each time she had declined, each time she had ignored his glances.

"And I think Bobby does, too," Tina added, her eyes looking beyond the football field where Bobby was walking back to join the rest of the football players.

Bette followed her gaze.

"Don't you think boys are silly?" Tina asked.

Yes, Bette thought, and I don't care either. All I know is that to be popular, I need to get attention from boys. That way they'll always remember you, Mother had told her. And there was Tina, a phase she hoped would pass.

Tina shrugged. "I'm not really interested in them yet."

"No?" Bette asked, wondering if Tina was jealous, or better yet, didn't much like boys, either.

"I don't know, really," Tina continued.

Walking through the field, Bette looked at Tina, her long blond hair, the liveliness in her eyes. All she knew was that she had an absence of feeling while with boys, but yet, had a fascination for the power she exerted over their wanting. It wasn't anything Bette had ever been told, more like something she knew deep inside, like a secret someone she had never met, but had told her in a dream.

"I'm like you, Tina. I guess the time will come," she said, hoping that this secret power would transfer to her friend. Especially, during sleepovers.

FOURTEEN

The Importance of Parties

Teddy walked through the front door of the frat house as a couple of the brothers wrestled a large table through the doorway.

"Where are you taking it?" he asked, grabbing a leg.

"It's getting ruined from the parties," one of the brothers replied. "We thought we'd better store it in the cellar."

He'd never been down there before, and imagined an old root cellar, dank and musty with the odd shallow puddle of moisture, but the lowest floor of the Psi Upsilon house surprised him. The ceiling was high, and the yellow and brown checkered linoleum floor was clean and dry. There were even two sinks against the back wall. The space was mostly empty except for a collection of old club chairs, a few rolled up carpets, and an assortment of tables.

It gave Teddy an idea.

Seated around a long formal table in the dining room, the members settled all outstanding business, concluding with the problem of dwindling reserves.

Teddy tentatively raised his hand. "I think I know how we can make more money," he said.

A couple of the brothers looked at him, puzzled. The young man had only been there for a few months. Teddy, aware of the danger of being perceived as pushy—arrogant even, had recalled his mother's lessons, on how to take the time to assess a worthy cause, that if one could improve the lot of many, as well as advancing one's case, it was best to proceed. His mother would have never become Secretary of the Institute had she never spoken up.

"We've got an enormous basement that's not being used," Teddy said. "I think we should build a bar down there, buy all kinds of liquor and hire a professional bartender who knows how to make any kind of drink, as well as keep an eye on the till."

Most of the men laughed.

"With what money?" the President asked.

"We'll approach alumni," Teddy firmly offered. "The war economy is booming, and if the alumni can't pledge any money, they could likely donate goods."

By the time the meeting was over, Teddy had all the brothers down in the basement. Excited, they studied the space, imagining it furnished, imagining the bar and its liquor—imagining the parties. The money.

Over the following week, the President drew up a list of alumni to contact. Every member of the fraternity would be responsible for approaching twenty of them, to have their name written on a chair so they could come and sit at the bar any time they pleased.

The President claimed it was brilliant.

Teddy said it would likely work.

The implementation of the plan swallowed up the last week of November, and most of December, but by the time Christmas rolled around, the Psi Upsilon bar was ready and open for business. The word was all over the campus, and everyone planned on making a stopover.

Teddy was up in his room cramming for a chemistry exam when the doorbell rang. He ran down the hall and slid down the banister as the doorbell rang again. A midsized, paneled van was parked in the driveway, and a burly fellow with a cap, a clipboard, and a stack of boxes leaned on the bell again. Teddy snatched the fraternity check book from the table and opened the door. "Hello."

"Liquor delivery," the man replied.

Teddy indicated to the door leading to the basement. "It goes down there."

The delivery man nodded, asking Teddy to make the check out for $35.00 and proceeded to carry the boxes of liquor down to the bar.

Following the man's departure, Teddy hurried down to the basement where boxes and boxes filled with everything his parents despised welcomed him. Uncontrollable laughter emerged from deep inside.

Things were certainly changing, he thought, walking around. I'm here living in this fraternity house, and signing for expensive liquor deliveries. He wondered, had Uncle Ed ever done anything like that? And who exactly had Uncle Ed been?

Looking inside the boxes, Teddy realized he had come to understand everyone had secrets, inevitably, to survive, he imagined. Uncle Ed must have had some of his own, just like him, the hushes in his life allowing him to breathe better; to live better; to survive his families rules, the weight of them. They're small minded, he decided, pulling bottles of whiskey out of the boxes and carefully lining them on the shelf behind the bar. Once finished, he turned around, letting his finger walk over its top, and he smiled. The bar, a stainless-steel structure lined with slightly used stools, shined in the subdued lighting Laura had recommended.

Her home economic classes sure have been good to us, he thought, remembering how she had designed and decorated the space on a budget.

"Women had to do without during the Depression," she said, "and necessity meant that they had to be resourceful."

He surveyed the room, noting the full, comfortable sofas, and club chairs clustered around low slung mahogany coffee tables.

Before exiting the basement, he looked once more, and felt proud: The bar was ready. Turning to the stairs, he glanced at the red neon sign that glowed the letters of his fraternity, Psi Upsilon. He turned the light switch off.

Everything was perfect.

Laura arrived at the party accompanied by Agnes and Ross, as Teddy was too occupied setting up the bar to have escorted her. One of the brothers flung open the door to greet them, and a group of party goers, still in their coats, filled the foyer.

"Where's Teddy?" Laura asked.

One of the fellows said he was down in the bar making sure the liquor supply was adequate.

Ross and Agnes started chatting with another couple as Laura walked to the stairs leading to the basement. The basement itself was packed with nicely attired young men and women busy discussing current events, such as the war effort, exam preparations, Tommy Dorsey playing Maple Leaf Gardens and the Americans development of what they were calling the 'A bomb'. What had troubled Laura most was the news concerning the existence of concentration camps. The Germans were rounding up homosexuals, gypsies, and Jews, and any group Hitler deemed inferior to him, or his race. It struck Laura that she had several Jewish professors—especially her beloved chemistry professor—the one said to be 'light in his loafers.' Convinced privacy was privacy, that what anyone did privately was nobody else's business, Laura always had made a point to voice her opinion on the matter.

Hearing a group of Psi Upsilon brothers laugh and talk at the bar, she looked up, and thinking Teddy in the center, she moved between the tables, wanting to reach him, and yet, before her, seemed to stand another Teddy, one wearing a new jacket and pleated grey trousers, with spectator shoes. He appeared different, like a new man. The shoes startled her. She'd seen them before, but never as shiny, never with the brilliant luster that met her eyes now. She remained looking, still wondering, and as a lock of his dark hair dropped over one eye, he thrust his hands into his pockets, and smiled, wide and endearing. Teddy lights up the room, she thought, with such confidence and assurance. Why haven't I noticed before? And she thought, some young woman would be very lucky to have him, but who?

Suddenly, the boys hoisted Teddy high on their shoulders, as the President of the chapter proclaimed, "From this day forth Theodore Barnes shall be known as Master of the Revels."

The crowd cheered, and as it did, something moved inside of Laura, bringing her back in time, to that moment at the Royal Winter Fair when Teddy had won first prize for that bird—Hannibal, was it? She'd forgotten about the rooster and the ribbons. Ed Barnes, his death, had erased her memories of that day, until now.

Agnes, coming out of nowhere, appeared and took Teddy by the chin and turned to Laura. "Look at him, doesn't he look handsome?"

Laura smiled—her heart, beating a different beat, most certainly agreed. And suddenly, she couldn't wait for the holidays.

Teddy had promised to visit on New Year's Eve.

FIFTEEN

Christmas

"How many pancakes do you want?" Bette called upstairs. Teddy's eyes opened. He'd been tired from the late night caroling at the church and had slept right through the morning chores. Quickly, he went down the stairs dressed in his pajamas and robe.

"Dad," Teddy said, dropping into his chair. "You should have woken me up. You need help and I'm already skipping off."

Charlie, dressed in his overalls, cheeks pink from the cold, said, "It's Christmas boy. You need a break."

Teddy was about to respond when Bessie patted his shoulder. "Don't contradict your father. If you're going to get through this next semester, we've got to get you all rested up. Now, how many pancakes?" she asked.

"Three to start, please," Teddy replied, pouring himself a cup of coffee.

Taking a deep breath, he saw the red poinsettia his mother had placed in the centre of the table, surrounded by a nest of pine boughs.

"Mother," he said smiling, "the house smells like it was made of Christmas trees."

Bessie smiled back, and after serving the pancakes, slowly took her seat, looking tired, or was it age? Teddy thought.

"Good pancakes, Bessie," Charlie said, shoveling in another mouthful.

"Thank you, dear.".

"Say Mother, did you ever think of trying dry roasted coffee?" Teddy nonchalantly asked, finding the coffee bitter. "I think they sell some in town."

Bessie's head turned. "Something's wrong with my coffee?"

Teddy swallowed. "No, no, no," he quickly said, wanting to soften his comment. "I just got into the habit of the other stuff at school, and wondered if you'd ever like to try something different, that's all."

His mother cleared her throat while Bette looked at Teddy with an eye roll that said, "What did you go and do that for?"

Teddy sipped his coffee, assessing the sister before him, no longer the girl he had left when he'd first went off to medical school. She's so beautiful and tall, he thought to himself, eyebrows raised, and wondered if she needed to wear her sweater so snug?

"Bessie," Charlie asked, "why don't you pour me another cup of that *fine* coffee?" He looked at Teddy. "Just because you're living in the city doesn't mean we have to be picking up fancy ways."

"No, sir," he said. There was no point trying to explain, they wouldn't understand. "You make the best pancakes in the world, Mother," Teddy said, forking another three onto his plate.

"Better than the city?" she asked.

"Oh, yes," Teddy replied. "Nobody can cook like you."

Bessie's smile returned. "Well now, you children hurry up with your breakfast, so we can open the gifts."

Bessie turned to Charlie, her eyes tired, and said, "Honestly, Charlie, I don't know what's wrong with my energy today. I've just been feeling flat."

"Take another pancake," Charlie said. "Your blood sugar is likely low. Isn't that so, son?" he said to Teddy.

Teddy simply nodded, not wanting to get involved. Hadn't he done enough damage with his opinion about coffee?

They walked to the living room, excited for the gift distribution.

"Oh, Dad, we're too big for you to wear the Santa hat!" Bette said, as her father happily trotted out of the pantry wearing his ratty old red and white striped cap.

"Nonsense," Charlie said, sitting down on a petit point stool, and reaching under the tree. "Now who is this for?" he said with a jolly laugh. "Why look, it says Mother and Dad," and he handed the package to Bessie.

Careful not to tear the paper so she could reuse it the next year, Bessie slowly opened her gift.

"Hurry up, Mother," Bette said. "I've got to go tobogganing. The kids'll be here soon."

"You just settle down," Charlie said.

Teddy stretched his legs out, anxious for his mother to open the present he had gotten her.

"Oh, Teddy," Bessie said, "you shouldn't have."

Beaming at her son, she held up a box of Turtles, deciding right then she would serve them to Mrs. Moffatt and Mrs. Little for tea the next day. A perfect occasion to brag about how her 'son the doctor' had given them to her.

"Can we have one?" Bette asked.

"No, you may not," Bessie replied, patting Teddy's hand.

Charlie picked the next gift from under the tree. "This one says it's for itty bitty Bette," and he held the gift out to his daughter.

"Oh, Dad," she said, snatching it out of his grasp and tearing the wrapping paper. "A new pencil case. Thank you, Teddy!" she said, hugging her brother. "Look Mother, it's from the University."

Charlie smiled, handing a package with Teddy's name on it. "Why don't you open this up, son?"

The label read: From Mother, Dad, and Bette. After thanking each one of them, Teddy tore the paper away, revealing a new white dress shirt.

"It's the perfect size," said Teddy, and he kissed his mother lightly on the cheek and patted his dad's back. "This is exactly what I wanted. Here, Dad," he said, handing his father another gift. "It's time for you to open something."

Charlie opened the card, and silently read the words Teddy had carefully chosen: "To Mother and Dad, to help keep the correspondence coming. I truly appreciate the financial aid and especially your letters. Love, Teddy." Placing the card down, Charlie proceeded to open the parcel, uncovering a beautiful Cross pen and pencil set.

"Oh, Teddy," Bessie said, delighted, "You shouldn't have."

Charlie abruptly put the set down, startling everyone in the room. "What exactly are you doing spending your money on fancy gifts, when you should be spending it on school?"

"I saved," Teddy replied.

Charlie's anger was becoming unleashed, and as he went on about spendthrifts, and how a modest man doesn't need to impress people with showy gifts, Teddy felt every ounce of Christmas cheer seeping out of his body. He didn't want to be here anymore, and he didn't want to listen to his father continue about money. He hated it.

Looking at his mother's worn-out Christmas dress and recalling how his father couldn't afford to replace the old Dodge, acidity flooded his stomach. How insensitive and wrong of me, he thought, to bring them these types of presents.

"Don't fuss, Charlie," Bessie said, anxious to put a happy face back on the family affair. "It's a lovely set and I'm sure it didn't cost all that much. Now what about Bette, isn't there something over there in the candy cane paper with her name on it?" Bessie, rummaging beneath the tree, said, "Why, yes there is," and she handed Bette the gift.

Bette removed the wrapping paper, wanting to look excited by the new turquoise sweater she was unfolding, but the mood had been broken.

Charlie tugged off his Santa hat and sat in his chair while Bette and Bessie handed out the few remaining gifts. Eventually, the doorbell rang, and Bette bounced to her feet. "That'll be Jimmy," she said, running to the door.

"Jimmy?" Teddy asked, turning to his mother.

"That's Jimmy Clyde. There's been quite a battle going on between him and Bobby Riddell to see who Bette is sweet on."

"Isn't she a bit young for that?" Teddy asked.

"That's what I say," Bessie replied. "But your father thinks it's all well and good."

"They're just off to a church sledding party," Charlie replied, eyeing the pen and pencil set. "They'll be chaperoned."

"That's right," Bette said, coming back into the room in her coat and hat. "I won't be too long. And then I want to hear everything about your landlady and your room in Toronto," Bette said, giving Teddy a kiss on the cheek. "You never really talk about the city, and I can only hear so much about school." She walked out of the room, laughter filtering into the parlour until the outside door slammed shut.

"She's right," Bessie said. "How's the new landlady? Is the food any better?"

"She's okay," he nervously replied, standing up.

"She's giving you three square meals a day, isn't she?" Bessie asked.

"That's what we're paying for," Charlie added, shifting in his chair, making a point to turn away from the pen and pencil set.

"It's fine. It's just that nothing compares with mother's cooking. You know that," he said quickly to his father. And wanting to escape the subject, Teddy decided to go out for a walk, invoking some fence was down by the pasture.

Bessie and Charlie nodded their heads as Teddy went up to change. Climbing the stairs and hearing his mother compliment the pencil set, Teddy rushed to his room, not wanting to hear his father's reply. He felt bad enough already.

Bette wrapped her legs around Jimmy as the two of them straddled his Red Rocket sled. She pointed to the steeple of the Presbyterian church far in the west, telling him to look at the horse drawn wagon carrying straw in the north. "It's so tiny," she screamed in laughter, "like an ant."

Around them, fourteen teenagers milled around the top of Baden Hill, excited to breathe in the fresh air, and that Christmas had arrived.

"Who wants to race?" Jimmy called, his heels slamming into the crunchy snow to keep him from sliding down the hill. Bette jumped on behind him.

"I will," Bobby said, throwing his sled down beside Jimmy.

"Okay!"

"Come on, Tina, be my partner," Bobby said, patting the back of the sled.

The decision was a torture to Tina, as she was terrified of heights. Reluctantly, she left the group of girls standing around in a circle talking to one of the chaperones.

"Why don't we start a little lower?" Tina asked, nervously peering down.

"Don't be such a scaredy-cat," Bette teased.

"Oh, all right," Tina said, hopping on behind Bobby.

The two boys rocked their sleds back and forth, gaining as much momentum as possible. A short boy with yellow hair removed his blue toque, waving it up and down for the countdown. "One, two, three … Go!"

And the two sleds shot down the hill.

Jimmy and Bette's sled ran into a rock, sending Red the Rocket into the air, and yet, it miraculously landed back down, bouncing hard off the surface of the hill. Threatening to spin out of control, Jimmy expertly maneuvered it back into place. Let me see, Bette thought, as she looked on to assess how far ahead Tina and Bobby sled was. From afar, she could still hear Tina screaming, and it made her feel good: She had never screamed in her life, and felt, she didn't know how.

A group of skiers scattered out of the way as a little girl flopped over on her side, poles sliding down the hill, her father shaking his hand, yelling to look out, that, or something like it, but Bette couldn't hear over the rush of the wind. She clamped her hands around Jimmy's waist and told him to go faster. "I don't want them to beat us," she yelled in his ear.

"Too late," Jimmy replied, pointing to the bottom of the hill, "look, Bobby is jumping out of his sled."

The boy rushed to Jimmy and Bette's sled, oblivious to Tina.

"Let's do this again!"

Tina, pale and silent, stared at Bobby.

"Sure, but this time we don't hit a rock," Jimmy said to Bette.

"Now, Bette rides with me," Bobby said.

"Okay," Bette replied, looking for a reaction.

Jimmy looked over at Bobby, not understanding. Tina frowned, puzzled just as well.

The boys started to race one another back up the hill, their sleds bouncing along behind them.

"What are you doing?" Tina whispered, out of breath, trying to keep up with Bette. "You came here with Jimmy."

Pretended she didn't hear, Bette listened to the boys ahead fighting over her. "It's up to the lady," Bobby said, looking over his shoulder at Bette.

"You're going steady with Jimmy," Tina continued, a little bit louder this time, yanking Bette's coat sleeve to get her attention.

"I'm not going steady with anyone. Besides, what's the big deal about riding on somebody else's sled?"

Tina pulled her hat tightly down over her ears and walked down the hill.

Why is she getting herself in such a tizzy over a race, Bette asked herself, but seeing Tina wasn't going to stop, she ran after her friend.

"Hey where are you going?" Jimmy called.

"I'm cold, Jimmy."

"But your ride—" Bobby said, standing on the middle of the hill grasping the rope of his sled.

"I'd like to go home."

Tina, glanced over at the boys, then watched Bette's silhouette trudging down the hill. She smiled, seeing Bette had changed her mind.

Absent-mindedly, Teddy, polished a glass, watching Mrs. Moffatt and Mrs. Little struggle through the snow in their ankle high, fur lined boots toward the front porch.

"Teddy," his mother called from the parlour. "Company is here."

Teddy, folding the dish towel over the rack, turned to his father. "Do I have to?"

It's not that Charlie didn't pity Teddy, having to listen to Bessie and the neighbourhood hens peck through all the news, but it troubled him Teddy would deny his mother this simple courtesy. Bessie had been going without new dresses, and even a new winter coat, all so that her boy could attend university. He placed his hands on the table, "It's all your mother asked of you. Is it really that much trouble?"

"I have schoolwork, Dad, and my shoes and my suit have to be ready for the Gillespie's New Year Eve party tomorrow night."

Feelings of resentment emerged, confusion as well, invading his mind. Images of Uncle Ed's death appeared. Why was he thinking about that horrible event right now? Dad must have known, if not suspected, that Mother had sent Uncle Ed to his death, chasing him from the house. And while wondering why his father hadn't forced the police to take Uncle Ed to the hospital, some truth finally wiggled its way out. Like everyone else around him, Dad was afraid of his wife, something Teddy had long forgotten, all of it flooding back to him. He resented it, his father's weakness. He paused, suddenly gripped with guilt. He was afraid of Mother, too. It wasn't only Dad. It was so long ago, he tried to rationalize, wasn't it? Why should it still matter still? He recalled his parent's suffering, the divide that had ensued, weighted down by all that went unsaid. How could he have forgotten the long strain his parents had known following his uncle's departure? They are happy now, he thought, regaining some control, they are putting me through school. I have no right to complain, none at all.

"I expect you to go in there and make your mother proud," was all his father said as the kitchen door swung shut behind him.

"And what are you learning?" Mrs. Moffatt asked, as Bessie passed around her silver tray filled with an assortment of homemade Christmas cookies and shortbread.

"Medicine," Teddy replied.

Bessie radiated pleasure, handing the tray to Mrs. Little. "And how is Rusty?" She loved to bring up Mrs. Little's no account son, especially when she could compare his life efforts with Teddy's.

"He's in the barn helping his father," Mrs. Little replied. "He likes to do heavy work."

Bessie set the plate down a bit harder than necessary. "Coffee?" she asked.

Mrs. Moffatt quickly changed the topic. "Teddy, what do you make of your mother's low energy?"

"I'm fine. I just need some blood thickener is all," Bessie replied, asking Mrs. Little how many lumps of sugar she'd like.

"No, you're not all right. You haven't been yourself in quite some time. What do you think, Teddy?" Mrs. Moffatt asked again.

Teddy shifted his coffee cup to the other knee and looked closely at his mother. It was true. She did look tired. Christmas activities, he thought.

"What are you ladies doing for New Year's Eve?" Teddy asked, still thinking of his mother.

"I imagine we'll be attending the dance at the Highlands," Mrs. Little replied. "It's what we've done every year."

"Mr. Moffatt and I are going to the movies," Mrs. Moffatt said. "We want to see 'Our Vines Have Tender Grapes.' It's meant to be very good. And you, Teddy?" she asked.

"I'm going to a party at the Gillespie's," he replied.

"Now doesn't that sound splendid?" Bessie said, returning with another plate of cookies and a fresh pot of coffee. "They're such lovely people. More coffee?"

Mrs. Moffatt shook her head, no, as Mrs. Little extended her cup, and said, "How is Bill? Nobody's heard hide nor hair from that boy."

"He's at war," Bessie said. "I imagine he's got more important things to do than to write letters," she added.

"I still say it's odd. His mother and father rarely hear from him, and he never writes to his sisters. What about you?" Mrs. Little asked.

"Now and again," Teddy replied.

"Teddy, do tell. What is it like studying to be a doctor?" Mrs. Moffatt asked.

The opportunity to boast had arrived, launching Teddy into a vivid account of what university life was like as Mrs. Moffatt listened raptly. The intended effect materialized. Mrs. Little starting to wiggle on her chair, and trying to hide her growing jealousy, pretending not to care.

Bessie sat back, contentedly nibbling on her shortbread, grateful for the son Teddy had always been.

Teddy raised the Gillespie knocker, letting it drop on the stopper. From inside came piano music, and the sound of laughter. He heard footsteps running down the front hall. When the door opened, Laura and Janet appeared, pulling him into the house. They tugged off his overcoat and told him to put his hat on the rack.

Once into the hall, Laura's sister grabbed him by the hand. "Come," Anne said, "I want to introduce you to some of my nursing friends."

Following her, he felt amused, he had always seen her with a white cap on dispensing pills, and wisdom, too. Now, Anne was teaching, and her friends teased her, claiming she had become no less than a tyrant, even if a kind one.

So much is changing, he thought, passing by the fire crackling in the hearth.

With Teddy's hand still in hers, Anne pulled him to the piano bench. "Teddy, meet Sue, Jack's wife. Sue, meet Teddy."

The woman, all dressed in red, nodded hello, and continued to play Deck the Halls. As the crowd gathered, and started to sing around the piano, Teddy caught Mr. Gillespie's eye. The man nodded, sending a feeling of relief through Teddy. Still, there was a discomfort, in both their looks, an extension that went back to that horrible night of the rally.

They'd exhausted every song Sue knew when Mrs. Gillespie rose, telling Laura, Janet, and Anne she needed their help in the kitchen. The dumplings had already been made, Sue had said, but the pigeons needed to be attended to.

"Come on," Joe said to Teddy. "I can't do this myself, not tonight."

The barn was pitch black when they opened the doors. A few birds fluttered by in the night forcing Teddy to duck.

"What do we do?" he asked, knocking feathers from his hair.

Joe explained the procedure: He would shinny across the rafter, and then Teddy would flick on the lights to see where the pigeons were. Once Joe had located them, he'd crawl across the beam, grab the birds, lock their wings, and drop them to the floor.

"That's where you pull their heads off, and then Sue here, she skins them."

"Then they get dropped into pastry and right into the oven," she added, nearly gleeful.

"Okay," Teddy said. "But I'll lock their wings. You pull the heads off," he said to Joe.

To gather, kill, and skin twelve pigeons was the goal Sue had given them.

Teddy climbed the ladder, and standing on the edge of a barn beam, high above the floor, saw the upper haymow on the other side was alive with the birds. Taking a step, he slipped, just as Joe yelled for him to watch out. Regaining his footing, Teddy carefully continued his way to the other side. Leaning down, he snatched his first pigeon. He fanned its wings, quickly locking them so the bird couldn't fly, and dropped the bird down onto the floor below. Joe picked it up and quickly ripped the bird's head off so Sue could begin to skin it. Laura walked into the barn just as the last pigeon hit the floor. Looking up, she saw Teddy.

"Why do you have him doing that?" she asked Joe.

"We needed the help," he replied, ripping a pigeon's head off.

Teddy came down, and chased Laura outside, not understanding. What was she so upset about?

"You're here as a guest," she said, kicking through the knee-high snow toward the house. The look of disgust on her face struck him. "You shouldn't have to do that."

"I don't mind it, Laura. I just wanted to help."

She paced, her face distorted by something that escaped Teddy.

"It makes me sick to eat food like that. Those poor birds, it's ... so cruel ... too cruel. Maybe there was a time when we needed to do that, but now Dad has enough money. So why?" She turned to Teddy, "And you could have fallen out of the mow, you know."

"Laura, I've spent my life in barns. I know what I'm doing," he said, trying to calm her, "and besides, my name is ... Teddy Barnes."

Laura smiled. "It's just that it's stupid. I hate that stupid pie," she muttered, as they reached the door.

"I see your point, Laura," he replied, not fully convinced it was true. Pigeon pie seemed exotic to him, so different from his mother's traditional roast chicken. Knowing there was no point explaining, he kept his thoughts to himself.

They continued to walk, not talking until they reached the house.

Bette Barnes, eager to celebrate New Year's Eve on her terms, invented a story about going out with Tina so her mother would let her go, unsuspecting of anything.

Come with me, Bobby had insisted, you broke my heart when you wouldn't ride on my sled that day on the hill. You owe me a date.

Really? she had thought, and she had kept it to herself since she'd only accepted his offer because Jimmy was too broke to take her out. For Bette Barnes had learned, youth was not something to be wasted, which meant, penniless boys were not for her.

Walking through the Galt movie house, Bette admired the rich burgundy carpets where Oriental yellows swirled, the light sconces like seashells clinging to the walls, and she felt light, victorious. She had fooled her mother and in doing so, she had carved a fine evening for herself.

Popcorn in hand, the couple headed down the main hall toward the neon sign that read, Balcony. "Those are where the best places are," Bobby said, and they climbed the stairs to take their seats.

"Did you see that?" Mrs. Moffatt asked.

"Did I see what?" Mr. Moffatt asked, clearly annoyed.

Bobby, hair slicked back, and wearing a new Christmas shirt under his school football jacket, had caught her eye. Accompanying him, Bette Barnes.

"Over there," Mrs. Moffatt said, trying to stay out of Bette's sight. "That's the Barnes girl. She's with Bobby Riddell," she whispered.

"Mind your own business," Mr. Moffatt said, half-indifferent. But Mr. Moffatt did look at Bette. The girl, wearing her new turquoise sweater with a matching ribbon in her hair, was becoming a fine-looking young lady. "A friend might mention this to, Charlie." Mr. Moffatt said, adding, "but it rarely pays to get involved."

Mrs. Moffatt straightened her hat as Bobby and Bette disappeared up the stairs, into the balcony.

"Just a minute," Mrs. Moffatt said, "is that Rusty Little?

"Oh, for pity's sake, be quiet," Mr. Moffatt replied.

"That girl's too young to be out at the movies with a boy. I bet Bessie doesn't know." She peered at the balcony again. "It *is* Rusty Little."

"Enough," Mr. Moffatt told his wife, "the movie's starting."

The entire Gillespie Christmas party was seated around an immense wooden table draped in a white linen tablecloth. The sight was a joyful one, with colourful vegetables filling fine china bowls, light from the candlesticks dancing, bouncing from the silver cutlery, and water glasses.

The holiday spread was magnificent.

Teddy, a starched linen napkin resting on his lap, thought the pigeon pie was delicious. Feeling Laura staring at him, he pretended not to be impressed.

The war, so current and present in everyone's mind, fuelled the table conversation. Wilton informed them Jack was no longer stationed on the front, that he had been moved to a hospital in England, specializing in shell shock victims.

"He says it's just terrible," Sue said, taking another bite. "Jack says they can sew up the fellows who get shot, but it's the ones who are psychologically damaged that are the real challenge."

"Yes," the minister said, with sadness in his eyes. "It took my father years to recover from the Great War."

"The good thing is," Anne added, "terrific advances in prosthetic limbs are being made."

"The war is becoming more efficient from a medical standpoint," added one of the other nurses.

"If you can ever call war efficient," Laura said, looking at Teddy.

"I'm sorry, dear," Wilton said, realizing they hadn't allowed for his daughter's feelings given Bill was fighting on the front.

Mrs. Gillespie quickly changed the topic. "We've got some news tonight that I'm keen to share. News that certainly deserves a toast." She turned to Sue. "Is this all right with you?"

Sue nodded.

"Fill your glasses," Mrs. Gillespie said, motioning Sue to stand. "Ladies and gentlemen, please raise your glasses. We just found out today," she reached over and took Sue's hand into hers, "a baby is coming to bless this family."

Sue, beaming, sat down, acknowledging everyone's congratulations, while around her, backs were clapped, and hands were shaken as shouts of joy rang around the room, and up to the sky, over the fields, and across the ocean, surely—to where Jack Gillespie was fast asleep, in a bunk bed, somewhere in England.

It was cold outside of the movie house, but Bobby hadn't even done up his coat. Bette rushed along behind. He got in the car and slammed the door shut. "Let's go."

"What's wrong with you?" Bette asked, getting in beside him.

Several more cars passed them by as the snow continued to fall.

Bobby stared at her, his fingers wrapped tightly around the steering wheel. "You're a tease," he said.

The words were out, and Bette's temper flared. She was a tease if she accepted a date and wouldn't make out? What kind of arrangement was that? "You're just being mean because I wouldn't kiss you."

"Are you coming?"

"I don't know," Bette replied. Now she was the one who was annoyed.

"I'm going,"

"Well, I'm not going anywhere with you."

"Fine, then don't." Bobby turned the engine on, threw the car into reverse, and left Bette looking at the car lights fading ahead of her, panic beginning to rise, attacking her chest. All will be okay, she told herself, regaining some ground.

Buttoning her coat, and pulling on her gloves, she walked back to the theater. There, she would call her mother and father and make up some sort of excuse. As she looked inside her purse for a nickel, she heard the voice of a man call, "You want a lift?"

Bette looked up. Rusty Little was pulling out of the lot in his mother's car.

"Hi Rusty. Were you at the movies?"

Rusty nodded. "I'm heading back home, and I can drop you."

"That would be great," Bette replied, running around to the passenger door, counting her blessings.

"What did you think of the movie?" she asked, as they drove down Water Street past the family church.

"I like an Edward G Robinson movie, but I prefer gangster pictures. I like action," he said.

Rusty became quiet, and Bette welcomed the calm, wanting to understand what had happened in the theater. Bobby had tried to wrap his arm around her, wanting to kiss her, and she had refused. Confused, she wondered, was kissing the price for a movie entry? It didn't seem fair to her, or right. Still, it gnawed. Was she doing something wrong? Did going on a date cost something like a chocolate bar or bestowing a very unwanted kiss?

"Rusty?"

"Yes?" he replied, as they were driving down Cedar Creek Road, near where the road dipped low by the river.

"Have you kissed a lot of girls?"

His smile, like a slow flicker that would remind her of a wolf—later.

"Have you kissed a lot of boys?" he asked back.

"No," she replied, instinctively tucking her purse into her stomach. "I want to save everything for my husband."

"Funny, that's not what I hear."

The car was slowing down.

"Are the roads icy?" Bette asked, wanting to change the direction of their talk.

"I hear you've kissed most of the boys in North Dumfries, so why haven't you kissed me?"

The car slowed even further, and Bette could see the clearing by the river up ahead. Rusty pulled in and turned off the engine.

"What are you doing?" she asked, knowing they were miles from home, and wondering if the car was broken.

He put his hand on the back seat and slid over to her side. "Everyone says you're so friendly, I thought you could be friendly to me," he said as he grabbed her by the neck and pulled her face to his lips.

Bette stiffened, her body wanting to push the shock away. The taste of Rusty's mouth sucking at hers, a taste of sweet licorice and burnt popcorn that was nauseating. The feel of his hard bristles scratching her face, the stink of skin not meant for her, and she tried not to gag.

Rusty fumbled at the buttons on her coat as he kept kissing her and telling her how pretty she was. His hand slipped inside the coat, his fingers, strong and icy, reaching for her breasts, tugging at her sweater. Bette tried to fight back, with her hands, with her body, but Rusty kept saying this was what she wanted, what she'd been asking for. She tried to turn away, reaching for the door. When she did, Rusty held her tighter, pushing himself onto her.

For the first time in her young life, Bette screamed, not recognizing herself, like the birth of some form of loss. But the young man just laughed, saying he'd heard all about her games.

Bette screamed again, still to no one, for they were miles away from town. She started to sob between her screams as Rusty pulled up her new turquoise sweater. But then, the driver's side door opened and a rush of cold air entered as a large, dark shadow yanked Rusty out of the car.

Amidst the sound of Rusty screaming, Bette drew her knees to her chest and began to shake, not understanding why Lily Moffatt was there talking to her.

"Come," she said, helping Bette out of the car.

Bette let herself be led, crying, as Lily helped her through the snow toward the Moffatt's pickup. Once there, Lily tucked a blanket around her, and helped the girl settle into the truck.

Adam, his foot planted on Rusty's chest, saw his wife and Bette's silhouettes cross through slants of moonlight. He wondered, how could a man force himself on a girl like that?

Rusty moaned, and saying he was sorry, so sorry, that it was all a mistake, but Adam continued kicking him. In the back and aiming for the kidneys. Three in the stomach. Over and over, again and again, Adam kicked. He left Rusty's face alone. Adam bent to one knee and seized Rusty by the hair, yanking his head up. "Listen," he said, looking Rusty dead in the eye, "if I ever hear of you spreading one word against this girl, I'll rip off your pecker and feed it to my hogs."

He let go of Rusty's head, leaving it to land hard in the snow.

Feeling sad for Charlie, his girl, Bessie, and their family, he walked back to the truck and wondered what the world had come to.

The banging of the door sent Bessie to her feet. She and Charlie were still up, knowing Bette should have been home at least an hour ago.

Bessie opened the door and saw Bette in Adam's arms, her face contrasting with her hair, paler than the moon.

Bessie stared at of them, confused.

"I stopped to call Doc Ramsey on the way over," Mr. Moffatt said. "He'll be wanting to examine your girl."

Lily and Bessie had taken Bette up to bed, while Charlie and Adam, not wanting to intrude, had vanished into the barn. Doc Ramsey slowly sat down beside Bette taking her hand and asked her what happened? Bessie and Lily stood nervously behind, looking down at the girl, now nestled beneath a pile of warm blankets.

The moment Doc touched her, Bette broke into sobs, apologizing for what she'd done. The doctor insisted she'd done nothing wrong, and quietly explained that sometimes, certain men couldn't control their urges, and that Rusty, apparently, was one of them.

Watching the doctor examine her daughter, Bessie remembered Ed, their kiss in the barn. Her stomach roiled. Did she have difficulty with her own urges? Had Ed been like Rusty? Then she recalled Edward's tenderness, the safety she had felt when in his arms. Edward had never once behaved like Rusty.

Doc Ramsey slowly lifted Bette's nightgown, gently examining her thighs for bruising, and asked if Rusty had touched her anywhere beneath her belly button.

Bessie flinched, glancing away at the sight of her daughter's milky white skin. "No, he only tried to take my sweater off," Bette said.

"All right," he said, bringing a pill to her mouth and handing her some water. "Let's get you some rest while I talk with your mother."

He tucked her back in, and left the room, the two women following.

"Are you sure you won't have a cup of coffee, or maybe some cake?" Bessie asked, as the Doc removed a packet of pills from his medical bag. He shook his head no.

"I'll be back tomorrow. If she wakes up, give her another one of these," he said, handing Bessie the packet of tablets.

"Thank you," Bessie said, slipping them into the pocket of her dress.

"She'll be fine," the doctor added. "It'll just take a little time."

Mrs. Moffatt let the doctor out, and Bessie immediately sank down on the lowest step of the staircase, her head in her hands. Mrs. Moffatt sat beside her, worried. She had never seen Bessie in such a state, and the Lord knew the family had been through a lot.

Bessie finally asked, "Do you think we should call in the law?"

Mrs. Moffatt took Bessie's hand. "No," she said firmly. "He didn't really touch your girl."

"He was going to rape her," Bessie said, her voice rising. "If you and Adam hadn't shown up, God knows what would have happened."

"But it didn't," Mrs. Moffatt replied. "It's Bette's word against Rusty's, and you know the way folks talk."

Bessie raised her head. "What do you mean?"

"They'll say she brought it on herself," Mrs. Moffatt said quietly. "It's always the boy's word over the girl's. Unless of course—"

Lily was right, Bessie thought. If Rusty had raped or killed Bette, his behavior might have been met with serious consequences. As it was, Bette was simply a tease who got what she deserved. It had always been the boys over the girls, the men over the women, that was the truth of the world they lived in, and there was no point denying it. Even though her daughter had almost been raped, she'd have to be content with the beating Adam put on Rusty, that, and grateful Adam had guaranteed the boy would preserve her name.

From her hidden perch on the top step, Bette leaned against the banister to rest her head while she listened more. She had heard the women say they should call the police, that the boy deserved to be punished by law. And it made her feel good, imagining Rusty getting his due, as a feeling of warmth wrapped around her shoulders. But now, Mrs. Moffatt had said Bette had brought it on herself, leaving her mother to become silent.

Mrs. Moffatt's words rang in her head, a voice now singing a different song—no, they shouldn't call the police, the girl had misbehaved. She didn't understand. What had she done to deserve what Rusty did?

And did her mother share Mrs. Moffatt's opinion of her?

The house became a worrisome quiet as Bette brought her arms to her chest, her thinking gradually turning into a conclusion she would carry like a misunderstood burden. Bobby had said she was a tease, and Rusty thought he could do what he wanted. Doc Ramsey was wrong, what had happened that night *was* her fault. If Rusty had been deemed guilty, her mother and father would have raced over to the Little house with the police, and rousting Rusty out of bed, they would have dragged him off to prison.

Slowly, Bette rose to her feet and tiptoed down the hall to her bedroom. She slipped between the sheets, turned off the light, and closed her eyes as tightly as she could. Nestled in her bed, she thought more about wrong and right, about truth. Maybe one day, she hoped, I will make Rusty pay. Because nobody it seemed, would.

It was nearly three in the morning when Teddy and Laura, along with other guests, slid their coats on, ready to leave The Gillespie household.

"Thank you so much for having me," he said to Mrs. Gillespie.

"And thanks for taking such good care of Laura while she's at school," Mrs. Gillespie said. "I'm sure it helps Bill sleep better knowing his friend's got his eye out."

Laura started to slip her galoshes on to walk Teddy to the car.

"You needn't bother," Teddy said, indicating the boots.

"It's no bother," and calling back to her mother, she said, "leave the light on. I'll be right up."

The door closed behind them and they walked across the veranda, down the steps, and across the driveway to the car. Teddy began brushing the snow off the windshield with the sleeve of his coat.

"You need a scraper for that," Laura said, "or you won't be able to see." She grabbed one from the back seat of her father's sedan and began helping Teddy clean off the Dodge.

"That's wonderful news about Jack and Sue," Teddy said.

Laura nodded her head. "Dad was thrilled. This is the first grandchild. It'll happen to you one day," she laughed.

"That's a good ways off."

"Don't get nervous," Laura said. "Nobody's looking to lock the gate."

"Not like you, huh?"

Laura shrugged.

"When Bill's back, I imagine you'll be getting married right away."

"We didn't really talk about it, but I think that's what he's got in mind."

"Don't you talk about it in your letters?" Teddy asked, wondering how a man like Bill, fighting overseas, would forget a girl like Laura was waiting at home—for him. Wasn't she the perfect motivation?

"No," Laura replied. She stopped scraping for a moment. "I haven't heard from him in well over a month, and I don't know what to think," she added, her voice beginning to shake. "Oh shoot. I'm sorry. Don't pay any attention to me. I'm just being stupid," she said, starting to scrape the snow again.

Teddy reached over, grabbing her hand to stop her. "You're not being stupid."

A light layer of white dusted her auburn hair as they stood in the snow holding hands.

"I'm confused is all. Come on, let's get your car cleaned off," she said, taking back her hand to brush the tears away.

They quickly finished the job and Teddy thanked Laura for the best New Year's Eve he'd ever had.

"Well, then we're going to have to get you out more often, Dr. Barnes," Laura replied.

Teddy said goodbye, his eyes locking onto Laura's, and he stepped into this car.

Driving back home, he decided to take the slow route, wanting to think and savor every moment the night had brought. So grand, he thought, so perfect.

Mrs. Moffatt filled up the hot water bottle and slipped it between the sheets. Adam, already in bed, and wearing his old flannel pajamas was already heating up, prompting Mrs. Moffatt to snuggle beside him for warmth. It was a cold night, and her bones had a deep chill.

"That was a terrible thing," she whispered. "Thank goodness you insisted on following him. You saved that girl."

At first Mr. Moffatt grunted, but then he said, "I think this makes us more than even."

"What are you talking about?" she asked.

"You gave them the egg money, and I saved their daughter, so I think that means we're square for that bullet," he replied.

Mrs. Moffatt blinked in the night.

"You think I didn't notice all that money gone?" he asked.

Mrs. Moffatt lay still, anticipating her husband's reaction.

"You did the right thing, Lily," he finally said.

Mrs. Moffatt couldn't believe what she was hearing. The man she married admitting he'd been wrong. "Oh Adam," she said, turning over, and throwing her arms around him. "You're a good man," she continued, her kisses endeared by the sound of his words, their meaning.

"Don't be giving me your germs," he said, trying to roll over. But Mrs. Moffatt, insisting, quickly pinned him with her thigh, and kissed him again.

This time, Mr. Moffatt didn't resist.

SIXTEEN

The Killing Machine

It has already been a year, I think. Or maybe two. Since Teddy.

Since Mother and Father.

Since Laura.

All of them, buried in my mind, from before.

Wet, hunkered down in a clump of trees deep within the Reichswald forest, I feel tired— of the rain, of the emptiness—of death.

Artie peers out from up ahead and signals for me to follow his lead. I mindlessly nod. On my belly, I crawl through the thick mud.

We are the only two left.

The rest are dead.

I don't recall what happened. It is enough to follow Artie. It is everything. The rain continuing to beat down—will it ever stop? And a flash triggers my mind, bringing me back to this beginning.

My first battle.

I was ready. I was fresh and green and I was ready. The gutting of a man. The feel of his blood on my body. The first one. A burning of a uniform. Mine? I don't know. I walked on, I remember that, spraying machine fire at German boys.

How many?

Fallen bodies.

Many, they said, and they baptized me, giving me a new name—The Killing Machine. I don't want it now. I didn't then.

I am barely able to put one foot in front of the other, but there is nobody to notice.

We had no radio contact, but the Gerrys had no problem. Days before the battle, Hitler youths ran telephone cable through the forest.

My unit tried advancing, slowly. A Panzer powering through the forest, laying down tracks, laying waste to anything.

I take a small sip of water from my canteen. It is nearly empty. My breathing, I am aware of it. That's a good thing, I tell myself. A good thing.

Artie turns to me, his finger to his lips and points up ahead. I don't care what it is. I want to sleep. Artie signals for me to get behind the tree, stand guard. My walk is slow, unsteady.

I see Artie removing his rifle from his shoulder, checking for shells. I watch him rise. He is all mud, mixing with the trees in this darkening gloom, creeping, like we do, amongst the death in the foliage, everywhere, to the edge of a foxhole. I am no longer here; I feel gone from myself. There are flashes, sudden and blinding. Artie. Three short barks have silenced the lives of three young Germans. He turns to me, points, and I realize then—I forgot to stand watch. Our eyes lock but for a moment, animated by the fear of soldiers who know, and now I watch chunks of Artie splattering trees.

I hear the turret on the tank turn. I hear the reload mechanism.

All else is silence.

One year. Two?

Since Teddy.

Since Mother and Father.

Since Laura.

A blessing comes, numbness leaving my body, and I charge the Panzer.

For Artie.

For the others.

Feeling my rifle drop from my hand, I look at the tank gun turning at me.

In the silence of everything else, I open my arms, and there are no faces any longer buried in the back of my mind. Smiling, I embrace the violence of the yellow blast of light.

The Killing Machine, will kill no longer.

SEVENTEEN

The Pall of Grief

Laura was walking back to the residence when she noticed her father's car in the drive. Has something happened to Mom? Running through the foyer, she burst into the common room. Her father, coat on and his hat in his hand, was sitting in a leather chair. She stopped. "What is it, Dad?" she asked.

Wilton Gillespie stood and crossed the room. He took Laura's hand. "I'm so sorry, dear," he softly said.

Her eyes remained on him, not even asking.

He looked down. "It's Bill."

Laura turned her head away, understanding. "He's been killed."

"I'm afraid so."

Folks from three counties arrived at Ayr United to attend the memorial service.

Huddled on the church bench with his family, Teddy looked at Laura's black hat ahead of him. Seated on the MacMillan family pew, flanked by Bill's sisters, she sat motionless, the sounds of her crying reaching him.

The minister signaled, and the choir began to sing "How Firm a Foundation." Multicoloured shafts of light poked through the glass stained-glass Rosetta, and as voices soared, pushing up to the top of the church, Teddy's throat constricted, his disbelief leaving with the voices. "I will never see you again," he whispered to himself.

Mr. MacMillan slowly unfolded from his seat and walked to the lectern, eulogy in hand. All watched in silence, and as he climbed on, Bette began to whimper. Teddy took her hand and squeezed it. Momentarily forgetting where he was, he focused on his sister, wondering why she hadn't been herself since Christmas? Mother had said it was nothing more than growing pains, but Teddy suspected something wasn't right. He knew his sister. Puzzled, he held her hand tighter, and turned his attention back to the pulpit.

The family grave was at the top of the hill sheltered by a line of ancient Scots Pines. Beside it, a red Canadian Ensign fluttered in the wind. Laura stood with the MacMillan family, the group in black edged against the brightness of the blue sky, watching Bill's casket disappear into the earth. A Scottish piper in Highland attire stood on a nearby hill. The bag inflating with a sorrowful moan, he began to play.

Laura held Mrs. MacMillan's hand, listening to the sweet, sad notes of the family's distant home. As the older woman sobbed, Laura suddenly wondered, had Bill been afraid of death? They had never talked about these things, she now recalled. Thinking more of Bill's recklessness, of the sparkle he carried in his eyes, she asked herself, can such a spirit be killed? She stared down at the cold dark earth, and sensing tears coming, she closed her eyes, looking for Bill's face in the dark.

The minister picked up a handful of snowy earth and tossed it on top of the casket. "Ashes to ashes," he intoned, as the rest of the family filed towards the grave, bending to pick up their handfuls of earth.

Laura gathered a fistful of hard soil in her hand, and with her tears rolling off her cheeks, she released the soil from her hand, her tears following. She stood, watching the earthy snow fall away, just like our plans, she thought, a life filled with children, laughter, and joy. Gone.

At first, Tina followed Bette up and down the school hallway, probing, and insisting she sit beside her at lunchtime, but Bette wouldn't talk. Not at home, or at school. With anyone, not even her. Bette had learned to stay still, that sharing about the assault was as useless as it was dangerous. Keep attention away from yourself, she now thought. Help Mother wash the dishes. Do your house chores. Keep your grades up. Blend.

At the sink, with Bette by her side, Bessie thought of the strangeness that had taken hold of her daughter. Of the changes she could not seem to penetrate.

More than a month later, Tina arrived at the Barnes's front door, determined to speak to her friend.

"She's up in her room," Bessie replied, very happy to see Tina. "Why don't you give her a surprise."

When Tina opened the bedroom door, Bette was sitting on her bed crying. Quietly, she tiptoed over and sat down.

Bette looked up and began to dry her eyes. "What are you doing here?" she asked, with fury and embarrassment. "I told you that we weren't friends anymore."

"What happened?" Tina asked.

"Nothing," Bette said. "I just don't like you anymore."

"I don't believe you," Tina replied, taking Bette's hand. "Don't you know how much I care about you?"

"Nobody cares about me," Bette said, yanking her hand away. "Just go."

Tina wrapped her arms around Bette, and holding her close, she asked Bette to talk to her, telling her, no matter what, she would understand. They were best friend, and always would be.

Bette broke into a deep sob and finally shared her story of Rusty's assault, and her guilt. Even Mrs. Moffatt thinks I am a tease, that I string boys along, and that I had it coming.

"You've done nothing wrong," Tina said.

"I don't know, Tina. Sometimes I even think my mother and father think the same, too."

Tina kept her arms around Bette, rocking her softly.

"I only feel good when I'm with you," Bette finally said. "Safe."

Upon hearing those words, Tina lightly kissed Bette's cheek, quieting both their thoughts. Bette, in Tina's arms, rolled both of their bodies onto the bed.

"Are you okay?" Tina asked, feeling the touch of Bette's hand on hers.

A long sunbeam stretched across the bed as the girls remained in each other's arms, not moving. Not needing to.

"Yes," Bette said, "I am now."

Standing in the kitchen, looking out the window at the fields expanded before her, Bessie thought of her daughter hiding upstairs in her bedroom, sorting through her life, the meaning of it, since Rusty.

Bessie thought of Ed and … their own transgressions. Why couldn't Bette do the same, take the memories and push them away, bury them somewhere that can't reach her? Was her daughter, too, trying to wrestle demons into a closet and lock the door?

Yet, Bessie knew of the mind's permeability, letting memories spill out, fresh and clear as the day they happened. The day Ed had kissed her.

She walked to the oven and pulled a cake out and set it on the sideboard to cool. Sitting down, she stared at it. I've sinned, she thought, so many times, haven't I?

It started the same way, the guilt-filled thinking. She rationalized, Edward had been a good man; a clever man; a handsome man, even though he'd been driven by … go on, she thought, say it. And even though no one ever said it out loud, she knew, by pushing Edward out of the house, she had killed him.

Her thinking, like now, always wavered between remorse and rectitude. One minute she felt as though God approved of her choices, Edward had been a communist, after all. Then, the weight of honest reality on a heart shaken by the discovery and loss of true love.

She thought of May's arms around Ed's neck, of how she'd ruined the young woman's name, driving her out of town in the middle of the Depression with nowhere to go. She pretended, didn't she? To do the right thing, showing the world she was, after all, a woman of good standing, loyal and faithful to her family, and filled with Godly principles. But in truth, she nauseated herself. I am evil, I am sin—and still, I want Edward back. I want him alive.

A voice, sweet and sad. Mom, is the cake ready?

She looked. Yes, Bette, it is.

Teddy decided to stop by the residence and ask Laura out for Sunday brunch. It was nearly Easter, and Bill had been dead for months, and yet, Teddy still hadn't really spoken to her. They had occasionally seen one another on the train home, and there had been the odd coffee at Murray's, but something had been broken in her. Perhaps, between them too.

He missed her. He missed their walks through Queen's Park, and their discussions about politics and religion—everything. The Laura he had known.

About to knock on the door, Agnes appeared in the doorway. "She won't accept any visitors," she said, "and I don't like it any better than you." It's true, Teddy thought, Agnes has to share a room with Laura, and the pall of grief had to be oppressive.

"Ross thought one of the parties at the house might help lift her mood, and Laura nearly took his head off."

"Grief," he said, remembering Uncle Ed's death, "it will change you. You leave to go somewhere you've never been, and then you come back different. Not the same."

"She's not gone forever, I know … it's just that—"

Teddy reached out and touched Agnes' hand. "I know. Thanks, Agnes. I hope to see you soon."

Walking back to his room, he wondered, about Laura, about him, about the type of man he was becoming. While he was heartsick over Bill's death, a part of him was already wanting to stake a claim on Laura, his best friend's girl.

The train pulled into the station at Ayr, and Laura stepped from the car onto the ground.

"Hello Laura!" her father called, catching sight of her.

"Thanks for taking the time to come and get me, Dad," she said as they walked to the Chrysler. "I know you're busy."

It was rare Wilton Gillespie had the time for such a task, but since Bill had died, he had become worried, as he hadn't seen Laura so much as smile.

"Where's your kit?" he asked, searching for the purser.

"I didn't bring one. I don't need anything dressy, I won't be going out," Laura replied.

Her father looked at her, concerned. It's been over four months, he thought, as he opened the car door. He missed his daughter, yearning for Laura to beg him for the car keys, and take the car for a spin, just like before. Her teasing, her insistence on doing things her way, none of which was here with them today.

Laura, ignoring her father's sad eyes, slipped into the passenger seat and sat quietly staring straight ahead for the entire drive.

Reluctantly entering the chicken coop, Laura found her brother covered in feathers with blood on his overalls.

"Welcome home, Sis!" he said, grabbing a squawking chicken by its feet and walking toward a slaughter room located at the back of the coop. "Mom wants three killed, plucked and drained for Sunday. We've got a full house coming."

Laura looked at the birds clucking and cooing on their nests. It wasn't as if she hadn't done it before, she'd been killing chickens since she was ten, but she despised the task—hated it.

Quickly, she slipped her hand under the biggest bird's chest cavity, yanked it out, and tipped it over before it could peck her. She watched Joe snap the neck on his bird, and quickly plunge the chicken into a pot of scalding hot water to ease the plucking of its feathers.

As flurries of white and red down floated around her brother, she listened to him talk about Sue, how she'd been a real trooper. "What are you doing?" he asked, pointing to her hands. "Making friends with that bird? Come on sis, just do it."

Laura looked down at the chicken, and refusing to think about what she was doing, quickly wrung its neck. The bird did a small dance, flopped over and died. Laura quickly dunked it in the hot water and started to pluck.

"Have you been out to see the Leaf's play?" Joe asked.

"Not this year," Laura said, "I don't feel like hockey."

"Too bad. If I lived in Toronto, I'd go and see every single game."

Joe stopped plucking and looked at his sister. "Laura, with all due respect, you know, with what happened to Bill, you've got to try and snap out of this funk. Mother and Dad are worried sick about you."

Laura didn't answer. None of them could understand, she thought. This other thing in me, what I've done.

"They think you're spending too much time alone. You don't talk."

Laura tried to ignore him. She hadn't been able to stop thinking about Bill since the day her father had arrived with the news. But it wasn't Bill's death, there had been something else. The moment she'd heard the news, she realized, she'd stopped thinking about him long before. She had no longer dreamt of Bill and their future life together. No, instead, her thoughts had been of Teddy. But what she wasn't sure of, and couldn't stop thinking about, was when did that happen?

Laura pulled the final feathers out from the bird's back and reached for its breast. As she yanked a handful of feathers, the bird suddenly began to kick, stumbling off the table, and starting to run around, clucking hysterically. Joe began laughing, running around the room imitating the chicken.

"Stop it!" she yelled, horrified, shoving her younger brother against the table.

The half-plucked, near dead bird ran out of the slaughter room. Running across the farmyard, Laura thought, maybe it was Bill's spirit? Looking up, she almost ran into her father.

"What's wrong?" he asked.

Laura, unable to contain herself anymore, shouted, she hated the farm, that it was base and hideous—killing everything! "We're above that!"

Her father grabbed her by the shoulders, "We're farmers, Laura Jean Gillespie, and wasn't this life the one you were planning to live with Bill?"

Her heart broke at the look on her father's face. "I'm so sorry, Dad!" Laura said, dissolving into tears, her father helping her into the house, down the hall, and into his study.

"Sit down," her father said, and he pulled a chair close to him. "Let's talk, Laura."

And for the first time since Bill had died, Laura opened, about Bill, about the guilt of having forgotten him before he was gone.

"I loved Bill, Dad, but in the time that he was away, I felt I was falling for somebody else, somebody who doesn't want the kind of life Bill was offering me. I never wanted to be a farmer's wife ... Toronto, the city life, that's me."

Her father listened, not interrupting her.

"I should never have agreed to marry him one day," she said. "But I loved him then."

Wilton Gillespie surrendered to the moment, just like Laura was, and shared his own hopes, and his own dreams, the ones he had never been able to reach. "You know, there was a time in my life when I had planned on buying a ranch and having at least 4,000 acres to live on. But then, my father died, and they called me back home. There were no other choices. Not then, anyway."

"I should be in mourning for at least a year," she said. "Don't you think it's my duty?" She laid her head on her father's lap, and they talked more, about Bill, the war, about the world's expectations, about the expectations humans place on themselves, to please others. "Don't you think it's my duty to grieve more?" Laura asked again.

"Duty keeps us in line. It keeps us honest. Moral. But too much duty also binds and traps" he said, the Barnes boy on his mind. He hadn't liked him, thought him a radical guided by a communist uncle. Yet, he'd also seen the great care the young man bestowed on his daughter, how hard Teddy worked at his studies, and how good his prospects were likely to be. Whatever his uncle might have done, he realized, didn't matter anymore. The boy was as good as they came. "I don't care what people say," Wilton replied as he stroked Laura's hair. "And neither should you. You've done nothing to be ashamed of."

EIGHTEEN

The Bad Penny

Bessie and Mrs. Little sat on the bench at the edge of Watson's Dam watching the swans and waiting for the girls to come back from bartering for tomato seeds.

"Such a beauty, your Bette," Mrs. Moffatt said. "Shame for her to be a spinster."

"She's only sixteen, Lily. That's a fair way from spinsterhood," Bessie replied, annoyed by the comment. But feigning unconcern, she thought of how Bette and Tina were always together, at school, at church, all their weekend sleepovers that were now occurring during the week as well. Bessie wondered at times if she'd inherited a second daughter. She liked Tina, but she still wished for her daughter to find herself a beau.

As she and Lily continued talking, Mrs. Little's blue car pulled up in front of the Mercantile.

"Look," Bessie said.

"Hello ladies," Mrs. Little said, bowing her head in greeting. "How lovely is it that you have the time to rest on a working day."

"Indeed, it is," replied Bessie, with light acid in her tone. "We are truly fortunate."

"I thought I'd buy my son some ice cream," Mrs. Little said. "Since he works so hard and the day being so hot."

"But the weather is cool today," Bessie replied. Glancing toward the car, she saw Rusty seated, staring out at nothing. Because you are nothing, she thought.

"Won't you join me?" Mrs. Little asked Mrs. Moffatt.

"Surely Mrs. Barnes as well," Mrs. Moffatt replied, eyebrows raised.

"We have matters to discuss," Mrs. Little continued, adjusting her jacket. "That don't concern her."

"Make no mind. While I'm waiting, I can visit with your son." Bessie said, looking back at the car.

"The boy's tired," Mrs. Little said.

"Nonsense," Bessie replied. "From doing what? And anyhow, he's a fine strapping young specimen, your boy, isn't he?"

"Very well. Come along, Mrs. Moffat," Mrs. Little said, failing to assess the threat inside the moment.

As the women closed the door behind them, Bessie walked to the car, fire burning inside of her.

"What are you doing here?" she hissed, as she slid in the driver seat.

Rusty remained sullen and still.

"You know you're not to be seen," she added.

"I'm bored," he replied.

"You nearly rape my daughter and you're *bored*?" she asked, her voice rising, as Bette and Tina emerged from the exchange carrying two large bags of seed.

Rusty stared at her daughter, "not anymore, I'm not," and smiled.

A tide swept over Bessie, one carrying the fury of a mother's rage. "You stay away," Bessie said, wagging her finger in Rusty's face. "You stay away from my girl, or I'll kill you myself!"

Upon seeing Rusty, Bette nearly dropped the bag of seeds.

"What's happening?" she whispered to Tina, "why is my mother in the Little's car?"

Unaware the girls had returned, Bessie got out of the car, slamming the door as hard as she could. Mrs. Little and Mrs. Moffatt, just emerging from the Mercantile, and watching the scene unfold, said nothing.

"Lily," Bessie said, "take Tina home. And you Bette, in the Dodge, now. We're leaving."

"But I want to stay with Bette," Tina said.

"You'll go with Mrs. Moffatt," Bessie replied, annoyed by the girl pushing back.

"I want Tina to stay," Bette implored, taking her best friend's hand. "She's supposed to sleep over."

"Not tonight," Bessie replied, taking Bette by the arm.

Seeing Bessie's state of mind, Mrs. Moffatt intervened, taking Tina's hand. "Come along dear. You can see Bette tomorrow."

Bette was trembling. "What were you doing with Rusty?"

"I told him I would shoot him if he ever came near you again," Bessie answered, opening the car door.

"You did?" Bette said in disbelief, getting into the Dodge beside her mother.

"What else was I to do?" Bessie asked.

"I'm so tired of being scared of him," Bette said, dropping her head onto her mother's shoulder. "I just wish Tina was here."

Bessie walked into the barn. "Rusty's back in town."

Charlie dropped the pitchfork. "I'm going over there."

"What good would that do?" she asked, "and so you know, I told him I'd kill him if he'd ever come close to Bette. Right there at the Mercantile. In front of everyone."

Charlie walked to Bessie and remembered, this was the woman he'd married, the strong woman with whom he'd built a good, solid life. "I am

245

so proud of you, Bessie," Charlie said as he took her in his arms. Taking her face between his hands, he moved to her—her lips, moving his one hand to brush over the contours of her body. "How about we go up while Bette is out planting her own seeds in the garden," he said with a smile.

Teddy was about to walk across Bloor Street when he heard someone call his name. He looked, and he saw Laura waving from the marble steps of the Home Economics building. He squinted his eyes, trying to make out what she was saying, but her voice was lost in the din of car and truck horns.

Suddenly, he saw, all around him, movement, like a wave. To his left, several fellows had leapt out of their vehicles, jumping on their roofs and bouncing deliriously. To his right, maids, all dressed in white, were flying out of the Park Plaza Hotel, dancing with their dusters and brooms as crowds of students began to swell through the gates of Philosopher's Walk, hooting and cheering.

Laura ran toward him, her arms up and yelling something he couldn't hear. Behind her, Ross burst through the doors of Murray's with a trio of waitresses behind him.

"The war is over," Laura gasped, out of breath.

"What?" Teddy said.

"Hitler's dead. The war is over!" she said again.

Understanding the weight of her words, Teddy swept Laura up in his arms, and began to twirl, his body pressing against hers, and when he stopped, he looked at her. Surrounded by men, women, and children celebrating the end of an era, the start of another, Teddy kissed her mouth, and she was willing, and more, wanting.

Finally.

They stood amidst the hooting riot of happiness, oblivious to everything and everyone around them, arms wrapped around one another, not wanting to let go.

Murray's was packed.

"Jack's coming in on the five o'clock train!" Laura said, sliding into the booth beside Teddy. "Finally, he's going to meet his baby boy!"

"Baby Hugh Gillespie," Teddy smiled.

"Did you know Dad offered the newborn a cigar," Laura said, shaking her head.

"Why am I not surprised?" Teddy replied, amused. "Sue must be thrilled?"

Laura acquiesced, explaining how Sue had been strong and patient. "She's the best sister-in-law anyone could ever have, and funny, too. Jack's a lucky man."

Like me, he thought. Looking over at Agnes and Ruth seated on the other side of the table, he recalled telling them about Spring Fling at the Psi Upsilon House. He had wanted to ask Laura, but now, he'd had been upstaged by Laura's news about Jack.

"I've got to go down to meet him," Laura said, shaking him from his thoughts. "He's here to change trains, before catching the next one home."

"Do you want some company?" Teddy asked.

"Yes, I would." she replied.

Shoved into a rattling streetcar, Teddy and Laura headed down Bay Street for Union Station. "Do you remember?" he asked her, traveling back to the time they'd been looking for Uncle Ed.

"Yes. Strange how long ago it was." She looked out the window at the growing skyscrapers. "So much has happened since then, hasn't it?" She looked back at Teddy. "How different do you think Jack will be?" she asked. "Do you think war will have damaged him?"

"There will likely be a period of adjustment, Laura, like it is for all the boys," he said. "But Jack has a new baby, and a wife to come home to. Plus, he hasn't been fighting on the front line, so ..."

The car lurched to a halt in front of Union Station, and they moved along with the press of bodies, all heading for destinations of their own.

"There he is!" Laura called, waving at her brother, tall and thin, dressed in a medical officer's uniform, stepping off the Montreal train.

"Oh Sis, you look terrific!" he said, picking Laura up by the waist and twirling her around. "It's awfully good of you to come. Hi Ted," he said, shaking Teddy's hand.

"Of course, I'd come," Laura replied, carefully checking Jack over for any signs of damage.

"I'm fine," he said. "I heard about Bill," he added, his gaze soft and sad.

"I'm all right," Laura said, lowering her eyes. "Dad's been a big help." She looked at Teddy. "And so has this one."

"Then tell me about Hugh," Jack added, swinging his arms around both Teddy and Laura's shoulders. "And Sue, too."

Later, walking alone, just the two of them, Laura said, "He does seem well, doesn't he?"

"I thought so, too," said Teddy.

They walked across Bloor Street toward her residence, and though the party was less than a week away, he still hadn't asked Laura. "Why am I always such a dolt?" he muttered to himself.

"What?" Laura asked.

Teddy shook his head. "Nothing."

Laura looked at him wondering why his sudden quietness had become so frequent. Is it me, she asked herself, is he bored with me? He hasn't made a serious move since he kissed me on VE Day. She didn't understand. Both Agnes and Ross had already told her to expect an invitation to the party. Yet, Teddy remained mute.

"You've got to call that bandleader," Laura said as they climbed the stairs.

"Oh yes, Clara's nephew," Teddy said as he checked for the number in his pocket. "I'll phone from the fraternity."

"You can call from here if you like," Laura replied, opening the door.

Teddy nodded and followed her into the foyer as she pointed toward the phone.

"I'll wait for you in the room," she said.

Agnes, lying on the sofa and studying, lifted her head looking for a sign, hoping Teddy had finally done his deed. Laura sadly shook her head lip syncing, no.

"Thanks Laura," Teddy said, joining her back in her room. "I got them lined up. Lucky too, because it's last minute."

He looked at Agnes, tentative. "I better leave you to your studies," he said, backing up toward the door.

It was plain to see, Agnes told herself, the boy is crying for help. "Say, Teddy," she said, trying to conceal a smile, "are you taking anyone to the formal?"

Teddy stood there, and sputtered that no, he wasn't.

Agnes turned to Laura, this time smiling the smile of a friend who knows, "And you, Miss, are you going with anyone?"

"No," she said looking at the carpet, "I don't have a date, either."

If you can't summon courage, Teddy thought, then maybe it's the courage that summons you.

"Would you do me the hon—"

"Yes, yes I will," Laura blurted out.

"Well then, you two pathetic people are going together," Agnes said. "Pick her up at eight and don't be late, Teddy Barnes. Now shoo because we've got an exam in the morning."

Laura smiling, walked Teddy to the door, gently squeezing his arm. "See you soon," she said, as she kissed him on the cheek.

Looking past Laura, Teddy mouthed a thank you to Agnes.

Teddy and Ross were on their way to pickup the girls when Ross suddenly suggested stopping by Murray's.

"No," Teddy said. "I don't want to be a second late."

"It's good to keep them on their toes, Teddy, you want to establish who's the boss right at the beginning, " Ross said with a laugh.

Teddy hastened his step.

"No running," Ross said, as Teddy went faster. "It signals desperation!"

Teddy, looking back at him, rolled his eyes and broke into a sprint.

It was exactly eight when Agnes opened the door.

"Hello," Teddy said, looking over Agnes's shoulder for Laura.

"Don't you both look handsome," Agnes said.

Ross handed Agnes her corsage as Teddy clutched his in his hand.

"Laura will be down in a moment," Agnes said. "Go on in and wait." She and Ross stayed on the stoop, while Ross pinned the corsage to Agnes's gown. "Now don't prick me," she said.

"Then stop squiggling," Ross said, kissing Agnes's cheek.

Teddy walked across the foyer, corsage in hand when he saw a couple of the girls giggling as they worked on a puzzle. They paused, looking above him. Teddy followed their gaze. Laura was coming down as if floating, dressed in a full-length, sleeveless, cream satin gown. The light from the chandelier reflected on the bodice, making her sparkle with every step. She was stunning. No one would have ever known Laura Gillespie was attending her first formal—wearing her first full length gown.

Holding the corsage, he watched her descend carefully, each step studied.

When she reached the bottom, she stood, hoping her posture told Teddy it was time to advance to her, to help her not fall.

And he did. Walking across the room, he never once took his eyes from her. "I've never seen anything so beautiful, so perfect, in my entire life," he told her, as he took her hand.

"I was afraid to trip until I saw you," she said. "And you look quite dashing yourself."

Teddy, hair combed back, all straight and tall and wearing a tuxedo, looked suave.

"Is this for me?" she asked, pointing to the box in his hand.

Reaching into it, he removed the corsage, and gently pinned it to her bosom.

He wasn't shaking. He wasn't scared. Neither was she.

"There he said," as he extended his arm.

Laura glanced at him from the side as they walked together out the door on their way to the formal.

"I'm MC'ing tonight, Laura, I'll be gone for little while," Teddy said as he hurried to the stage. "Wait for me on the dance floor."

Joining Ross and Agnes near the back, Laura observed the man Teddy had become. The way he talks, the way he holds himself. She listened to him welcome everyone and deliver the official Psi Upsilon toast, impressed.

All this ease Teddy was displaying, an assurance he carried there for all to see. Where did it come from? she wondered. She didn't know, remembering the boy, and his face, the one that had watched his uncle being kicked to death.

Teddy stopped here and there, acknowledging the guests as he walked to Laura standing in the middle of the dance floor waiting for him.

"Will you dance with me, Laura Gillespie?" he asked, extending his hand.

She simply slid her hand into his.

"Look up," he said. Above them, a string of Christmas lights twinkled and reached through the branches.

"The night is a success," she said in his ear, and as she did, they continued to dance, understanding of their own stars, and how they, too, would shine.

"For the love of Mike, woman, he's not the King!" Charlie said, scolding his wife for expending so much energy.

"I just want him to be proud," Bessie replied, standing on top of a step stool carefully inspecting the top of the windowsills for any sign of dust. "Teddy is coming back, and I want this house to be perfect."

"The house is always clean Bessie, and to be honest, I'm worried that you're working yourself too hard."

Both Bette and Charlie nodded. Bessie had been a bit peaky of late and had dropped considerable weight.

"Just slow done, Bessie, there's no race going on here."

"You'll never stop, Mother," Bette said, on her way out to the chicken coop.

Bessie continued cleaning, ignoring their words.

Walking along the gravel road, Bette wondered about her future—her past, too. After the shock of seeing Rusty, after witnessing her mother threaten to shoot the son of one the biggest families in town, something inside the girl had shifted.

It became clear—she would never marry. The negotiations between men and women were too complex, and when there is a rule, everything favors men. Hadn't Rusty gotten away with what he did to her?

So many times, she revisited that moment in the car with Rusty. Maybe she shouldn't have accepted the ride and hopped in his car. Maybe. And maybe it was wicked to have simultaneously flirted with Jimmy and Bobby. Still, none of this seemed right, or fair, and she wanted nothing more to do with it.

She carefully collected the eggs, thinking about her mother, this mother of hers, of the strength that lived inside her core. "I want to be like her," Bette said to no one, "as strong, and as principled … but … different."

Returning to the house with her basket swinging from her forearm, she wondered, how can I make it happen?

The answer presented itself one late spring day.

Bette and Tina were sitting on the steps of the Mercantile Café when Anne and her nursing friends from London General came running up the stairs.

"What are you doing in town?" Bette asked, her ice cream cone in her hand.

"I wanted to show them baby Hugh," Anne said, pointing to ladies dressed in white. "And we had an urge for sugar, " she added, pointing at the shop.

Nodding, Bette looked over to her side. "This is my friend, Tina."

Tina smiled her bedazzling smile. "Best friend," she added, squeezing Bette's arm.

The girls looked at one another, a look Anne didn't miss. "Mind if we join you?"

"That would be swell," Bette replied, glancing at Tina to see if she agreed.

"We are off duty and hopped in the car to see the baby," Anne explained.

Off duty, Bette thought, suddenly more aware of the perks of being a nurse. As far as she could see, these women were professional women who ran their own finances and controlled their own destinies. Thinking nurses couldn't get raped either, their status a shield, she felt a switch flick inside her head.

She started to listen more, better, and asked questions: What is the nursing course all about, what do they learn, how is the work?

"You know, Bette, me and a couple of the girls are planning a trip to Scotland next summer, by boat."

Bette stopped licking her cone and looked at Anne.

"And if you want," she said, seeing Bette's interest in her profession, "I'll lend you a few of my nursing textbooks."

"Are you afraid of blood?" one of the nurses asked.

"This girl isn't afraid of anything," Tina blurted.

Bette played with the rim of her cone thinking it was true, not much frightened her. She had seen most everything Mother Nature had to offer in her nearly seventeen years on the farm: birth, death, sickness, and injury.

"Most men are suspicious of professional women," the oldest nurse explained. "They won't marry a woman who has her own career. They want a woman who puts their needs and the needs of the family first."

"If you put on the cap, you give up all likelihood of finding a husband?" Tina said. Turning to Bette, she whispered, "it's perfect if you don't want a family. Perfect for ... us."

"Can we stop by on our way home," Bette asked Anne. "We'd like to start studying the textbooks as soon as possible."

Anne said, that yes, they could, that she would be waiting for them at the farm.

Bette and Tina remained seated on the steps of the store, watching the nurses walk to their car.

"What do you think?"

"We're brilliant in science," Bette said. "Aren't we?"

"We can't begin right now, Bette, we're not nineteen yet, but … "

"But there's no reason for us not to prepare," Bette added. Lost in her thoughts, contemplating this new avenue, a real one made of real possibilities, to leave, to be more, to be like her mother, yet different. And then, Bette saw him—Rusty, looking at her from across the street, laughing with a couple of his friends. She backed up against the step, desperate to cover her breasts with her hands. Tina followed her eyes until she, too, saw the man.

She shot to her feet, only to have Bette pull her right back down. "Don't cause a scene," she whispered to Tina.

The girl reluctantly complied, staring at Rusty.

"Let's go home, Bette. Sleepover at my place tonight."

Relieved, Bette's fingers, intertwined with Tina's, pressed harder against hers. "Okay."

Tina's family had gone to bed over an hour before, but the girls were still up in Tina's room talking.

"You can't let Rusty bully you like that," Tina said, lying on her bed.

"What do you think I should do?" Bette asked, holding Tina's hand.

"Personally, I'd like to shoot him," Tina replied.

"Well, we certainly can't do that," Bette said, nearly shocked Tina would propose that kind of solution. "But we can get away. What do you think about nursing school?" she asked, propping herself up on one elbow. "I like the idea of it. The freedom. What about you?"

Tina smiled. "I'd still like to kill him, but you're right, I don't think prison would be much fun."

"So would you ever consider it?" Bette asked. "That way we could go to school together."

"I would," Tina replied. "But only if we're roommates."

A sudden silence falling over them, the girls remaining, their fingers interlocked.

Bette looked over at Tina, feeling a wave sweeping over her, and looking more, not asking anymore, she flipped Tina over, holding her fast on the bed. "I think I might love you."

As if Tina had waited for this moment, prepared for it even—born for it? she wrapped her arms around Bette's neck, opening her legs, and pulling Bette's thigh to her own, that intersection. Slowly the girls began rocking back and forth, letting their body take the lead, understanding the nature of its demand, until they both exploded, collapsing into one another.

Just then, amidst delight and laughter, a knock came at the door. It was Tina's mother. "What are you girls doing in there, Christina?"

They looked at one another. Did Tina's mother know?

"Just laughing," Tina replied.

"Then go to sleep. It's past one in the morning. You've got chores first thing in the morning."

As they slid underneath the covers, Bette started to giggle. "Come on, go to sleep, Miss *Christina*, you've got chores to do."

Holding hands and feeling the world had opened a door, widening its entry, they fell asleep.

Bessie was on the platform wearing her new yellow dress, a white hat and matching gloves, scanning disembarking passengers, looking for Teddy. "There he is, Charlie!" Bessie yelled. "There's our boy!"

Teddy wasn't sure if it was her love of intense colours, or simply that his mother's spirit was such a vast one, but … there she was, and she'd seen him. She'd lost weight, he noticed, offering Laura his arm as she stepped out of the train.

While the couple waited for the porter to bring them their suitcases, Bette, Charlie, and Bessie pushed their way toward them.

"Take my arm," Bette said, seeing her mother had become unsteady.

Bessie, quickly regaining her composure, discreetly pushed Bette's hand away. "I'm fine," she said. "Stop fussing."

"Teddy!" Bette cried. "Finally!"

"Son," Charlie said, and he shook Teddy's hand. "Welcome home."

Bessie looked him up and down, claiming he looked scrawny, and she'd need to fatten him up a bit.

"Mom!" Laura called, seeing her parents had arrived. "I'm so glad to see you, but I could have gotten a ride home with Teddy."

"Nonsense," Mrs. Gillespie replied. "Mrs. Barnes, Mr. Barnes," she said, turning to greet Charlie and Bessie.

Bessie, puffing up her chest at the sight of Mrs. Gillespie, looked around the platform to see if anyone she knew was watching. "I wanted to thank your Anne for lending Bette the nursing books. We can't keep her down in the parlour in the evening," she said.

"It's so interesting," Bette excitedly said. "I've found my calling."

"What's going on?" Teddy asked, not having heard a word about Bette's latest plan.

"Anne and the girls have been on a recruitment drive," Laura said.

Teddy tipped the porter for retrieving the luggage while Charlie watched, clearly questioning the amount. "There's going to be another medical professional in the family," he said, as the porter pocketed the change. "Those fellows must make a good living."

"Medicine?" Teddy asked, momentarily confused.

Bette picked up Teddy's suitcase. "I'm going to become a nurse. So is Tina. We're going to go together."

"That's terrific," Teddy replied, pleased at his sister's choice.

"It's terrific if you like spinsters in the house," Charlie said.

Bessie gave Charlie a sharp look.

"Those girls are never apart," Charlie continued, ignoring his wife. "I'd like to get some board."

"Let's go home. Mother's made a pie," Bette said, grabbing her brother by the arm.

Teddy looked to Laura who looked back. "I'll call you?"

Laura nodded, a sparkle in her eyes, and turning to her family, took her mother's arm. Charlie looked on with a slight smile as he detected a change between Laura and his son.

Charlie was at the kitchen table leafing through the paper as Bessie cut her raspberry pie.

Teddy took a drink of milk. "Mother," he said, "I was wondering if you'd mind if I didn't stay for supper?"

"Is that pie ready?" Bette asked, opening the screen door.

"You won't be home for supper?" Bessie asked.

"Your mother's been cooking and cleaning all week, getting ready for your homecoming," his father said, dropping the paper. "I'd think you'd want to be close to the farm, no?"

Teddy sat down, shifting uncomfortably. "Laura wondered if I'd like to go over there for a bite and get a look at that new baby."

"You're just home and you're already on the scram?" Bette asked.

"What kind of talk is that for a young lady? On the scram? Is that what they're teaching you in school?" her father asked, obviously annoyed Teddy wanted to leave home minutes after he'd finally arrived.

"Don't get yourself all worked up, Charlie," Bessie said, carefully placing the pie onto the plates. "That's fine, Teddy. You go to the Gillespie's. We'll hear all about your adventures another time."

"Thanks, Mother. Say Sis, when did you get interested in Nursing School?"

"Eat up," Bessie ordered, feeling her heartbeat change. "It'll get cold."

Bette took a bite of her pie, and thought of Rusty. In her mind, there was no need for Teddy to know about him, or—the other events that had unfolded at Christmas time.

Teddy obediently cut a piece out of his pie when Bessie suddenly shot up out of her chair and shouted "the ice cream" as she remembered leaving it on the porch to soften. Once out, she saw a cat licking the inside of the tub. Preparing to kick it off the porch, Bessie suddenly became woozy. Reaching for the railing with her right hand, she felt her legs buckle beneath her. Everything turned bright white.

"What happened?" Bessie asked, looking up.

"You fainted, Mother."

Bessie, lying on the pale green Victorian sofa underneath the big front window, tried to get up, feeling embarrassed.

"You stay put," Teddy ordered. He looked carefully into his mother's eyes. "Bette, run upstairs and get my medical bag."

"Has this happened before?" he asked his father.

Charlie shook his head. "Not that I know of," he replied. "But your mother has been off for a while, you know."

"Can you get a glass of water?" he asked his father when Bette returned with the bag.

Bette watched her big brother remove a stethoscope and a blood pressure wrap from the medical bag. Fascinated, she watched Teddy take his mother's vital signs.

"What about the weight loss, Mother?"

"I've been dieting."

"When did you start believing in diets?" Teddy asked as he rechecked her pulse. "It's all normal," he reported, handing Bette the equipment.

Almost reverentially, Bette returned them to their proper places.

"Of course, it is!" Bessie blustered. "I'm as healthy as an old horse."

Charlie arrived with the water and set it on the coffee table.

"Use a coaster," she said, no longer looking pale.

Charlie smiled to himself. Bessie was clearly returning to her normal self. "What do you think caused your mother to faint?" he asked Teddy.

"Did you eat today, Mother?"

Bessie couldn't recall. She was certain she must have, why she had fed Charlie and Bette hadn't she? Then she remembered, no, she hadn't, having lost track of time.

The four of them stared at Bessie and reprimanded her for not taking better of herself. Walking to the kitchen, leaving her to rest in the parlor, they all agreed—Bessie was simply tired.

NINETEEN

Will You Be My Girl?

C harlie turned to his son. "Bette and Tina are always up in her room. How much studying can two girls do?"

In his mind, Charlie knew courting was an equally important part of growing up, as much as studying was. Then again, maybe they were still too young. He shook the thought away. They'd have time enough for that later.

"It's hard getting accepted into the best school," Teddy replied, aware something was amiss with his sister's love life.

"What's going on with you and the Gillespie girl?" Charlie asked.

Teddy went quiet for a moment, and then sat down on a cedar railing. "I think I'm in love with her." The secret was out.

"Does she feel the same way about you?" Charlie asked, sitting down beside him.

"I have to say, Dad, I'm not sure."

"No sweet talking at all?"

"Not really."

"Did you ask her to go steady?"

Teddy shook his head, feeling somewhat defeated by the line of questioning.

"Well, then what are you waiting for? Get going, boy," Charlie replied, annoyed by his son's lack of movement.

Charlie slid in beside Bessie. "Love is in the air."

"What?" Bessie asked, turning over to flick on the bedside table light.

Charlie grinned, kissing her cheek. "You heard me. Our boy's in love."

Bessie sat upright in the bed. This was the first she'd heard about it. "With who?"

"With Laura Gillespie," Charlie replied, giving Bessie's thigh a slight pinch. "He's got good taste, like his father."

Bessie slapped Charlie's hand saying that he was full of nonsense, and quickly got out of bed.

"Where are you going?" Charlie asked.

"To talk to Teddy," Bessie replied, walking over to the chest to root something out.

Teddy's studies were interrupted by a sharp knock at the door.

"Come in," Teddy said, wondering who possibly could still be awake at this time.

His mother entered and sat down on the end of the bed, holding a small, but long and narrow blue velvet box. "You're still studying?"

"I want to get a head start on the next term."

He'd always studied like that, preparing over the holidays, reading all the text term books. "You've always been a good student," she said. "Worked harder than most."

Teddy played with his pencil, rolling it over the top of his desk. They don't know I work hard so I can get away from this place they love so much, he thought, guilt in his chest, and then he thought of his Uncle Edward, in the room between the two of them. Forgiveness, he thought,

262

will I ever be able to truly let it go? He didn't know. Teddy glanced at his watch. "You should be in bed, it's kind of late."

"I know you're wondering about why I'm here," she said nervously. "Your father told me about Laura. That's why I'm here."

Teddy's eyes widened as he rose to his feet. "Now Mother," Teddy said, his tone dry. "There's no reason to start going on about how I'm not good enough to date a Gillespie."

Bessie, startled, rose to her feet as well, placing a hand on Teddy's shoulder. "No son, you're a professional man. You're plenty good enough for that girl. It's us farmers that aren't good enough. But I think I might be changing my mind about that."

They stood quietly while Teddy tried to make sense of his mother's change of heart, when Bessie remembered her reason for coming in. She handed Teddy an old box. "Here, you'll need it."

As he inspected it, Bessie told him the story. "Granny Hunter brought it over on the boat from Scotland, and so you know, she strapped it under her skirts so thieves wouldn't steal it during the crossing. Once she arrived at the homestead, too busy with work—hard work—Granny never opened the box, never mind wearing what was inside. When she went to her reward, she left it to me, for my hope chest." Bessie paused, her finger brushing against the used velvet of the box. "You see, Teddy, I, like her, never really had the occasion to wear them either, so … I want you to have them."

Teddy listened, hope rising.

"Open it," she said.

Teddy complied, revealing the box's content. Inside, on a bed of creamy white satin, there was a strand of beautiful pearls.

"I think these might make a nice gift for Laura," his mother said. "What do you think?"

Teddy's voice began to shake. "They're beautiful. Thank you." For the first time since he was a little boy, Teddy instinctively moved to hug her.

Her discomfort palpable, but beginning to dissipate, she smiled. Her son was hugging her.

"I'm sure she will love these." Teddy said quietly, moving back, looking his mother in the eye. "And thank you, again, Mother."

"You're a wonderful man. She should be proud to have you."

He watched her walk out the door, and then carefully lifted the pearls, examining them under the light. Like Laura, he thought, they were flawless. Now, he thought, all I have to do is find the right moment.

While they drove through the night, Teddy pointed to the sky, identifying constellation after constellation. "Uncle Ed taught me," he said to Laura. "We used to lie in bed for hours and he'd point out the stars."

"You learned a lot from him, didn't you?"

Teddy nodded. "Uncle Ed has made me the man I am today. He taught me about history, language, and science, filled the parts of my soul that were never satisfied from life on the farm."

Laura took his hand.

"He made me believe there is something more out there." Away from here, he thought.

They'd reached the top of Trussler Road when Teddy pulled off to the side.

"Look," he said. "If you're absolutely still, the entire countryside appears to be on the move."

And so, it did. The moon moving past the church and onto the grain elevators. The starlight dancing on the water, and one by one the farm lights flickering off, as the two of them sat together.

Teddy put his arm around Laura's shoulder, holding her as she leaned against him. He had found his moment. Pulling the jewelry box from his pocket, he opened it. "I'd like you to have these."

Laura looked at him, then down at the pearls. Her mouth opened.

"And I was wondering if you'd be my girl?"

He placed the necklace around her neck, and carefully closing the clasp, told her he was happy. So very happy.

"You couldn't stop me from being your girl. They are beautiful, but not nearly as precious to me as you."

He leaned forward and kissed her. A kiss that marked time, all of their time—from that moment forward.

Bette and Tina were laying down by the creek, staring up at the clouds.

"That's a cumulus," Tina said, dropping her head on Bette's shoulder. "With some stratus high in the east. And there's a thundercloud too," she continued, pointing to the west.

Bette looked to the sky as the wind picked up, and not caring about the approaching black anvil, concentrated on the feel of the prized possession in her pocket. Teddy had given it to her when she was ten, having won it while playing Milk Bottle Knock Down at the fall fair. Never interested in sport, Teddy was still an excellent pitcher—Bill had called him Dead Eye.

Memories of Bill, his voice mostly, ran in her head, telling her to reach for what she wanted. That's what Bill had always told her. Go for anything that mattered. She touched the precious ring, and terrified, but equally determined, pulled it out.

While on a trip into Galt with her mother, Bette had snuck into a jewelry store and asked the proprietor to engrave a T on the blank space.

"This for your boyfriend?" the owner had asked, while grinding a perfect T into the metal.

"Yes," Bette had replied, thinking about Tina.

"We better make tracks," she heard Tina say. "Or we're going to be caught in heavy rain."

Moments are to be created, Bette thought. "I have something for you," she quickly said, as a rumble of violent thunder rolled overhead.

Tina, holding her breath, looked at the ring and immediately slipped it on. She lifted her head, meeting Bette's eyes. "Thank you, Bette. It fits perfectly. But I can't wear this in public," she quickly added, her face worried. "People will ask. My mother will want to know where I got it."

"Then keep it under your pillow and wear it at night. That way, you'll be with me. Every day and every night."

"Do you think this is unnatural?" Tina's voice was hesitant. Nervous. "Us?"

Bette's heart pumped. Maybe the ring was wrong.

"No. I think it's just a phase," Bette said. The wanting to soothe Tina, and also allay her own worries, was cramping her stomach.

"Okay, then," Tina replied, "if it's just a phase, then I can kiss you."

The skies opened and within moments the two girls were drenched. They didn't care about getting wet, and they didn't know, Teddy, looking for the girls, was standing close enough to see them kiss.

Lost to themselves, they never heard Teddy turn around and walk back to the house.

Laura stared into the floor length mirror in the foyer, loving the way the pearls nestled on her collarbone, the way they framed her neck.

"You gonna wear those things to feed the chickens?" Joe asked, sauntering down the hall in his overalls with an apple in his hand.

"Cut it out," Laura said, as he moved behind her. She had been wearing them nonstop since the night Teddy had given them to her. She shook her head, infuriated by Joe's teasing. Playing with the pearls, she thought about the future, wondering if Teddy would ask her to marry him. If so, what would she even say? She frowned at herself in the mirror. Marriage was too soon a thought to be entertained.

She looked at her watch. The family was having a party for Hugh's first birthday, and Teddy and his family; Tina too, had been invited. It was a casual affair, yet, with her pink blouse, dark slacks, and low pumps, Laura wondered if she was overdressed—and were the pearls too much?

Little Hugh sat at the head of the table beside Wilton, proudly waving a silver spoon back and forth in the air. It was clear to Bessie, Sue and Jack were going to have a problem with that child. To have a baby sitting at the head of a family meal was akin to lacking in judgement. Charlie felt the same way. It was hard enough raising children without them developing what his wife called "delusions of grandeur."

"This boy will never know the hardship we did," Wilton said, merrily feeding Hugh a piece of cake. He went on, expounding on how they'd all done without during the Depression, but stressing their children's children wouldn't have to. "This generation is going to have everything," he said, feeding Hugh another piece of cake.

And as the baby burbled happily away, licking at the icing, under the table, couples held hands, drenched in semi-secrecy. Laura wore her pearl necklace, Tina, boldly, her ring.

Jack stood, raising a goblet to make a toast. "First, I'd like to thank Mother and Dad for everything they've done for all of us, for the way they took Sue in while I was overseas and watched over her."

Mrs. Gillespie, tearing up, dabbed the corners of her eyes with her napkin.

"I'd also like to thank Dad for buying us the house in Windsor. I wouldn't be able to take the job position if you hadn't. Thank you."

Teddy caught Charlie's eye and gave him a tiny smile, knowing his father had probably started to think about what he couldn't give, and about what he had. He then looked at his mother, her mind judging, too, most likely, and comparing their worlds.

Bessie, feeling tired, tapped her husband on the hand. "I'd like to go home, Charlie,"

Bette and Tina were choosing gumballs in the Mercantile when Rusty walked up behind them. "Did you get me some?" he asked, slinging an arm around Bette's shoulder. "After all, we have unfinished business," he said, smiling his wolfy smile.

Tina grabbed Rusty's hand, and angrily threw it from Bette's shoulder as Rusty noticed the T on the ring.

"Now where did you get that?" he asked. "Some secret lover?"

Everyone at the Mercantile, noticing the commotion, looked, as Teddy and Laura walked over to break up the shoving taking place. Teddy turned to Laura. "Can you take Tina home?"

"Sure, but where are you going?" Laura asked.

"Bette and I need to talk."

Bette sat quietly in the Dodge, staring out the window at the countryside.

Teddy glanced at his sister. "I know what's going on with you and Tina."

"What?" she asked, shocked. "How?"

"I saw you two in the rain."

Bette shrunk down in the seat. "Are you going to tell Mother?" she asked, knowing that once her mother knew, she'd never be allowed to see Tina again.

"No, I won't." To Teddy's mind, as well as Laura's, homosexuals were people, too, even if they had to hide it. Laura had advised keeping it to himself, and quietly mentioned that Anne seemed to share the same inclinations. Laura hoped it could simply be a stage, yet wise enough the know she was lying to herself.

"What happened with you and Jimmy?" Teddy asked.

"I don't like boys the same way," she replied. "And besides, they always win, even when it's wrong."

"What do you mean?" Teddy asked.

"Nothing," Bette replied, staring at the white lines on the road. It was too dangerous to talk about Rusty, she thought, even with Teddy.

Teddy, confused, decided not to push the conversation further. He knew his sister. She would talk when ready. "Okay, home we go."

Bette found her mother in the kitchen. "Where's Dad?"

"He's in the barn," Bessie replied, noting the confused, angry look on her daughter's face.

"What is it?" she asked, sitting down.

"Rusty," Bette replied. "He's always in town. Staring at me. Likely talking about me and spreading lies. Do you think I could maybe live with Aunt Charlotte until I finish high school?"

"Well, I imagine that you could. I'm sure there's room for you at her house, and Galt's not that far," Bessie replied. "But that would mean you're letting Rusty win," she added.

"Of course, he's going to win. He's a Little. They always win, and eventually everyone will find out what happened, and they'll say I had it coming," Bette said, not only out of concern for herself, but even more troubled her girlfriend might take matters into her own hands. Tina's father owned several guns, and Tina was a good shot.

"Bette, you did not have it coming."

"Mother, everyone will know, and it will reflect on you and Dad and Teddy. All because I was stupid."

"I don't care," Bessie found herself saying.

"Yes, you do! Since day one. You've always said that standing is the most important thing in life. If this gets out, your name will be mud."

"You were not stupid. You are young. You are learning, and learning how to live in a *very* unfair world. Bette, do you hear me? You did nothing wrong."

"I got in the car."

"You needed a ride. You thought he was a friend. How is that stupid?"

"I don't know," Bette replied. "But I do know that I want nothing to do with men. Ever. And then your good name will be preserved, and I will become a nurse and make you and Dad proud."

Bessie reached out and took her daughter's hands, holding them tightly. "I've always been proud of you."

Bessie swallowed. "You always said standing was the most important thing in life."

"You are the most important thing. You, Teddy, and Dad," Bessie replied. "That, and never running away when you've done nothing wrong. That much even a woman can do. If she's strong enough." To run hard and fast, she realized, was the path she had taken, out of cowardness, out of misunderstood righteousness, and it was a path she did not want her daughter taking, no matter the cost.

"What should I do?" Bette asked.

Memories from her days at the London Ontario Normal School came, unannounced. "Screw your courage to the sticking place," she replied, recalling her favourite Shakespearean passage.

And Bette nodded, proud to be her mother's daughter.

TWENTY

The Fall Fair

Fair goers held pink and blue pyramids of wispy cotton candy as Laura and Teddy walked hand-in-hand through the bustling crowd. Around them, a world moving to the sounds and sights of colors: vendors selling stuffed animals, wooden toys, cap guns and homemade delicacies; small children clutching parents' hands, impatiently lined up to ride the colourfully painted ponies on the merry-go-round; older teenagers firing pellet guns at tin chickens for prizes; pink babies crying; a child vomiting; donkeys braying in unison while a wirehaired terrier danced on a ball.

A festival for the senses of those wanting levity.

"Let's see how the pie fight is proceeding," Teddy said, giving Laura's hand a squeeze.

Mrs. Little was carefully examining the desserts when Teddy and Laura approached.

"How do you do?" Laura asked.

"Very well, thank you," Mrs. Little replied, turning to Teddy, and carefully adjusting the veil on her hat.

Looking as if she was about to speak again, Laura quickly interjected, "It'll be interesting to see who wins this year?"

271

"None will hold a candle to mine," Mrs. Little called after them.

Walking away, Teddy looked back, "I hope her pie comes crumbling to the ground, and finishes last."

Laura laughed as they made their way toward Teddy's parents talking with the Moffatts.

"She's a nasty old busybody who gets her joy out of making other people miserable," Teddy said.

"Rusty's back in town," they heard Charlie say as they approached.

"Leering at Bette. Laughing at her," Bessie added. "The poor child is afraid to come to the fair."

"I'm heading over there later," Mr. Moffatt replied. "I told that boy to steer clear. Gave him fair warning."

"She'll handle this," said Bessie, her back straight. "A strong woman needs to learn how to hold her own, too. No matter how fearsome it might be."

Mrs. Moffatt nodded, and as she did, Bessie remembered when she had once crumpled in the face of shame. Again, she prayed her daughter would not do the same.

"There's Bette!" Teddy said, waving as Bette and Tina walked toward them.

Noticing her ring, Laura told Tina how much she liked it. Bill had given her one like that many years ago. "From a beau?" she asked.

While Tina nodded, smiling at Bette, Laura thought of Anne. She must also have a secret love. But would her sister ever talk about it? And if she did, what would Laura even say? Maybe some things were best left unsaid. Privately accepted and understood, but never discussed, preventing them from becoming real.

The judges stood at the front of the barn, behind a long table covered in a white cloth, an array of pies spread out before them.

Nearly everyone in the township was in attendance. Winning the pie competition had become one of the biggest annual competitions in the county, and everyone came to see who would win.

For over a decade, Mrs. Barnes had taken first place, Mrs. Little, second. While no one would openly admit it, her defeat at the fair had become everyone's secret delight.

Charlie saw Mrs. Little interrogating one of the judges, Rusty by her side. "The whole thing reminds me of the Last Supper, only now a group of women are running the show,"

Adam laughed, "Which one is Jesus?"

"I already know who's Judas," Charlie said, looking at Mrs. Little.

"You know," Mrs. Moffatt said, "Mrs. Little is trying a special recipe from France."

"Fat chance," Charlie said. "Nobody beats my Bessie."

"Lily is entering the contest for the first time," Bessie said.

Mrs. Moffatt smiled. "Bessie tasted my rhubarb pie and told me I had a chance."

"She's a real contender," Bessie said, squeezing Lily's hand. "It's one of the best desserts I've ever sampled."

Bessie felt the judges wouldn't break so radically with tradition— awarding the prize to Lily would create too much of a fuss, while secretly wishing that would be the case. Bessie hated to lose.

Teddy, Laura, Bette, and Tina were making their way through the crowd, when Bette noticed Rusty standing beside his mother. Quickly turning her eyes away from his, she continued to walk as if she hadn't seen him.

Bessie, seeing Bette had chosen to come after all, mouthed thank you. Bette smiled back.

As most everyone was watching the judges confer behind the microphone, Bessie, concerned, noticed Lily's pie had been positioned on the tablecloth next to hers. Would the judges break with tradition, after all?

Mrs. Little was also eyeing the placement of the pies. "I wouldn't put much stock in the order," she said. "My pie is from a French recipe. I've never made a better one."

"Doesn't matter," said Rusty. "You know it's rigged so they always win."

Rigged, Bessie nearly shouted. Inside her, a storm in the making was about to be released.

"They probably pay off the judges," Rusty continued.

Teddy moved away from Laura to join his mother and Bette, his anger rising.

"'Course, they probably can't afford that," Rusty said louder. "Maybe Bette pays 'em in some other way."

A collective gasp went through all within earshot.

The next few seconds were a blur to Bessie. Without thinking, she picked up her beautiful pie, the one that had taken her more than four hours to make, and with a piercing look, mashed it onto the sneer on Rusty's face.

Mrs. Little gasped.

The barn went silent.

"How dare you?" cried Mrs. Little, wiping away berries and juice dripping down her son's face.

"How dare I? How dare you! Your son is an animal!" said Bessie, shaking with fury. "He tried to rape my daughter. And now he's taunting her, too."

"Nonsense," said Mrs. Little. "You raised a tease and a tramp, and now you're trying to sully my boy's good name."

Bessie was about to reply, when Bette pulled away from Tina, and strode straight up to Mrs. Little. "You take that back."

"I certainly will not," said Mrs. Little.

"Your son tried to rape me. And if you don't believe me, ask the Moffatts," Bette snapped, turning to her neighbours.

Mr. Moffatt said it was true, and Mrs. Moffatt began providing details, Teddy absorbing the terrible ugliness for the first time.

All eyes were on Mrs. Little and her son. Needing to bring this situation firmly under her control, she turned to Bette. "Well, maybe if you hadn't been such a little slut, he would have been able to control himself."

Rusty, wiping pie from his face, laughed. "Like anyone would believe any of you."

Teddy moved to face him. So that's what had happened to Bette. That useless bully had gone after his little sister.

"What do you want, yellow belly?" Rusty asked, poking Teddy's chest, trying to shove him.

"Did you try to rape my sister?" Teddy said, not flinching.

"Nobody needs to rape her, she's more than willing."

Teddy cranked his arm back and punched Rusty hard in the jaw, sending the young man's body to the floor. Mrs. Little rushed to her son's side where Rusty lay semi-conscious.

Teddy looked down at Rusty. "Never say another thing about my sister, do you understand?"

Rusty, opened his eyes, staring.

"Do you understand?" Teddy repeated, more loudly this time.

Rusty slowly nodded.

Charlie walked up to his son. "You had no choice," he said. Then he looked down at Rusty, and said, "If you think that hurt, just trying speaking to my daughter again."

Laura took Teddy's arm. "You did the right thing," she said.

"Violence doesn't solve anything," Teddy replied, sickened by the act, thinking of Uncle Ed.

"That's right son," Bessie said, also remembering Edward.

"Somebody help me," Mrs. Little implored, looking up and seeing no one moving to help. "The boy needs medical attention."

People began to turn away as a voice came on over the loud speaker announcing, Mrs. Adam Moffatt's pie had won.

Mrs. Little hadn't even placed.

Driving home, Bessie looked out the window, listening to Bette and Tina in the back seat, chatting. They seem so free, she caught herself thinking. And why shouldn't they? After all, the world was changing; the war had created a whole generation of young women who wanted to work, who wanted more than she had wanted for herself. How her own daughter was choosing a profession, over being an upstanding wife. I've been terrified for years, that a man wouldn't claim her, and yet, the child does not care.

Once home, Bessie laid down on the sofa to rest her eyes. It had become clear to her, so very clear, the world would continue, with or without her approval, and besides, she was too tired to fight.

TWENTY-ONE

Beginnings and Endings

Laura was on her way home, dreaming of Christmas, when the train pulled into the Galt station. She glanced at her watch, she'd completely lost track of the time having day-dreamed the ride away. She pulled her compact from her purse, and looking at herself, quickly checked her rouge and applied a new layer of lipstick. Her hair, she adjusted, too, and smiling at her image, she closed the compact, its click satisfying to the ear. She made her way through the car and down the stairs to the platform, clutching her purse in one hand, and a new white vanity case in the other.

Wondering where her mother and Joe were, she scanned the crowd a little longer, not finding them. How odd, she thought, maybe they got the time wrong. Just then, she saw Teddy, almost running, making his way through the crowd, his navy fedora pushed back on his head, a long blue overcoat billowing behind him as he walked.

"What are you doing here?" she asked, kissing him on the cheek. "Not that I'm not delighted to see you."

"I told your mother I'd pick you up," he replied, taking her arm to lead her through the crowd. "Let's get you into the car."

The Dodge plowed up the hill and through the leaves as they traveled through an autumnal landscape of fiery red, sunshine yellow, and orange, the color of ripe pumpkins. Laura always had thought it the most beautiful time of year, one where the leaves slowly broke free from their branches and fluttered to the ground. It was as if nature was embroidering a quilt or making a carpet.

Looking at Teddy, she noticed his quietness, and saw something almost nervous about his manner. Her hand slowly went to her throat and rested on the pearls. Out of habit, she contemplatively rolled them between her thumb and index finger.

They were nearing the highest peak on Trussler Road when Teddy slowed the car down and turned off on the soft shoulder.

She smiled to herself, remembering, Teddy had brought her here the night he'd shown her his perfect view of the world. The night he'd given her the pearls.

He flicked the ignition off and placed his hands on the dashboard. He turned to face Laura. "I don't know how to say this," he began, taking a long pause.

His words caused a sense of panic in Laura. Had something horrible happened? Was there something wrong with Dad? "Whatever it is, just tell me," she said, reaching out to take his hand.

"I never thought I'd do this," Teddy said. "I never thought I'd meet anyone like you."

Everything had been going so well, but what if they weren't? she asked herself, not understanding Teddy's words.

Teddy read the panic in Laura's face and shook his head. "I'm doing a terrible job."

Confused, Laura watched Teddy fumble around in his coat pocket, searching.

BESSIE

"And it's just because I want to do it so well, Laura," he said, his hand now stable. "I've loved you since I first met you that night in the church."

Laura's heart began to thump as Teddy struggled to shift his frame from under the steering wheel so he could get down on one knee.

"We'll both be through school soon and I've been assured by the dean I won't have any problem securing a good practice," he said, as he opened a small box.

Laura's heart had understood before she did. And as she looked down at the most exquisite diamond she had ever seen, joy took hold of her heart.

Taking another deep breath, he continued. "What I'm trying to say is, Laura Gillespie, will you do me the extreme honour of being my wife?"

Laura, looking at Teddy, nodded, and nodded some more. Her man was there, eyes asking, an open ring box in his hand, a knee planted on the floor of his father's old Dodge, an adorable hat pushed to the back of his head, and a big coat twisted around him. She couldn't imagine being with anyone else.

"I would love to marry you, Theodore Barnes."

Teddy removed the ring from its case and slipped the ring on her finger. It fit perfectly. Motionless, they held hands watching the sun drop behind the horizon.

"We know where we're heading," she said. "Finally."

"And it's going to be a wild adventure, Laura Gillespie. I promise to make you happy."

"A good adventure?" she laughed.

He nodded; this time, more serious. "I still need to ask your parents for your hand."

"They think the world of you, Teddy. To them you're a marvelous young man who will take care of their daughter. You're a doctor—well soon will be. And besides, I love you. They know I do."

279

Teddy started the car and drove back to the sound of Laura's breathing, soft and peaceful.

They kissed goodnight, unknowing of the truths that waited for them, sometimes easy, often difficult.

Looking at the road on his way home, the warmth of Laura still floating in the car, he scratched his head wondering how on earth he had been able to drive the car at all? He didn't remember any of it. "Who was driving?" he whispered to himself, amused.

He parked the car and walked to the house wanting to share in all, his life, and about where he was headed, with Laura by his side.

Then he saw Dad running across the yard, yelling—something about his mother. "She's collapsed while crating eggs for Mooney, and I can't wake her up."

Teddy took the front stairs three at a time, running to the parlour. On the sofa, Bessie, a pillow beneath her head, was lying on her back. Seeing an ashen color had spread across her face, and hearing her breathing, shallow and quick, he immediately took her pulse. Something was wrong.

"Quick, Dad, get my medical bag."

Teddy pulled back Bessie's eye lids: The pupils were dilated. He undid her dress, his fingers expertly palpating her abdomen, and noticing the right side was abnormally distended, he pressed on the area directly below her rib cage. His heart sank. He could feel the presence of a large mass, a hard one.

When Charlie returned with the bag, Teddy quickly popped it open and removed an ampule of amyl nitrate. Cracking off the glass top, he waved it beneath Bessie's nose. She opened her eyes. "Hello Mother."

She looked around the parlour. "What's going on?"

"You had a fall," Teddy replied, turning to his father. "Get a couple more pillows and some blankets."

"Doc Ramsey should be here any moment, I called him before you got here."

"We don't have the time for that, Dad."

"What's all this nonsense?" Bessie asked, trying to rise on her elbow.

"We've got to get you to the hospital," Teddy replied, "Put your arms around my neck. I'm going to carry you."

Bessie was about to complain, but when the excruciating pain struck again, she realized something was terribly wrong. Teddy, carefully picking her up, was struck by how light she was.

Charlie, finishing scribbling a quick note to Bette in the kitchen, looked through the open door across the yard and saw Bessie, nestled loosely in Teddy's arms, her head swinging in the air like Bette's old rag doll.

Flat on her back staring into an unforgiving bright white light, Bessie listened to Teddy and the doctor speaking in a strange language about her condition.

A lump.

The lights hummed, her eyes flicked back and forth, and she thought, they've found it, just as she had, years earlier, underneath her abdomen. I couldn't tell Charlie. There was no money for medical care since all of it went for Teddy's board and tuition, and now Bette's dream of going to nursing school. No time for a silly lump. Mother Nature would take care of most everything else in her own sweet time, and that was how Bessie had dealt with the growing lump.

As other symptoms began their slow march, as fatigue, bloating, loss of appetite, and nausea became daily companions, Bessie had tried her best to ignore them, always pushing on, and pushing through.

"I already put in the call and the specialist will be here first thing in the morning. They needed to do a biopsy immediately."

Upon hearing those words, Bessie closed her eyes. It never had occurred to her that her body, always resilient, would ever let her down. Why then was she suddenly lying in a sterilized emergency room with a strange man prodding her stomach, and creating a hideous amount of pain? Because she had soiled her position in life? She had sinned? With Edward? Was God now here to exact his pound of flesh? She tried not to cry, wondering, was death synonymous with relief, was punishment the permissible exit?

Teddy and the doctors left the room, their voices fading, just as she was.

After conferring with the doctors, Teddy entered the waiting room. He was sick of secrets held tightly under the pretext of protecting others from pain. Even well-intentioned lies festering like the tumour in his mother's stomach. He sat down with his family and gently told them what he and the physicians suspected.

There was no hope.

Teddy felt the adrenaline stop coursing through his body. In its place, a sledgehammer of dread, pounding out a steady ominous beat.

When Teddy woke up, his head was on Laura's lap. "Tina called me, I know …" she said, her eyes meeting him. "And the doctor is here."

Remembering everything that had happened, he sat up. A tall thin man with a narrow face and an austere bearing, stood by the nurse's station, jotting notes into a patient's file. It had to be his mother's doctor. Teddy got to his feet, ran his fingers through his hair, and strode across the room. "Are you the oncologist here to see Mrs. Barnes?" he asked, extending his hand. "I'm her son, Ted Barnes."

The doctor told Teddy the attending physician had filled him in on everything, then quickly shook Teddy's hand, and asked him to come with him.

In silence, Teddy followed him down the long echoing white corridor, and stepped into the elevator that led to the basement. Teddy matched the oncologist step for step until they stopped in front of a tall stainless-steel door marked "Oncology Lab".

"I saw your mother at five this morning and did a sectioned biopsy. I've stained the tissue and want you to see the results," he said, as the door swung open to the lab.

Unforgiving fluorescent bulbs buzzed as Teddy peered into the lens of the microscope. There was no denying what he was seeing. The healthy cells had nearly all been devoured by rapacious cancer cells and the damage was astonishing.

"Can you operate?" he asked, knowing it was impossible, but praying he was wrong.

The oncologist shook his head no. The cancer had broken free from the original tumour and was marching through his mother's body, metastasizing at a frightening rate. There was nothing they could do.

"How long?" Teddy asked.

"A week, maybe two," the oncologist replied. "It really depends on your mother. I'm sorry Dr. Barnes."

And this first time, he thought, when a peer recognized another one––him, down in the bowels of a hospital, the smear of his dying mother's blood imprinted on his brain.

A memory made to last.

As they walked back to Bessie's room, the oncologist recommended using heavy pain medication to reduce her discomfort. He confessed he couldn't fathom how she'd lived with it so long, without a word of complaint. You don't know Mother, Teddy thought.

He didn't stop in the waiting room for Laura or the rest of his family. Teddy needed to talk to his mother while he had the nerve. He was soon to be a doctor, yes, but it was his duty to tell her, now, as a son.

Without knocking, he quietly slipped in expecting to find her resting. Instead, she was lying there, staring up at the ceiling with the strangest look on her face.

When she heard him enter, she quietly turned to him. "Sit down Teddy."

He pulled a chair up to the side of the bed.

"What did that nasty doctor say?"

Teddy gently patted her arm, a gesture telling of a truth loaded with the slow, chilling gnaws of a fear she didn't want to let in—a loss of control meant leaving everything she ever had been. All of it infuriated her—she didn't want to surrender, to expose this weakness.

"The patting doesn't help," she said, pulling her arm away. "Tell me what he said."

Teddy felt a sudden calm take hold of him. "He said you're dying. I saw the results. There's no mistake. I'm so sorry."

"I deserve it," she said.

Teddy looked at her. What on earth was she talking about?

"I killed your uncle," she explained. "And this is my punishment."

Words he needed to hear for the longest time, now seemed to mean nothing to him. "The past is the past, Mother."

She closed her eyes, and Teddy, shaken, rose quietly to leave the room.

Bessie, letting her thoughts drift to Edward, saw him standing in the doorway, and she heard herself saying, "We could have gone dancing, it would have been fun." Before she could understand any of this, a nurse appeared with a syringe in hand. A few moments later the pain receded, and Bessie floated away on a sea of morphine-fed forgetfulness.

A bright light woke her up.

"Bessie?"

She moved her head lightly, leaving curls of her hair stuck to the pillow.

"Charlie?"

"You've been gone for a while, Honey bunch."

Charlie looked tired. She placed her arms by her side, trying to prop herself up, but fell back, the weakness now having settled everywhere in her body. The oncologist approached the bed.

"You've been in and out of consciousness for a week now, Mrs. Barnes," she heard him say. "Your family is here." Lifting her eyes, she saw them all and smiled. She turned to Charlie.

"My dearest," he said, lightly stroking the rich black hair he loved so much.

She tried to smile and turned and looked at her daughter. "You're going to have to wait on school and help Dad with the farm."

Bette's fingers, wrapped around the back of a metal chair, squeezed it hard as tears fell. She nodded her head in agreement.

"I'm sorry if I wasn't a very good example," Bessie said, motioning for Bette to come and take her hand.

"What are you talking about, Mother?" Bette cried. "You're the finest woman I know. Shakespeare, those words, they live with me, because of you. The sticking place, remember?"

"Yes," she whispered, and nodded. "With no deep personal sticking place, you can be blown away by every storm that passes."

Keeping Bette's hand in her hers, Bessie beckoned Laura over to the bed. "Take care of my boy," she said softly. "He loves you very much."

"I will, Mrs. Barnes. I promise." And as she wiped away her tears, Teddy stepped forward, taking her hand. All these years of medical school, and there was nothing he could do to help his own mother.

"I'm proud of you," Bessie said. "The first professional man in the family."

And now his tears came, and reaching out, he took his mother's hand. "Without you..."

Bessie didn't push back—not this time, wanting—needing, to feel the comfort of her son's words. His touch, the warmth, she was now finally permitting herself to feel.

Looking at one another, their eyes filled with an understanding, one that spoke of her ways, and of his, too. Of how love reaches, and can stay, forgiving. Needing.

She twisted her body, another wave of pain cresting. When she opened her eyes, Bessie took Charlie's hand back in hers, and heard Teddy ask the nurse to administer another dose.

The liquid entered her vein like a compassion-filled heat, spreading through her, and this tide of forgiving—of herself, was wide and deep and carried her far beyond anything she had ever known. But before she could enter, she looked back at her family, looking back at her. She smiled, hearing ever so faintly their words, spoken with sadness, and spoken with love: Bessie, please no.

And then she was gone, and she was in peace.

Edward there, waiting ... for the next dance.

CODA

Teddy's black graduation gown fluttered in the wind around his legs, and he had to clap a hand over his scholar's cap to keep it from lifting off. He was taking over a practice from a retiring doctor in a growing village. Laura was particularly fond of the idea because it was close to the city of Hamilton, so she could shop and they could see the odd show, and it was only an hour's drive home to visit her parents.

Bette and Tina were applying to McMaster's nursing program, with Teddy and Laura's full support. Even Charlie seemed to be somewhat getting back on track without Bessie. A few widows from the area had started appearing at the house with casseroles, anxious to feed him. Teddy knew that while his dad complained they were a nuisance, he enjoyed the female companionship.

Family and friends of the graduating class clustered on the steps of Convocation Hall, cameras at the ready to take photos of the students waving while marching up the marble stairway through the high archway into the magnificent round hall.

Before he reached the steps, Teddy could see his father, Laura, Bette, and Tina waving from down front. Knowing his dad, they'd been there for at least an hour to secure the best spot. Mother would have insisted.

His mother. That was the space, the gap in what should have been one of the happiest moments of his life. Teddy thought back to all the years he'd resented her. He'd blamed her for his Uncle Ed's death, but now he knew, that she, too, had blamed herself. Yet with this final gift she had given him, and herself, they were both set free.

Walking past Laura, he reached out his hand to hers, their fingers brushing, and in that moment, the sun shining down upon him, he heard his mother saying to him: How I love you. How proud I am of you. My son.

Acknowledgements

The thanks for the publication of this novel go far and wide. My many friends and extended family supported this work. Chicken breeder John Tilt (yes, Mr. Tilt was based on a real person) took an afternoon to show me his prized birds and gave me a behind the scenes look at the intricacies of the chicken competition in the 1930s. Uncle Hugh regaled me with exciting stories about The Royal Winter Fair, while cousin Bill "Big Daddy" explained how the cheating was done. Aunt Sue Maus and cousin Margaret Thomson also kindly offered their help. Since so much of this book is based on memory, I wanted everything to be just right.

My brother Richard and his wife Catherine, voracious readers of fiction, offered me a great deal of insight. As did my brother Paul and his wife Michelle. I must also thank my cousin Laurie McGugan who very patiently read so many drafts along the way.

Sascha Hasting, Nora Young, Caroline Martin, Sue Hilborn, Ernest Hillen, Diana Young and Sasha Darling are but a few of the many people who advised, edited, and offered unwavering support. Also kudos to Susan Swan, Janice Zawerbny and Patrick Crean who provided me with background information regarding the publishing industry.

Special thanks to my editor, the very talented Elyse Friedman who aided enormously in the story's structure and tone. And then there is Don Oravec, the wonderful former Executive Director at the Writer's Trust of Canada. Don and his partner Jim Harper both firmly believed in Bessie's story, even when I truly feared that I'd never be able to get it published. They invited me down to Florida to discuss Bessie with an extremely funny and smart book club. Which resulted in even more consideration and editing. Thanks guys.

And finally, the saviours of the day, Christian Fennell and Nathalie Guilbeault, informed me that The Montreal Publishing Company would like to publish my work. These two incredibly skilled writers are committed to seeing that all good books get a chance. Not only the very few that get the backing of the big houses. Chris and Nat, I can never thank you enough.

Montreal Publishing Company publishes works of
poetry, drama, fiction, and non-fiction.
We seek writers that dare, and make us think—reconsider.

Relevance Without Fear

Montreal Publishing Company
montrealpublishing.com

Manufactured by Amazon.ca
Bolton, ON

38555614R00180